PRAISE FOR THE LORI ANDERSON SE...

'Sharp, thrilling and one hell of a ride. This series just gets better and better!' Chris Whitaker

'*Deep Dirty Truth* is an exhilarating and addictive read. Every time I put the book down to do stuff in the real world, I couldn't wait to pick it back up again to see what else was in store for the characters and myself. A compelling and thrilling read with a kick-ass protagonist readers are going to love' By-the-Letter Book Reviews

'WOW. The third instalment of the kick-ass bounty hunter Lori Anderson series was the best one yet! Tense and exciting with no let-up from the very first sentence' Ginger Nut

'I've just finished *Deep Dirty Truth* and I think I need some oxygen as I'm all out of it! Breathless stuff. Best Lori yet, and that's the *deep dirty truth* of it' Beardy Book Blogger

'Best book I've read in 2018 – amazing, fast-paced thriller!! Download t...

'*Deep Dirty* ... nable, and I am already l... his fantastic series!' Book ... after Book

'While most of the narrative concerns Lori, you also get to see what is happening with JT, Dakota and Red. Each time it switched I was anxious to go back again, the timing is that perfect. I read a lot of books that have more than one narrative and it takes a great author to get it as perfect as it is here' Steph's Book Blog

'It's a thriller with bite, grit and attitude. If you love punchy dialogue, break-neck speed and unrelenting action, then this is the book for you ... Lori Anderson is THE bounty hunter/all-round crime fighting, no-nonsense hero that you need' The Book Trail

'Fast, confident and suspenseful' Lee Child

'Like *Midnight Run*, but much darker ... really, really good' Ian Rankin

'A real cracker ... Steph Broadribb kicks ass, as does her ace protagonist' Mark Billingham

'This is romping entertainment that moves faster than a bullet' Jake Kerridge, *Sunday Express*

'If you like your action to race away at full tilt, then this whirlwind of a thriller is a must' Deirdre O'Brien, *Sunday People*

'Stripper-turned-bounty hunter Lori, with her sickly young daughter in tow, gets into high-octane escapes when she sets out to bring her former lover and mentor to justice. Lively' *Sunday Times* Crime Club

'Sultry and suspenseful, it marks a welcome first for an exceptional new voice' *Good Reading Magazine*

'A bit of everything – suspense, action, romance, danger and a plot that will keep you reading into the wee small hours. I loved it' *Daily Record*

'Bounty hunter Lori Anderson returns in this instalment of the high-octane US trilogy. Gutsy Lori is tasked with bringing in an on-the-run felon, her only chance to save her daughter's father from jail. Fresh, fast and zinging with energy' *Sunday Mirror*

'As Anderson follows Fletcher's trail to California, she faces insults, attacks, and deceptions from a host of people connected to the fugitive, including his brother and his lover, with grit and determination. Readers will cheer her every step of the way' *Publishers Weekly*

The constant juggling of work and motherhood, aggression and affection, danger and domesticity make Lori a seductive star, excitingly extraordinary and yet still identifiably ordinary. The result is entertainment all the way… don't miss it!' *Lancashire Evening Post*

'The non-stop twists and turns draw in readers like a magnet and keep them hooked to the action right up to the emotional conclusion' *Burnley Gazette*

'Another electric humdinger of a read. Bounty hunter Lori is thrown in the deep end when she agrees to hunt down a murderer in order to strike a deal with the FBI. The clipped, almost unsentimental tone allows the fast-paced story to explode from the get-go' Liz Robinson, LoveReading

'Lori Anderson is back with a bang … a sharply written, fast-paced thriller with bucket loads of heart. With a heroine who jumps off the page and a fantastic supporting cast, this series is a sure-fire winner for anyone with a pulse' S.J.I. Holliday

'Another adrenaline-fuelled, brilliant thriller from Steph Broadribb. Trouble has never been so attractive' A.K. Benedict

'Pacey, emotive and captivating, this is kick-ass thriller writing of the highest order' Rod Reynolds

'A relentless page-turner with twists and turns that left me breathless' J.S. Law

'Fast-paced, engaging and hugely entertaining' Simon Toyne

'Brilliant and pacey' Steve Cavanagh

'Excitement and exhilaration flies off every page' David Young

'An explosive, exciting debut' David Mark

'A hell of a thriller' Mason Cross

'A setting that zings with authenticity' Anya Lipska

'Fast, furious and thrilling' Graeme Cameron

'A series that will run and run' Howard Linskey

'A blistering debut' Neil Broadfoot

'If you love romantic suspense, you'll love this ride' Alexandra Sokoloff

'A stunning debut from a major new talent' Zoë Sharp

'Perfect for fans of Lee Child and Janet Evanovich' Alex Caan

'Powerful, passionate and packs a real punch' Fergus McNeill

'Delivers thrills at breakneck pace' Marnie Riches

'Assured and emotionally moving' Daniel Pembrey

'Crying out to be a Hollywood movie' Louise Voss

'High-octane and breathlessly paced' Ava Marsh

'One of my favourite debut novels for a long, long time' Luca Veste

'A fast-talking, gun-toting heroine with a heart of gold' Claire Seeber

'A top crime talent! Unputdownable' Helen Cadbury

'Relentless, breathtaking and emotionally charged' Jane Isaac

'A gritty debut that will appeal to Sue Grafton fans' Caroline Green

'Great action scenes and great atmosphere' C.J. Carver

'Crazy good ... full-tilt action and a brilliant cast of characters' Yrsa Sigurðardóttir

'Broadribb's writing is fresh and vivid, crackling with life … an impressive thriller, the kind of book that comfortably sits alongside seasoned pros' CrimeWatch

'Delivered with both energy and colour. Lori is an unusual protagonist, and Orenda Books' venture into action-thriller territory proves (in Broadribb's capable hands) to be as successful as the company's moody Scandinavian offerings' Barry Forshaw

'Fast-paced, zipping around the south-eastern US with chases, fights, ambushes and desperate escapes … There's a sensitivity in the telling of Lori's struggle to save her daughter that gives this a bit more depth than other action thrillers' Crime Fiction Lover

'Steph Broadribb has written a fast-paced action thriller … I'm loving this series – it's fresh, fun and a rollercoaster read each time' Off-the-Shelf Books

'Steph Broadribb has created a genuinely authentic, kick-ass, realistically flawed heroine who I will now follow anywhere – a breath of fresh air on a hot summer's day blowing right through the thriller genre and turning it on its head … Addictive, fun, bang on the money from first page to last!' Liz Loves Books

'Nerve-wracking and so fast-paced you won't have time to even stop and breathe. This is a one-sitting kind of a read, so think carefully about when you are going to pick it up. Once you start, just like Lori facing down her target, you won't want to back away until you turn the very last page. A totally cracking book three' Jen Meds Book Reviews

'This was a superb novel that I thoroughly enjoyed reading. It is a thrilling, action-packed read that once you pick up you find hard to put down' Hair Past a Freckle

ABOUT THE AUTHOR

Steph Broadribb was born in Birmingham and grew up in Buckinghamshire. Most of her working life has been spent between the UK and USA. As her alter ego, Crime Thriller Girl, she indulges her love of all things crime fiction by blogging at www.crimethrillergirl. com, where she interviews authors and reviews the latest releases. Steph is an alumni of the MA in Creative Writing (Crime Fiction) at City University London, and she trained as a bounty hunter in California. She lives in Buckinghamshire surrounded by horses, cows and chickens.

Her debut thriller, *Deep Down Dead*, was shortlisted for the Dead Good Reader Awards in two categories, was a finalist in the ITW Awards, and hit number one on the UK and AU kindle charts. The sequel, *Deep Blue Trouble* soon followed suit. *My Little Eye*, her first novel under her pseudonym, Stephanie Marland, was published by Trapeze Books in April 2018.

Follow Steph on Twitter *@CrimeThrillGirl*, and on Facebook at *Facebook.com/CrimeThrillerGirl/*, or visit her website: *crimethrillergirl. com*.

Deep Dirty Truth
Lori Anderson Book Three

Steph Broadribb

**ORENDA
BOOKS**

Orenda Books
16 Carson Road
West Dulwich
London SE21 8HU
www.orendabooks.co.uk

First published in the UK in 2019 by Orenda Books
Copyright © Steph Broadribb 2018

A catalogue record for this book is available from the British Library.

ISBN 978-1-912374-55-7
eISBN 978-1-912374-56-4

Typeset in Garamond by MacGuru Ltd
Printed and bound by CPI Group (UK) Ltd, Croydon CR0 4YY

For sales and distribution, please contact *info@orendabooks.co.uk*

In memory of my wonderful Dad – Jim Broadribb.
I miss you every day.
With love, always.

1

I never saw it coming. Got totally blindsided. That's the God's honest truth.

See, we've gotten ourselves into a routine of sorts – me, JT and Dakota. Living all together in my two-bed apartment at the Clearwater Village complex, playing our version of house. It's still a little awkward, with each of us taking time to find our rhythm in the shared space of each other's lives. But, you know, all that domestic stuff? It's starting to feel real good, kind of natural. I should've known something bad was lurking around the corner, and some kind of evil was about to storm in and mess it all up.

Because that's what happens when you've a dirty secret in your past, and a price on your head from Old Man Bonchese – the head of the Miami Mob crime family – because of something he's discovered you did ten years back. Someone you killed: a lying, cheating, murdering mobster. Thomas 'Tommy' Ford; my wife-beating, son-of-a-bitch husband.

First they thought JT was responsible. Nearly had him killed a couple of months back – multiple stab wounds, busted ribs, punctured lung and a heart attack. But he's strong. A fighter. And he's convalescing well.

But they wouldn't let it go. Word was they'd got new information and were now gunning hard for me; raising the bounty, getting every low-life, bottom-feeding asshole to think they should chance their luck.

As it was, they waited until September 19th to make their move. The day started with a shared breakfast of bagels and cream cheese, followed by me taking Dakota to school and leaving JT to do the dishes before his physical therapy appointment. It seemed like a regular day; just like the day before, and the day before that. But the schedule got changed up. Our rhythm violently disrupted. And by 08:29 that morning our world was shot to shit.

2

It's mad busy outside the school, and I can't squeeze the Jeep into the drop-off area, so I continue along the street a ways before finding a spot that's clear. I glance in the rearview mirror at Dakota as I shove the gear into park. She's fiddling with her cellphone, brow creased and front teeth biting her lower lip in concentration, playing whatever game is the latest craze.

'Come on, honey. You don't want to be late.'

She nods, but doesn't look up. Jumping out, I run around to her side and open the door. She puts the cell into her bag and I gesture for her to get out. She's got a coy expression on that usually means she's revving up to ask something.

She takes her time unfastening her belt and gets her bags together real slow. Clears her throat. 'So JT said it would be okay, Momma, and you know how much I love the Tampa Bay Rays.'

Her love of the Tampa Bay Rays is new. It started the moment JT said they were his favourite local sports team, second only to the Yankees. I lift her science project – a papier-mâché model of the planets in the solar system – out of the trunk.

'Sweetie, hurry.'

She dangles her legs out of the Jeep. Her knee socks are scrunched around her ankles, her shoes are new, but the toe of the right one is already scuffed. 'So can I?'

They've been talking about it the last three weeks. JT wants to take her to a ballgame at Tropicana Field and she's keen to go. I want them to have some father-daughter time, even if we haven't yet told her that

JT is her father, but I'm worried the trip is too soon. Not for their relationship, that's doing just fine, but for JT's health. He's still healing, and although the external bruises have faded now, he's no way close to being back to full strength. Standing for any length of time makes him dog-tired and he still can't walk any kind of distance.

'Maybe, honey.'

Dakota sits on the edge of the seat. She pushes her strawberry-blonde bangs out of her eyes and looks up at me through long lashes. 'But why only maybe? Why not yes?'

I smile. She's persistent. Determined, just like her momma. 'How about soon?'

She frowns. 'It's better than no, I guess.'

I laugh. 'Yes, it is. Now, scoot.'

She grins, and slides out of the Jeep. Swinging her bags over her shoulder, she takes the science project and trots towards the school gates. I stand on the sidewalk in the morning sunshine, leaning on the trunk, and watch her join the flow of kids rushing into school. She's been through so much in the past year, yet she seems happy. She's been abducted, seen men die and been in fear of her life. That's stuff no nine-year-old should ever have to experience.

As Dakota reaches the school gate she turns, waves and disappears inside.

I watch her, daring to hope the psychological scars are fading. The guilt that what happened to her was because of me, because of my job, remains heavy in my chest, and I know I'll never forgive myself for it. But I have to push through. Move on and stay focused on the future. We all do.

On the street close behind me, a vehicle brakes hard, pulling me from my thoughts. I hear a door slide open and glance over my shoulder, glimpsing a van with blacked-out windows that's stopped, butted up against my Jeep, blocking me in.

I start to turn. 'Hey, what are you...?'

Two men with shaved heads jump out of the vehicle. Hands yank me backwards. Fingers dig into my shoulders and hips, pinning my arms. I kick back, fighting hard, but they're pulling me off balance. I can't get any power into my blows.

The voice in my right ear is low, menacing. 'You keep wiggling, you'll only die tired.'

I pay their warning no mind. As they haul me across the blacktop I'm screaming, bellowing, frantically looking for someone who can help. But there's no one; the other parents are inside the school gate, out of sight and oblivious. I'm too far away.

'Let me go ... get your goddamn hands off—'

Tape is slapped across my mouth, silencing my shouts. Trapped inside, my screams and curses echo in my head. Rough hands hood me. The black material turns the world around me dark.

Then I'm off the ground, lifted up and back. I'm still fighting, punching, bucking against them, but I'm outnumbered and they're too strong. I'm losing the battle. Seconds later they release me. Gravity drops me onto the floor of the van. Pain shoots through my hip, my knee, my elbow. My face hits something solid and I hear my jaw crack. I taste blood in my mouth.

The door slides shut. The engine fires, and we're moving.

Less than fifteen seconds from start to finish.

I doubt anyone even knows I'm gone.

3

WEDNESDAY, SEPTEMBER 19th, 08:31

Panic never helped no one, and I'll be damned if it'll get the better of me.

Heart punching in my chest, double-speed, I take stock of the situation. I'm on my back – not a good position as it leaves my stomach exposed, my vital organs vulnerable to easy damage, so I arch my back, turn myself over.

My captors have other ideas. One grabs me, pulling me across the van floor. I kick hard at them. Feel my toe connect and hear a grunt. The moment of triumph doesn't last. I feel more hands on me, flipping me onto my side and clamping me still. My arms are yanked behind me and I feel tape against my skin, binding my wrists, then my ankles. Next moment they've gotten me hogtied. They're are fast, practised and methodical. This isn't their first time.

So I make a choice and quit fighting. Conserve energy. But I'm sure as hell not giving up. I'm harvesting data; every sound, every bump in the blacktop, every gradient in the terrain, is a clue about where they're taking me.

I close my eyes. Listen real hard. At first I mostly hear the thump of my pulse gunfire loud in my ears, but as I force my breathing to slow, clearing my mind of panic, more sounds start to register.

The muffler's rattling and the air conditioning is dialled up high. I hear low voices, male, up front. I can't make out their words, but I can tell that there are two of them. Wondering how many others there are, I move about the van floor, act restless and try to push myself up with my elbow. Rough hands on my shoulders and my hips force me down hard. My face slams against the floor. Pain shoots through my forehead.

A third hand presses down on me. The same voice as before snarls in my ear, 'Quiet down, bitch.'

I don't appreciate his tone, but I've got me my answer: there are two people riding in the back with me, so with the pair up front that makes four in total. Four guys sent to grab one woman.

Numbers like that tell me these people take no kind of chances.

We come to a stop, at an intersection I'm guessing. Over the blowers of the air conditioning, I hear a blast of Miley Cyrus. It's to our left, likely coming from another vehicle. Then the van's engine guns hard, and we take a left, leaving the music behind.

I need to get my bearings but it's tricky without any visual references. I think back to the route we've taken, run through each of the turns made since leaving Dakota's school. I feel about-faced, but figure we're maybe going north-east. Heading out of town. Question is why; is this a random snatch, or am I their target?

Right now, there's no way to know for sure.

My captors are silent. The blacktop is smooth, the turns minimal. The van coasts on at a steady speed, doing nothing that might attract attention.

I concentrate on my breathing. Try to ignore the musty stench of the hood, the oppressive gag of the tape and the sweat running down my back. I push away thoughts of Dakota and JT, and the fear that I'll never see them again. There might be four of these guys, but I'll never go down easy. I'll wait it out, looking for my chance to fight back.

Minutes later the van brakes and we start to reduce speed.

I flinch as a hand grips the back of my neck. 'No noise, no tricks.'

We're almost at a stop. I hear the buzz of a window being lowered and the clatter of coins hitting metal. The hand around my neck squeezes harder.

'Have a nice day.' A woman says from outside the van. There's a pause, followed by an electronic ping. Then we're moving again.

The window buzzes back up and the pressure on my neck releases. I know where we are. The woman was in a teller booth. We've just passed through a toll.

My captors used coins – they don't have a resident's sunshine pass that would've allowed them to use the lane for automated toll payments, and that means they're most likely from out of town.

As the van reaches cruising speed two things are real clear: we're on the freeway, and we're not in Clermont anymore.

Not a car jacking.

Not robbery.

Not rape, at least not yet.

Then what the hell is it that these men want with me?

Again I run through the turns we've taken since leaving Dakota's school. I concentrate hard on the direction we're taking along the freeway. I think about the enemies I've made during my time as a bounty hunter, and the threats I've gotten since. The realisation of who could be behind this slithers up my spine and into my mind like a copperhead.

I clench my fingers together. Grit my teeth beneath the tape.

I've seen the faces of the two men with shaved heads, and I'm clear about what they're capable of. If I'm right, if these men work for who I think they do, then my situation is way worse than a random abduction. If I want to live, I have to figure out a way to get free. I need to be ready. Stay vigilant for any opportunity. Because one thing's for sure: these men are playing this game for keeps.

If they get their way, I won't get out of this alive.

4

We take a right turn off the highway. The wheels judder across the uneven track. The muffler rattles louder. I wince as my ribs bash against the van floor. The men up front are talking in low voices. I figure we've reached our destination.

Minutes later we brake to a halt. Doors open. Heat floods the vehicle. There's shouting, new voices, then I feel hands grip my ankles and I'm yanked across the floor of the van and dumped onto the dirt outside.

They cut the hogtie but keep my wrists and ankles bound. As they haul me to my feet I feel sensation start to return to my limbs. Pins and needles stab at my muscles, waking the nerves that went numb hours ago. My mouth's as parched as a storm drain in the dry season. I could really use a drink.

Doesn't happen. My captors keep me gagged and hooded. Powerless. Disoriented. That tells me that they're still being careful, not taking chances. The hood blinds me to my surroundings, and if I can't see where I am, I can't figure out the best escape route.

'Barn two,' a man says. His accent has a hint of New York about it. I search my memory, but I come up empty. 'Get yourselves to the house when it's done.'

I inhale sharply. *When it's done* – what does that mean?

The hands grasping my arms lift me off my feet and drag me across the dirt. I want to fight back, but that's not the smart play here. I have to conserve my energy, pick my moment real careful. So I go limp, make them work harder at moving me. Tell myself to bide my time and hope to hell I have time to bide.

The guy on my right mutters under his breath about me being heavier than I look, and the one on my left grunts in agreement. Even through the hood I can smell his cheap cologne; it's vinegary and applied overzealously. The scent of a low-rank foot soldier aspiring towards a style they know nothing about.

They continue dragging me across the dirt.

I hear the distant clank of machinery. The sun's high and hot. This morning, in my hurry to get Dakota to class, I forgot to put on sunscreen, and now the rays burn my skin. The air is still, no hint of a breeze. I figure it must be near on lunchtime, and I wonder if JT is worried yet.

'Here?' the cologne-wearer says.

'Yeah.'

I smell them before I hear them. Way stronger than the cologne, and a whole lot nastier. Then I hear the stampede of cloven feet across baked earth, and the grunts and snuffles getting louder.

Pigs.

I tense. Dig my heels into the dirt and swallow hard. If they toss me into the pigpen I'm a goner for sure. Hooded, with my arms and legs bound, I'll stand no kind of chance against a herd of hungry swine, and, from the noise they're making, they sure sound hungry.

The guy to my right laughs and jabs me in the ribs with his elbow. 'You can smell 'em then, our little pets?'

I try to get my heart rate under control and think logically. It makes no sense to snatch me and drive all those hours just to feed me to these beasts. If they wanted to get me dead right off the bat then a bullet in the head would've done the job real nice. They're messing with me, but I don't think they're going to kill me, not at this moment anyways. So I force my body to relax, release my heels from the dirt and wait to see what happens.

We keep going, past the pigs and a few hundred yards further. Moments later, even through the material of the hood, I can tell from the change in light that we've passed from sunshine to shade. The stench of the pigs is replaced with sweet meadow hay. I figure we're inside barn two.

Seventeen steps later the men spin me around and push me backwards against a pillar. The wood is rough and splinters rub raw against my skin. Cologne guy holds me upright, as close to the pillar as he can make me, while the other one ties me. They use rope this time. I feel him loop it tight, around my neck, my waist and my legs. My wrists and ankles are still bound with the tape. They leave the hood on.

The one with the growly voice slaps me on the shoulder. 'See y'all later, blondie.'

'If you're lucky,' cologne guy adds.

I say nothing; the tape over my mouth is keeping me silent. I hear their footsteps retreat, and the bang of a door slamming shut. Then I'm alone.

It doesn't take long for the discomfort to set in. My muscles ache right from the get-go and before long they're burning from the forced immobility. My head throbs like a bitch. My mouth's dry and I feel nauseous – a sure sign of dehydration.

They've tied me real snug. I feel along the rope where it's closest to my hands, but there are no knots for me to try to loosen, and the tape around my wrists is too high for me to get a finger through. I bend my knees and try to slide down the pillar, but I'm stuck; the noose around my throat won't shift.

I'm all out of options. All I can do is wait.

Time passes. The fire in my muscles intensifies. The temperature rises and I sweat rivers, my clothes turning damp against my skin. I need the bathroom bad.

No one comes.

I withdraw inwards, using memories to distance myself from the pain. I think of how my morning began, and it seems like a world, a lifetime, away: waking snuggled against JT with the light streaming in through the window; his lopsided smile as I kiss him awake; the feel of him inside me as we make love in the shower – getting clean and being dirty all at once; then later JT, Dakota and me having breakfast – bagels, juice and coffee – JT and Dakota chattering about Tropicana Field, me smiling at the easy way they banter with each other. The concentration on JT's face as he tries to braid Dakota's hair for school; the way she thanks him even though his best effort is a clumsy, half-assed job. Me laughing and telling him practice makes perfect. Him looking at me all serious with those old blues of his and telling me he'll keep on practising; and how in that moment I knew he was talking about more than just the braids.

In the couple of months we've been playing house we've never made each other any promises. I've said before, a promise is just a disappointment bought on credit, but that don't mean I'm not curious, maybe even a touch hopeful, to see how things play out. I want to give us a chance. After everything we've been through, we owe ourselves that.

I clench my fingers together. Grit my teeth.

So, whatever else happens, there's one thing I'm sure about.

I refuse to die here.

5

WEDNESDAY, SEPTEMBER 19th, 16:58

I come to with a jolt.

I'm choking. Disorientated. Blind. I try to cough, but my lips are locked closed. I claw for my throat, but my hands won't move. By body feels numb, my limbs heavy and alien. Panic grips me. My pulse thumps in my ears. I can't get enough air.

A door bangs. Men's voices come closer.

'You still here, blondie?' one growls.

His mate laughs.

The stench of vinegar-like cologne makes me remember. I'm in a barn, held captive by these people; my mouth is forced shut by tape, there's a noose tight around my throat. My legs aren't supporting my weight and I've slumped forwards onto the noose – that's what's choking me. I coax my muscles into action and push back against the pillar, ignoring the bite of wood splinters in my flesh. The grip of the noose loosens a fraction and I inhale through my nose. Feel my heartbeat start to return back to normal and wonder how long I've been unconscious. Wonder what the hell will happen next.

I don't have to wait long to find out.

They release the noose, cut the tape around my ankles, and I drop to the ground, my legs too numbed by cramp to hold me. With my hands still bound behind my back there's no way to break my fall and I face-plant onto the dirt floor. The impact knocks the breath clean out of me.

The men laugh.

The growler prods me with his boot. 'On your feet.'

Asshole. I don't move. Refuse to flounder at their feet. I can't get up with my hands tied, and I can't tell them that because of the gag. They're going to have to figure it out for themselves.

It takes a minute, but they catch on. I can tell by the smell that it's cologne guy who hauls me to my feet. Shoving me in my back he says, 'Walk.'

I stumble forwards, but don't fall this time. Force one foot in front of the other, wobbly as a minutes-old colt. One of them grabs my arm and pulls me along faster. It's all I can do to stay upright.

We pass from the darkness of the barn back into the light, but the sun is weaker than before, and the heat's not as intense. I want to ask where we're going, but I can't. All I can do is keep going forwards as directed, hating the feeling of powerlessness.

The man on my left growls a command: 'Step up.'

I do as he says and my feet land on wood. The heels of my cowboy boots clonk across boards and I wonder if we're on a porch. A few steps later and I hear a door creak open. They push me inside.

I smell fresh bread and gardenia blooms and wonder where the hell I am. Cologne guy is still behind me, pushing. I keep walking.

'Stop.' Growler says, grabbing my elbow. 'This is you.'

I hear another door open, and Growler pulls me hard to the left. The door closes again, and I hear a bolt scraping across wood.

Growler releases my arm. 'Hold still now.'

I do as he says.

He removes the hood first. The light is unbearably bright and I snap my eyes shut, then start to blink rapidly, trying to adjust. Next he rips the tape from my mouth.

I inhale hard. Open my eyes. See I'm in a bathroom that's decorated in more shades of pink than I'd ever realised existed. 'What the—?'

'No cussing.' Growler cocks his head to one side. 'Ain't that kind of house.'

'You're kidding, right?' My voice is rasping. My throat's dry as the desert. 'It's okay for you to abduct me and hold me here as your captive, but damn me to hell if I dare to take the Lord's—'

The blow comes fast and hard to the side of my head. Oftentimes

I'd have moved with its momentum and stayed standing, but I'm too weak and groggy, so I crumple to the floor, landing on my ass on the fluffy bath mat.

Growler looks down at me. 'I warned you, this is no place for bad language.' Rubbing his knuckles, he shakes his head. Looks almost apologetic. 'This pains me as much as you. I sure do hate having to hurt a woman.'

I glare at him. My hands are still bound, but I feel around on the mat behind me, searching for anything I could use as a weapon. 'Trust me, honey. I've taken worse than your little-girl punch.'

He watches me a moment then shrugs. 'Guess that's okay then.'

I find nothing of use. Keep staring, appraising my enemy. Growler's about six foot tall and medium build, real tan with cropped dark hair, and older than I'd reckoned on – nearer fifty than thirty – wearing cargo pants and a white wife-beater with a plaid overshirt. I take note that underneath the shirt he's got a gun in a shoulder holster, and note the bulge around the left ankle of his pants – a back-up piece is strapped there, for sure.

'So what now?'

Growler doesn't answer. He steps behind me and kneels down. I tense. Get ready to scoot forwards. Then I hear the rip of tape and my wrists are free. I rotate my arms gingerly. Wince as I massage my wrists where the tape has cut into them.

I glance over my shoulder at Growler. 'You don't like to hurt women, huh?'

'Freshen up. There are clean towels in the closet and toiletries in the rack.'

'I'd rather you took me home.'

'Not my call. Right now, I need for you need to get washed and presentable.'

I shake my head. 'For what?'

He steps back around me, heading to the door. He raps on it twice in quick succession. As the bolt slides back, he turns to look at me. 'Do as you're told, and don't think about trying anything funny.' He nods towards the window. 'There're bars on the outside. You've got no way to get free.'

I wait until he's out of the room and the bolt's been drawn back into place on the outside of the door before I move, not wanting him to see how unsteady I am. Easing myself to my feet, I stagger forwards and grip the washbasin. My head's spinning, and my vision's blurred. I lied to Growler; his punch was pretty damn hard.

I splash cold water over my face. Feeling half crazed with thirst, I duck my head down and let the water run over my lips. I take a mouthful and swallow. Cough from the liquid hitting my parched throat, and spit it out. Try again, but it still makes me gag. I try smaller sips and manage to keep some water down.

There's banging on the door. 'Hurry up in there, you hear? Get in the shower.'

They're listening to me. I glance round the bathroom, wondering if they're watching too, but see no obvious cameras. It doesn't make sense, this change in the way they're managing me. Why tie me hooded in a stress position in the barn for hours without any interrogation, and then bring me into the house for a shower? It's like no kind of abduction technique that I've ever heard of.

The move inside this house has given me a bunch more information, and there are things bothering me a whole lot more now than when these men were treating me mean. This bathroom has bars on the window and a lock on the outside of the door. Unless it was put there for my benefit, it seems they have a habit of taking prisoners into this bathroom. And Growler saying he didn't like it when he had to hit women makes me think they could be in the business of abducting women against their will; sex trafficking. Making my abduction about my gender rather than me personally.

But that doesn't ring true. If my hunch about where we are geographically is right, then the people holding me dabble in sex trafficking, drugs and a whole lot more bad business. But the reason for them snatching *me*, and *my* being here, will be personal. Dead personal.

I shudder. The only way to know for sure is to play this through to the end.

Moving across the room to the closet, I open the doors. Inside it's stacked with towels, aligned into sizes and sorted by colour. I pick two red ones and close the closet. Stepping across to the corner closest the door, I fold my clothes into a pile on the wicker chair and step into the shower, pulling the smoked-glass screen closed behind me.

The shower is powerful. I let the water cascade over me, washing away the sweat and dust. I find shampoo in the rack and wash my hair. I'm rinsing away the soap when I hear a door bang. Spinning round, I peer through the glass, but it's too opaque and I see nothing. Heart thumping, I shut off the water and reach for a towel, wrapping it around me before opening the shower door.

The bathroom's empty, but someone has been inside.

My clothes and boots are gone. In their place on the wicker chair is a glass of orange liquid and a bag of cosmetics. Hanging from the mirror is a dress: a floaty, cute chiffon number with blue flowers on cream. There's a note pinned to it. Reaching out, I rip off the paper and read what it says.

Wear this. Make yourself pretty. You've got ten minutes.

6

Wear the dress. Look pretty.

This kind of sexist bullshit drives me bat-shit crazy. I pound on the bathroom door. 'Give me back my clothes. I'm not wearing a damn dress.'

I recognise cologne guy's snigger. 'It's the dress or nothing.'

Son-of-a-bitch. I'm tempted to go with nothing just to throw mud in their eye, but I know that could be inciting more trouble, and I'd do best to avoid that, given the situation. I towel myself dry and reluctantly put on the dress. It's low cut at the front and virtually backless; the skirt is long and will be difficult to run in, which is a problem, because I need to run.

I take a black eyeliner from the bag and draw it across my lids, trying to ignore that my hand is shaking. Staring into the mirror, I force myself to face the facts. Growler took off the hood, knowing that I'd see his face. I caught a glimpse of the two goons that lifted me outside the school too. People who go to all this effort – plan a snatch and grab this thoroughly – don't make rookie mistakes. I've seen their faces because they either meant me to, or it doesn't matter a dime. And the usual reason for it not to matter is because they don't intend me to leave this place alive.

I inhale hard. Drop the eyeliner into the make-up bag.

I've lived a life, several lives. I was the daughter of a violent father, the wife of a violent husband; oppressed by weak men who only knew how to express themselves with their fists. Now, at thirty-two years old, I'm living something close to the life I hoped for. I've got a successful career on my own terms; I'm mom to Dakota; I'm lover to JT. I don't want things to end. Not this way.

There's a bang on the door and I jump.

'You decent?' Cologne guy calls. He laughs. 'Don't matter none anyways, I'm coming in.'

I hear the bolt being scraped back. Blinking away the dampness in my eyes, I grab the flat glass dish that holds the soap and slip it into the back of my panties. It's not much, but it's something. Because, whatever they're planning to do to me, there's no way I'll go down without a fight.

The door opens.

Cologne guy lets out a long whistle. 'Well, would you look at that?'

'Enough already.' Growler pushes past him. He looks me straight in the eye. 'Put out your hands.'

He's holding a pair of metal handcuffs. Damn. He puts them on me and my options will be a hell of a lot more limited. Maybe I should make a move now. I calculate the odds. Two on one and they're both packing heat. I have an soapdish. Even with luck on my side those odds don't look good.

So I do as he asks and watch him snap the cuffs around my wrists. 'Where are you taking me?'

Cologne guy sniggers.

Growler shoots him a look. Glances back at me. 'You'll find out soon enough. Now move.'

They lead me out of the bathroom and along a hallway to the kitchen. The place is neat and clean, furnished in a traditional ranch-house style, with freestanding wooden dressers and a huge dining table in the centre of the kitchen where places are set for eighteen. In the middle of the table is a vase of gardenias.

This is a home, with family pictures on the walls and notes for a grocery run on the chalkboard beside the stove. I glance at the photos as we pass but I don't recognise anyone. What I do recognise are a lot of the locations: they're all in Miami.

Growler and cologne guy take me out through the back door. There are a bunch of vehicles – pick-ups, SUVs and Jeeps – parked around back, and I see four men stationed at a high gate positioned this end of the long driveway. They all have automatic weapons.

A ways ahead of us along a dirt path are four huge barns, but they don't lead me that way. Instead we hang a left across the yard and walk around the house to a paved sun deck screened off by a white picket fence and high hedge. Beside me I can feel the two men becoming tense.

Weird. I glance at Growler. 'You sure we're going the right way?'

'Quiet,' he says.

We walk in silence. I case out the surroundings, alert to any opportunity for escape. Aside from the gardens we seem to be surrounded by some paddock land, and then a dense forest of trees for as far as I can see. There's no other property in sight. I'd be crazy to try and make a break for it now and I'm betting my captors know it. Handcuffed, with no vehicle, my only choice would be to run into the trees. Chances are, in their numbers, with all the vehicles and firepower at their disposal, these men would shoot me easier than they could a raccoon in a trap. I figure I need to hold on a while longer.

As we reach the far side of the deck, cologne guy opens a gate, gesturing for me to go through. Only Growler comes with me. We walk around the end of the house and then I see it. I see *him*. And everything falls into place.

I halt abruptly.

'Keep it going,' Growler says, taking hold of my elbow and dragging me forwards. 'He doesn't like to be kept waiting.'

That maybe so, but I sure as shit am in no kind of hurry.

Across the vast swimming pool, on the far side of the veranda, a table has been set for two with white linen, silver cutlery, and china plates. As we move towards the table, the man sitting there looks up.

I clench my fists. We've never met, but I can guess who he is. He's in his seventies, trim with the straight posture of an elder statesman and black hair, greyed only a fraction around the temples. He's wearing a dark suit with a white short-sleeved shirt, but as a concession to the heat he's removed the jacket and draped it over the back of his chair.

He nods to Growler, who removes my cuffs. Then watches him turn and leave, only looking at me when we are entirely alone. He takes his napkin from his lap, folds it neatly on the table, and stands, fixing me with his gaze. 'Hello Jennifer Lorelli Ford.'

I frown, unsure how to interpret what's going on here; the dinner placement versus the undertone of menace. 'It's been a long time since I've gone by that name.'

'Time to revisit the past then, I'd say.' He gestures to the chair opposite him. 'Sit, please.'

I stay where I am. My hands are free and I figure I could overpower him easy enough. 'And if I don't?'

He gives a little smile and sits down. Picks up his napkin again and spreads it over his lap, smoothing it free of creases, before glancing pointedly towards the gate that I came through, and then over to another gate on the other side of the house. I follow his gaze and see both gates have a man with an AK-47 standing behind them. 'Then I'll be disappointed that you chose for things to get ugly.'

Outnumbered and outgunned, I step towards the table and sit down.

He nods. 'Good girl.'

Patronising bastard. I lean forwards, close my hand tight around one of the silver knives. 'I'm not anyone's *girl*. You had me snatched off the street, strung me up in your barn and are making me wear this damn dress.'

He winces as I cuss. Closes his eyes like he's in pain.

'I want to know why the hell I'm here.'

He shudders as I say the word 'hell', then his eyes snap open and for a moment he looks at me with undisguised fury. Then the emotion is gone, the fury replaced by a neutral mask. When he speaks his voice is low, and his tone dead serious. 'Well, Jennifer, the way I see it, we're overdue a talk about how you trapped and murdered one of my boys – Thomas Ford.'

He smiles at me, and in that moment I know for sure that I'm a dead woman walking.

7

WEDNESDAY, SEPTEMBER 19th, 18:01

It's not always easy to spot a mob guy. They don't all look stereotypical gangster, and it's not like they wear buttons shouting about their allegiance. The foot soldiers might get inked, but those higher up the food chain, they're a whole other ballgame. Respectable, that's what you'd think if you saw them. And that's what I've heard folks say about the man sitting opposite me, Old Man Bonchese – that he's nice and respectable. But they don't know what business he's in.

I do though, and it sickens me; the drugs and the girls, the clubs, casinos and sweet-sixteen massage parlours. He's been head of the Bonchese family for more than thirty years, ever since his papa was executed gangland-style outside one of their clubs. Under the Old Man's direction the Miami Mob's empire has grown ever bigger, and the business it does has gotten more twisted. No matter what he looks like, he's a monster. And from the way he's treating me, it's clear he enjoys playing with his prey before going for the kill.

He gestures towards the platter of shrimp on the table. 'Eat, please.'

I fake like I'm not hungry, even though my belly rumbles at the sight of the food. I want him to get to the point. 'Why the dress, don't you believe women should be allowed to wear pants?'

Old Man Bonchese takes a shrimp from the stack. He stares at it for a long moment before ripping off its head with a swift, brutal movement. Looks back to me. 'I'm all for female equality, but I wanted you to feel like a woman for this meal, just in case it's the last one you have. The dress is a gift. A kindness. From me.'

'I feel like a woman whatever I'm wearing.' He's talking crap. The dress robs me of my own clothes, ones far more suited to fighting my way out of this place. He's using it to try to control me; same with the use of my married name. He wants to delete the person I've become and turn me back into the girl Thomas Ford used to beat on. But it won't work. 'So what is it you want to say to me?'

The anger flares in his eyes again. 'Your Tommy was like a son to me, and like a brother to my eldest boy, Luciano. He was important to the family.'

I'd seen pictures of what my husband did for the Bonchese family; of the people he beat because they couldn't pay their gambling debts, and the body of a man he'd killed for them. JT was the bounty hunter sent to find Tommy when he skipped bail before the trial for that murder; that's how we met and the pictures were what convinced me to help him. But Tommy found out and came back to take revenge for my betrayal.

'Tommy killed my friend, Sal,' I say. 'Shot her at point-blank range because she was calling the cops when he started beating on me. She was only seventeen – just a kid – but he didn't hesitate to pull that trigger.'

'Regrettable, I'm sure, but not really of my concern.'

I feel rage building in my chest. Clench my fists. I trained as a bounty hunter with JT so that I could find Tommy and take him to jail to serve time for what he did. 'He had to pay for what he did.'

'So you murdered him in cold blood.'

I shudder. Remember standing in the back yard of the cabin where we'd tracked Tommy. JT went in through the front but something went wrong. Tommy escaped through the back, and I was blocking his exit. When he saw me, he laughed. Said he didn't care none that he'd killed Sal. Lunged for me, saying that now it was my time to die.

'It was him or me. I shot him in self-defence.'

He narrows his eyes. 'Way I heard it was you emptied your gun into him.'

I hold the Old Man's gaze as the memory of Tommy's bloodied, bullet-riddled body slumping onto the dirt replays in my mind. Clasp my hands together to hide that they're shaking. 'I had to be sure.'

He closes his eyes and exhales hard. 'And so it's true what my son tells me: you were the one who killed Tommy. It wasn't the bounty hunter who claimed to have done it.'

I nod. JT had taken the rap for me, and had got a price on his head from the Miami Mob as a result, but I hadn't known that until ten years later. Recently though, the mob had somehow discovered I was the shooter. 'Yes.'

'Then the way I see things, it's just like the good Lord said – an eye for an eye. And that's what I want.'

An eye for an eye; my life in revenge for Tommy's. I slide my right hand across the tablecloth and clench my fingers around the knife. Think of my baby girl Dakota, waiting for me at home with JT, and know I have to try and get free and clear now, whatever the odds.

The Old Man sighs. 'I do hope you're holding that knife so you can butter your dinner roll.' He glances up towards the house. 'Aside from the sentries on the gates, my grandson, Angelo, has his gun trained on your back from the window of his bedroom on the second floor. Tommy was his hero. He took it hard when he disappeared. Angelo believes in an eye for an eye too.'

I keep hold of the knife. 'Then why haven't one of you killed me already?'

The Old Man sighs. 'My son, Luciano, sees things differently.'

I hold his gaze as I ease my feet out of my sandals, figuring it'll be easier to run barefoot than in these heels. 'How so?'

'Luciano is perhaps a little less traditional – he takes things less literally.' He picks up the headless shrimp from his plate, pulls off the tail and dips the fleshy pink body into cocktail sauce. 'He thinks you can pay your debt another way.'

'I'm listening.'

Old Man Bonchese puts the shrimp into his mouth and chews slowly. I wait, keeping my hand tight around the knife. He seems unbothered.

Swallowing the food, he dabs his mouth with a napkin before he speaks. 'Find Carlton North and bring him back to us.'

I frown. 'And who's he?'

'Someone who's somewhere they shouldn't be. Find him. Luciano says it should be within your capabilities.'

I remember the photographs of Tommy beating the gambler to death. If I did what the Old Man's asking that would most likely be Carlton North's fate. 'Find some guy just so you can kill him?' I shake my head. 'Honey, that dog just won't hunt. I want no part in anything like that.'

The Old Man looks at me as though I'm a backward child. 'I don't want North *dead* – he's my numbers man, I need him. But the FBI snatched him and have got their mind set on forcing him to take the stand against our cousins in Tallahassee around some unpleasantness with our accountant. The cousins acted badly, but North mustn't speak against them. It will cause a nasty situation – a split in the family. I can't have that happen.'

'So you do want him stopped?'

'I want *them* stopped and North back where he belongs. Here. He's like my son too.'

I stare at him, trying to fathom whether he's feeding me a line or the truth about his motives for wanting to find Carlton North. 'Seems a lot of people are like your son.'

'We're a family here, loyal to the death.' He takes another shrimp, beheading and detailing it before dipping it into the sauce and eating it. He gestures to me as he chews. 'We stick together, whatever the cost, and that's something you clearly have no concept of.' He looks genuine, but looks can be faked for sure.

'So I find him. Then what?'

'Bust him free of FBI custody, and bring him back here. The trial where he's due to give evidence starts Friday. He needs to be out before then.'

'That doesn't give me long.'

'Find a way.'

'You know where they're holding him?'

'If I did I wouldn't need you.'

I shake my head. 'I don't think...'

The Old Man reaches behind him into the pocket of his jacket, which is draped over the back of the chair, and pulls out a photo. He places it on the table facing me. I inhale hard. It's Dakota and JT. They're walking towards our apartment. Dakota is carrying her school bags, and JT has her planets science project tucked under his good arm.

I look up at Bonchese. 'You took this today.'

'This afternoon, yes.' He taps the photo with his index finger. 'I don't enjoy ugliness, but I need you to understand how serious I am. Like I said, Carlton North is like a son to me. You get him free and bring him back, and I'll consider your debt paid. A son saved for one lost. A twist on an eye for an eye.'

'And if I don't?'

'You die.' He takes another shrimp. Eats it before he speaks again. 'And your family dies too.'

8

They say you can't run from your past, and it's true, especially when the past is a murdering, unforgiving asshole. I hold the Old Man's gaze for a long moment. Think on my options – find Carlton North or sign a death warrant for me and my family. Whatever way I look at it, I'm over a barrel on this. So, reluctantly, I nod. 'Okay.'

He looks towards the house and raises his hand.

I hear a screen door open and shut, followed by footsteps approaching. Turning in my chair, I see a figure walking towards us. Tall, with dark, artfully mussed-up hair and wearing a designer suit, this man looks more model than mobster.

'My eldest, Luciano,' says the Old Man. There's pride in his voice.

Luciano nods at me. Stays standing and gets straight to business. 'We don't know exactly where the FBI have North but we expect it's somewhere in the Tallahassee area. He was grabbed six days ago from downtown Fort Lauderdale when he was visiting with some of our associates there. The word is the Feds have been moving him every day since then. We had a sighting at a motel in Ocala two nights ago, but if they were there, they'd cleared out by the time our men arrived next morning.'

I ignore the hostility in Luciano's voice. Concentrate on getting the intel I need to get the job done. 'So tell me about North.'

'Like I said, he's our numbers man,' The Old Man says. 'He's been with the family since he was a kid, like his daddy before him. Luciano and him grew up together. He's part of us. When his father passed, just before his tenth birthday, I took him in. He's been like a son to me ever since, and a brother to Luciano.'

Was it my imagination or did Luciano look tense when the Old Man talked fondly of North? I look up at him. 'Any rivalry between you "brothers"?'

Luciano doesn't meet my eye. 'No. Never.'

From the way he's acting, I'm not so sure. I raise an eyebrow.

Luciano ignores it, his expression unchanging. 'North knows everything about our business, all the financials. We need him.'

I understand. A man with the full picture of what's going on in the family business would make for a valuable FBI asset. I can see why Bonchese wants North out of the FBI's custody. 'You got a picture?'

Luciano pulls a folded photo from his pants pocket and hands it to me.

Unfolding it, I inhale hard. Look up at Luciano then to the Old Man. '*This* is Carlton North?'

'Yep,' Luciano says. 'Why, you recognise him?'

I stare at the black-haired guy in the picture and nod. It was a long while ago, back when I was married to Tommy – when he was hitting both the drink and me hard – but at one time Carlton North oftentimes used to drop round our trailer. I didn't know his name and Tommy said they had business together, but I never knew what kind of business. I guess now I do.

One time, maybe just a few months before Tommy killed my friend Sal, North came around when Tommy was out. He found me bleeding; Tommy had lost a big stack of chips gambling all through the night and had gotten home that morning in a bad mood. He'd smashed my head into the kitchen cabinet when I asked him about the game, and then took off. North arrived soon after. He was kind to me. Helped me get cleaned up, and said what Tommy did wasn't right. He gave me his number and told me to call him if I needed out.

That was the last time I saw him. I remember he was wearing mirrored shades and a leather jacket – maybe the same one he has on in this picture. I stare at his image. Ten years on, him and the jacket are a little more weathered, but still looking good. I glance back at Luciano. 'He was a friend of Tommy's.'

'Yeah,' Luciano says. His tone's hard and there's a muscle pulsing in his jaw. 'Tommy was a popular guy.'

I say nothing.

He shakes his head. Leaning forwards, he scribbles something onto the top of the picture and hands it back to me. 'When you find North, text me on this number before you go in to get him. If you get dead in the process, I want my people en route to have a second go.'

I fold the photo over and tuck it into my bra. 'Thanks for the vote of confidence. Are we done?'

The Old Man clears his throat. 'There's one more thing. You must do this alone. No JT. No other people flanking you when you break North out. Just you.'

'Why the hell...?'

'Because doing this is like a penance – a test to see if you're worthy of redemption.'

Well, shit. 'I don't need redemption.'

'Yeah you do,' Luciano says, his tone heavy with contempt. 'If you want this family to let you stay alive.'

⌒

Luciano walks me out. We leave the Old Man poolside, working on his shrimp, and head back around the side of the house towards the makeshift parking lot. As we round the corner I see my Jeep parked up beside the van I arrived in as a captive.

'You brought my car?'

'Figured you'd need your wheels,' says Luciano. 'If you took the job.'

'You got my purse too?' I glance down at the dress I'm wearing. 'And my clothes?'

'On the passenger seat.'

'Good.' I reach out and open the driver's side door then turn to Luciano. 'I'll do what I can to get North back.'

He shrugs. There's venom in his tone as he says, 'It doesn't matter to me so much as the Old Man. Way I see it I'll win either way. You find North for us, I win. If you don't, I get to kill you.' He smiles, but it doesn't reach his eyes. 'So I'm still winning.'

I've got no words. I climb into the Jeep and slam the door behind me. Firing up the engine, I pull out through the heavily guarded gateway and hustle along the dirt drive, keen to put miles between me and the godforsaken Bonchese family. As I turn onto the highway something occurs to me, and despite the heat I feel goose bumps spread across my flesh.

If Luciano figures he'll win, whether or not I succeed in bringing back North, then he can hardly give a damn for his so-called brother. If that's the case, why did he persuade the Old Man to send me to do this job?

I remember how Luciano looked twitchy when the Old Man said North was like family. There's something going on – jealousy, rivalry of some kind. Shit. I just want to find North and bring him back here, so I can get back to my family. Whatever's going on between Luciano and North, I hope to hell I'm not the one that gets caught in the crosshairs.

9

WEDNESDAY, SEPTEMBER 19th, 19:11

I pull over at the first rest stop I see. Grabbing my purse, I head into the store and get two bottles of water and a bag of corn chips. Back in the Jeep I eat as I trawl through my cell messages. Four texts from Dakota and a voicemail – each more worried than the last, asking why I'm not at school to pick her up, am I on my way, that she's gone back inside – the last saying JT is coming to get her and why aren't I answering.

I lose count of the voicemails JT's left.

I feel all kinds of awful to have put my baby through stress. I message her, apologising for leaving her hanging, telling her that I was on a job that went on longer than it should and that there was no cell reception. I feel bad for the lie, but I can't tell her the truth. She'll be mad at me, I know, but it's better than the alternative. I don't want her getting more worried.

The next message I send is to JT. I'm honest with him, but I don't want to get into a conversation. I need to tell him about the deal with the Old Man face to face, and right now I just want to be home. So I keep my message brief:

Snatched from outside D's school by Miami Mob. Taken to the Old Man's place. Forced into job. On way home now, will tell all when back xx

My cell starts ringing less than ten seconds after I press send. I stare at JT's name flashing on the screen before rejecting the call. I can't do this now. Not when I'm pretty sure I know how he's going to react.

A minute later a message comes through from him: *Okay.*

He always is economical with his words, but I can't help but feel irritated that he hasn't even asked me how I am. After everything I've been through today, I could do with a little bit of sympathy.

Eating the last of my corn chips, I think on my next move. By the time I get home it'll be late. Realistically I'll have a maximum of thirty hours to find Carlton North and get him out from under the FBI. Not easy. To make this work I'm going to need help. Sure the Old Man said I had to break North out on my own, but although this might be a solo mission, he didn't say I couldn't get others to feed me intel. Right now, there are two people I can think of who might be able to get me a location for North. One of them – Red, the retired private investigator who's helped me out on a job on more than one occasion – I'd trust with my life; the other – Alex Monroe – I trust a whole lot less than a gator with an empty belly.

Never trust no one, JT always says. That rule was written because of people like Special Agent Alex Monroe. But he's FBI and he owes me a favour for an off-the-books assignment I did, so I make the call to him first.

He answers after the third ring. His Kentucky drawl is as strong as ever. 'Lori Anderson? This is a surprise.'

'I need some information.'

'Yeah,' says Monroe. There's the sound of fingers tapping on keyboards and conversations in the background. 'And I need your help with that Chicago job I told you about, but I'm not noticing any answer being forthcoming on that.'

I'd been avoiding Monroe, putting off giving him an answer ever since he'd asked me to go to Chicago and help him with a sting to incriminate the head of the Chicago Mob.

'You owe me,' I say.

'And if I help you now, you'll owe me again.'

'Yeah.'

'So what is it you want?'

'I need the location of a federal witness, Carlton North. He's in protective custody for—'

'Shit, Lori, that's classified. What the hell are you up to?' There's rustling and Monroe's silent a while. The background noise switches from office sounds to quiet. When he speaks, the room he's in gives his voice an echo. 'North's Miami Mob. He's giving evidence about the family.'

I pick at the label on my water bottle. Just need Monroe to agree already. 'Yeah, under duress.'

'That's usually the only way men like that talk. Anyways, if he wasn't inclined to speak we couldn't make him.'

'I'm not the public, Monroe. I know how you guys work. Waterboarding and the rest can have a very persuasive effect on a person.' I take a breath, and soften my tone. 'Look, I need that location. You owe me, and you know why.'

There's a pause. Monroe knows I've got dirt on him. There's enough to sink his bureau career, and most likely put him in jail for a good while. We both know he wouldn't fair well inside.

'I'm not going to like what you'll do with the intel, am I?'

I rip the label off the water bottle. Scrunch it between my fingers. 'Unlikely.'

'Then I'm going to need you to agree to do something for me. Say you'll work the job in Chicago.'

Shit. I never want to work with Monroe again; the last time near killed me. But what choice do I have? He's got access to the data I need. With the time pressure I'm under, he's the best option I've got to help me find North. 'Get me North's location and I'll help you in Chicago.'

'Good. I'll see what I can do, but no promises.'

'I need it fast, Monroe.' I try not to let him hear the desperation in my voice. 'I'm on the clock here.'

'I'll be in touch as soon as I have something.'

I hang up and take a long swig of water. My throat's still burning from all the hours without drinking, my head's thumping and my body aches. Ignoring it, I fire up the Jeep's engine and pull out of the parking lot and onto the highway.

I have to get home and talk to JT. I need him in my corner on this job, and from his one-word message I'm thinking that isn't going to be easy.

Putting my foot on the gas, I push the Jeep up to the speed limit. I've a few hours on the road to get back home. By the time I arrive I hope I'll have figured out how to talk JT around to my way of seeing things. Because, even though I hate it, I have to do this job.

10

WEDNESDAY, SEPTEMBER 19th 22:54

I park in the lot and make my way up to our second-floor apartment. The concrete steps feel like a mountain. Every muscle in my body's got tight; it's all I can do to put one foot in front of the other.

Krista's place is closest to the steps. Her lights are on, the drapes open. As I pass, I see her teenaged son and his friends huddled around the television, X-box controllers in their hands, and hear them whooping and laughing as they shoot things on the screen. I think back to my captors, of Growler packing heat with his shoulder holster and ankle strap, and shudder. Virtual guns are a lot more fun than those in real life.

The blinds in my apartment's front window are drawn, but light leeches from around the edges. Putting my key in the lock, I take a deep breath and open the door. It's quiet inside; no sign of Dakota or JT. I close the door behind me and slip off the sandals I'm still wearing.

Before I take a step JT appears at the end of the hallway, big and sexy as hell, in jeans and a black tee, his dirty-blond hair a little on the long side and flopped down over his forehead. Our eyes meet and he frowns.

'JT, I—'

'Godammit, Lori.'

He takes seven strides, and then he's standing in front of me. Kissing me on the lips, he pulls me into a bear hug. I wince as he squeezes me tight.

'Where's Dakota?' I ask.

'In bed. She was worried until you messaged, but after that she was fine.'

I pull away slightly and look up at him. 'Thanks for getting her from school. They took my cell. I had no way of letting you know what'd—'

'No problem.' His expression is full of concern. 'What the hell happened?'

'They jumped me outside the school, shoved me into a van and bound and gagged me. Drove a few hours to the Old Man's place down near Miami and kept me captive in a barn for most of the day. Then they took me inside the house and made me freshen up and put this on.' I gesture to the flower-print dress I'm still wearing. 'And then I met the Old Man himself.'

JT's jaw is tense. He doesn't try to contain the anger in his voice. 'And what did he want?'

I exhale and use Old Man Bonchese's words. 'An eye for an eye. He knows I was the one who killed Tommy and he wants revenge, but his son, Luciano, persuaded him that there's another way. They want me to break their numbers man, Carlton North, out of FBI protective custody.'

'I sure hope you told them to go to hell.'

'You think I'd be here if I had?'

We stare at each other a long moment. Neither of us speak.

JT shakes his head. 'Shit, Lori. You can't—'

'I said I'd do it.'

He runs his fingers across his stubble. 'Why'd you go and do that?'

'Because they said they'd kill me if I didn't, and then they'd come after you and our daughter.'

'Well, shit, going after North is a suicide mission.'

I don't disagree. 'I've already spoken to Monroe. He's going to get me the location where they're holding North.'

JT cusses under his breath. 'You can't be serious? Now you're trusting that double-crossing son-of-a-bitch?'

'No, I'm not trusting him.' I harden my tone. 'I'm using him for his intel.'

'But at what cost?'

I don't want to get into that with JT right now. 'He owes me.'

JT's silent a long moment. Then he nods. 'Well, if this is happening, I'm coming with you.'

I put my hand on his arm. 'No. I have to do this alone.'

'You can't, Lori. Going in on your own – that's crazy talk. If North is a federal witness against the mob the Feds will be expecting trouble. He'll be heavily guarded with proper firepower. You go in alone and they'll shoot you to shit.'

'It's the way it's got to be – the Old Man's orders.' There's another reason too; one I'm not going to say to JT. It's only seven weeks since he was stabbed. He's still recovering from the punctured lung, the cracked ribs and the heart attack that trauma induced. I can't let him come with me. He's not strong enough. 'I'm going alone.'

'It can't happen that way.'

'Why, don't you think I can take care of myself? I managed without you just fine for the last ten years.' As soon as the words are out of my mouth, I regret them. I reach towards him. 'JT, I didn't—'

He steps back. Shrugs my hand away. 'Sounds like your mind's made up. Guess you best go get yourself ready.'

I can tell from the stubborn tilt of his chin and the look in his eye that there's no sense trying to talk to him. He's hurt by my comment, and it's sent him retreating back into himself. He's always been a man of few words, but at times like this he becomes a man of none. Right now, I wish he'd get over that.

I walk past him, along the hallway to our bedroom. Stepping inside, I drop my purse onto the floor and lean back against the closed door. It's been a hell of a day ... and this is just the beginning.

I plug my cell in to charge, and step over to the closet. Opening the doors, I reach down and pull out my footlocker. Inside is my battered but serviceable brown leather carryall – the 'go bag' I've used ever since I started in the bounty-hunting business. Lifting it out, I unzip the front section and check my equipment: my leather rig, a canister of extra-strong pepper spray, three sets of plasticuffs, a roll of twenties totalling five hundred bucks. I put the bag onto the bed and kneel down. At the bottom of the footlocker is my lock box. I take the key from my necklace and unlock it then lift out my X2 Taser and my Wesson Commander Classic Bobtail. I don't like carrying a weapon, but I've got a permit, and on my more recent jobs I've learned it's better to have it with me than to be in a situation where I regret not taking it.

I put the footlocker away, then peel off the dress that Bonchese made me wear, drop it into the trash and head to the shower. After I've freshened up I fix my hair and make-up and dress in my own clothes – jeans, blue tee, cowboy boots and leather jacket. I add clean panties and an extra change of clothes to my go bag. Then, taking my wallet from my purse and unplugging my cell, I put both into the pockets of my jacket.

Catching sight of my reflection as I walk past the mirror, I pause. There are dark circles beneath my eyes and a bruise is developing across my right temple; souvenirs of my time at the Bonchese place. Shit. Is JT right – am I making a mistake? I shake my head. Need to get this done. I pick up my go bag and carry it out into the hallway.

JT's waiting. He glances at my bag. Frowns. 'You're leaving right away?'

'North is due in court Friday morning. I don't have long to find him.' I step towards JT. Soften my tone. 'Look after our baby.'

He keeps frowning, disappointed. 'Yep.'

This isn't the way I want to leave, but what choice do I have? If I don't get Carlton North free of the FBI then this – JT, Dakota and me – will be at risk. Even if we ran, we'd never escape the Miami Mob. It's better this way. This way the price on our heads, the need to look over our shoulders all the time, goes away. Then we might have a real chance at being a family.

'Tell Dakota I had to go out on a job. Tell her I love her.'

He tenses as I say the word 'love' and I turn away. His feelings for me are strong enough, I think, but he won't tell me he loves me. He never does. The way I get around the pain of that is to never say it to him. Someone you care for not saying they love you back, why, that's more painful than a sucker punch to the heart.

I turn when I reach the door. 'I'll be seeing you then.'
He nods. Says nothing. The silence hangs thick between us.
I push the door open and escape into the night.

11

WEDNESDAY, SEPTEMBER 19th, 23:47

I head for Tallahassee. The heat of the day has gone, replaced with cooler night air. I turn off the air conditioning and wind down the Jeep's windows, hoping – Lord willing, and the creek don't rise – that the freshness will keep me alert.

It's an easy enough drive. Straight down I-75 and I-10. I turn the radio loud; perhaps the country music will stop me thinking on the look on JT's face as I left and the fact I'm missing my baby girl real bad already. I put my foot on the gas. At this time, with no traffic, I should reach Tallahassee by four.

I keep driving.

Later, a little ways past Madison, I see a rest stop and pull off the highway. The place looks deserted. The small store straight ahead is closed. There's a low-rent motel on the far side of the parking lot – the cream paint's flaking off the walls and some of the room numbers are missing. There are no lights on, which makes me doubt they're taking customers at this time of night, so I swing the Jeep into a space in the far corner of the lot between two sixteen-wheelers.

It's near on three-thirty. Still dark, and will be for a while yet. I take a swig of water and check my messages. I've got nothing new. There's no sense in getting any closer at this point. I need a location, and I need some rest. One of those things depends on Monroe, the other I can do something about.

I wind up the windows and set the alarm on my cell. Inclining my seat back, I stretch out as far as I can and close my eyes. My body aches, and my head's pounding. I try to ignore the pain and, after a while, start to feel myself drifting into sleep. I just hope Monroe has something for me by morning.

My alarm wakes me at seven a.m. The sun's coming up and it's starting to get warm inside the Jeep. I wind down the windows and take a long drink of water. I'm almost out. My head's still pounding, and I could do with the bathroom. I wonder if the store is open yet.

Getting out of the Jeep, I stretch and walk out past the trucks. Across the lot the store has lights on inside. I take that as a positive sign. Going back to grab my go bag, I lock the Jeep and stride towards the store. There's movement over by the motel, a couple of guys in shorts and ball caps are standing outside one of the rooms, mugs and cigarettes in hand. My stomach rumbles and I get a sudden yearning for coffee.

A bell jangles as I push open the door. It's an old-style place – mom and pop rather than chain owned. I'm relieved to see they have fresh coffee brewing behind the counter, ready to serve in go cups. I use the restroom first, freshen up as best I can and run my fingers through my hair to smooth it tidy. Then I pick out some supplies: more bottled water, a bagel for breakfast and some snacks. I find a map of Tallahassee and the surrounding area in the gift section and pop that into my basket too. I pay for my items and add a large black coffee to go.

As I head away from the counter I feel my cell buzz in my pocket. I put the bag down and pull out my cell. It's a message from Monroe: *Call me.*

12

THURSDAY, SEPTEMBER 20th, 07:37

Back at the Jeep, I call Monroe. 'You got something?'

'Good morning to you too,' he says, at this hour of the morning his Kentucky drawl a little more gravelly than usual. 'Where are you at?'

'On my way to Tallahassee.' I'm vague on purpose. I might need Monroe for his intel, but I sure as hell don't trust him. I don't want him knowing my location, because, although I'm pretty sure I've got enough dirt on him to make him play straight with me, if he does decide to flip the tables, I don't want him being able to tell his colleagues exactly where I am. 'What've you got?'

'Missingdon.'

'What?'

'The place they're going to be holding your friend, Carlton North, tonight. It's a small town about thirty miles from Tallahassee. They stayed somewhere else last night; they'll move him this morning.'

Grabbing the map I bought at the store, I spread it out across the passenger seat and scan the area around Tallahassee. I find Missingdon – a blink-and-you'll-miss-it town located part way between Waukeenah and Hampton Springs. 'Where are they staying?'

Monroe exhales hard. 'Now that I don't know.'

'Not good enough, I need a—'

'Wait up a moment, y'hear? The way it works is there's always three potential places the agents with a witness will chose from. There'll be bookings made at all three, then the agents in the field will make the decision en route about which to use. They don't tell anyone central their decision.'

Damn. 'What time are they moving him?'

'I don't know for sure, but usually they'd leave at check-out time and get to the new place a little after check-in opens. They won't want to risk the room not being ready and having to wait in the lobby.'

I nod. What he says makes sense. 'You got names for the three places?'

'Sure.' There's a rustle of paper, then Monroe continues. 'Hampton Lodge, Korda Motel, Missingdon Suites. They're all independent, no chains.'

Using a pen from the cupholder in the dash, I jot down the three names. 'So how do I figure out which he's at?'

'The places have been reserved by a pen-pusher in the office, not someone with boots-on-the-ground experience of the area. That means the three places are, in theory, what we need for a safe space, but the reality could be different. The agents with Carlton North will choose whichever one has most of the attributes on the list.'

'What list? Can you email me a copy?'

Monroe gives a hollow laugh. 'It's not an actual list, least I've not seen it written anywhere, but it's the things we know are needed to give us the best chance at guarding our witness.'

'So tell me.'

'Okay, so on this the FBI are predictable. If there's no permanent safe house available they'll look for somewhere that's mid-range and busy enough that they can blend in with vacationers. They'll need a room that has more than one potential exit – window, balcony, whatever – and have it located where they can get out fast to the parking lot. They'll want a good vantage point, so they'll only go for ground-level rooms if they're impossible to avoid. And they'll book three rooms in a row and use the central one for the witness.'

I make a mental note of the points as I repeat them back. 'Mid-range. Busy. Multiple exits. Vantage point. Got it.'

'As soon as they're in, they'll aim to set up some kind of counter-surveillance. Could be rudimentary, depending on their budget and time available, but you'll need to operate as if they have basic motion detectors and cameras in place.'

I nod to myself. 'That'll make getting close hard.'

'Yup.'

I think for a moment. I'm going to have to access each of the three locations that Monroe has given me, narrow it to one and do a more detailed search to try to find Carlton North, all undetected. 'So the agents with North, they'll aim to blend in with the other folks staying at the place, no suits?'

'They could be in suits. It depends.'

I glance in the rearview mirror at the parking lot behind. It's busier now, more people travelling meaning more people visiting the restrooms and the store. Turning my attention back to Monroe I say, 'On what?'

'The type of place. If there's people in suits there, they'll probably keep them on. The agents with him won't be undercover guys. They're used to dressing a certain way for work and they're like anyone else – they like the familiar. But if they'd stick out in suits they'll change, probably into hastily bought stuff.'

'Good to know. What about numbers; you got any idea how many of them they'll be?'

Monroe whistles. 'That's a piece-of-string question. It depends how much of the threat they think is out there. But seeing as your guy is a mob insider, I'm thinking they'll be cautious. Oftentimes two agents would be the charm, but there could be more. It's—'

'As long as a piece of string?' I shake my head. He doesn't know, that's real clear. 'I guess I'll learn that when I find them.'

'That's all I can give you, Lori. You're on your own now.'

He's right, but that don't make no difference. 'I always am.'

13

THURSDAY, SEPTEMBER 20th, 07:43

As I fire up the Jeep's engine, I think on what Monroe's told me. I need to get to Missingdon and work out which of the three places he's told me about the field agents with Carlton North have chosen. Then I need to break North out. I glance at the clock on the dash – it's almost a quarter of eight. That means I've got a little over twenty-four hours to get this done.

On the freeway, I stick to the speed limit and finish the coffee from the rest-stop store. The traffic's pretty clear at this time, and I make the drive in just over an hour, arriving into Missingdon a little before nine.

As I drive on in, I pass a wooden sign to my right bearing the words *Welcome to Missingdon – Home to the Wild*. It's faded and weather-worn, but the grass has been cut around it, and wildflowers bloom pink and blue around its posts. Keeping my foot gently nudging the gas, I coast into town.

Like I thought when I looked at it on the map, it's a real 'blink and you'll miss it' kind of place. Nestled into the side of the Aucilla Wildlife Management Area, vacationers here are most likely looking to get back to nature – going hiking and exploring rather than partying. I think on what Monroe said about the Feds and their fondness for suits; if they keep them on in this place, they'll stick out like a steer in a herd of mustangs.

The main street takes me towards downtown. I see a few homes dotted along the way, a sign for Zed's Autos that points along a dusty dirt track appearing just inside the town boundary, in a gap between the trees lining the highway, and another sign for Zimmer's which gives no clue to the nature of their business.

Rather than continuing straight downtown, I hang a left along the imaginatively called Boundary Road at the corner of Sixth, to circle around and get the lay of the land. A full circuit of the town takes me all of twenty minutes. What I learn is that the homes here are well kept – lawns neat, driveways tidy – but none are new builds. Their white and cream stucco façades gleam cleanly in the morning sunshine, the areas around their front porches filled with plants and flowers. Over medium-height fences I can see that some back yards have swing sets. But nothing about this place stands out or looks out of place; it's too everyman, too vanilla.

Places like this, they make me feel uneasy.

I head back downtown. There's a little more street traffic here and a few people on the sidewalks. Most of the businesses are positioned on the roads flanking a square of neat-kept grass, with a few benches and a large paved area where twenty or so fountain jets are firing water ten feet into the air in a synchronised display like a budget version of the dancing fountains at the Bellagio. A couple of young kids are playing chicken with the jets, their moms watching from the safety of the grass.

Slowing the Jeep to twenty miles an hour, I scan the shop fronts closest to me: there are a couple of grocery places, a hardware store, a laundromat and a bar. On the opposite side of the square I spot real-estate offices, a beauty salon and a diner. My cellphone's battery is dying, so I park the Jeep in a space outside Joe's Diner and head inside.

It's a basic set-up: no booths, and the wooden tables and chairs blend in with the cream, marble-effect linoleum floor, the pale-cream walls and brown wooden blinds.

A fifty-something lady in a checked yellow dress and white apron steps out from behind the greeter's desk and approaches me, a broad smile on her pink-lipsticked mouth. 'Welcome to Joe's, table for one?'

Her name badge says *Cherie*. I return her smile. 'Yes please.'

She leads me across the diner, past a family group – two parents and two kids, who are fighting about pancake toppings, and a guy on his own reading a newspaper – and gestures towards the empty tables at the window. 'Any preference?'

I pick one with an uninterrupted view of the door and the window, and a power outlet beside it. I hold up my cell. 'Is it okay if I charge this?'

Cherie smiles again. 'Sure, no problem. Menus are on the table. I'll be back once you're settled to take your order. Would you like some coffee while you're deciding?'

'That'd be great.'

As I sit down she moves across to the service counter and collects a pot of coffee. Returning, she fills my mug. 'Just holler when you'd like a refill.'

'You can count on it,' I say. Taking the menu from behind the little china vase of yellow gerberas, I scan the food for something that'll give me energy for my hunt. I've been lucky getting food so far, but once I'm back on the road I can't guarantee when the next opportunity will come. So, although I'm not massively hungry, I order pancakes and bacon.

As Cherie tells me I've made a good choice and bustles off to put my order in I scan the diner. Less than a third of the tables are occupied – by a mix of vacationers and people who look like office workers getting in a good breakfast before starting the day.

Pulling the charger from my go bag, I plug it in and set my cell to charge. There's a sign on the wall giving the wi-fi password, so I log in and open the internet browser. Googling each of the places on the FBI's list of accommodation options for this town – Hampton Lodge, Korda Motel, and the Missingdon Suites – I check out their websites. Like Monroe said, they all seem to be mid-range, non-chain places. It's hard to tell whether they fulfil the other criteria, though, which means I'm going to have to visit each one.

According to its website, the Hampton Lodge check-in opens at noon, the others both at two. I glance at my watch; it's almost nine-thirty. Realistically that gives me just over two hours to recon the three places and make a decision about which I think is the most likely candidate for housing Carlton North.

Cherie comes over. 'You all done here?'

I nod.

She nods towards my half-empty coffee mug. 'Want a refill?'

'No, thanks, I'm good.'

I think about how Monroe said the Feds like a place with a good occupation level, to allow them to come and go without standing out. I figure that, in a town like this, that'll more likely than not be the most popular place.

I look up at Cherie as she's turning away. 'I'm looking for a place to stay. Where would you recommend?'

She thinks for a moment, head cocked to one side, her hand on her hip. 'Hampton Lodge. Out-of-towners seem to like it and they have smoking rooms as well as non-smoking.'

'Thanks.' I smile. 'Can I get the check please?'

As I watch her stride away I decide Hampton Lodge will be the first place on my list to visit. Smoking rooms aren't the norm these days, but I know someone who might well appreciate one.

Back when I knew him, Carlton North smoked thirty Camels a day.

14

THURSDAY, SEPTEMBER 20th, 09:54

I find Hampton Lodge on the edge of town closest to the wildlife management area. Set back from the road, with the parking lot in the front, it's a two-storey motel set-up. Pulling into the lot, I park a little ways along from the lobby and get out.

The place seems pretty quiet. In the lobby there's a couple of people in line waiting to check out, but there's no bustle about the place and the ageing guy in the black wife-beater and chinos behind the desk seems in no kind of hurry.

I wait in line until he's dealt with the two in front of me, then step up to the desk. 'I hear you've got smoking rooms?'

He gives me a half-hearted smile. Although his tone is friendly enough it's obvious he's just going through the motions; hired help rather than owner. 'We do. How many nights are you looking to stay?'

'I'm not sure yet. I'm going hiking today and I'll decide after that.' I point outside, towards the forest. 'You got any good trails around here?'

'Yes ma'am, we do. Silver Point Trail starts right behind us and takes you all the way along to Carter Lake.'

Interesting. 'I didn't see that on the map.'

He shakes his head. 'It's not on there. Man-made, less than a year ago. Good place for camping. Popular with out-of-towners.'

'Thanks, I'll check it out.'

He gestures towards the map in my pocket. 'I can draw it on there for you if you like?'

Figuring it could come in useful, I hand him the map. 'Sure.'

Leaving the lobby, I walk around the white stucco building, counting the numbers on the green doors of the rooms. There are twelve at ground level and another twelve above; twenty-four in the front, twenty-four out back. On the corner there's a laundry room and a vending machine with soft drinks and snacks. The place seems basic but well maintained, and I'll bet the rooms are clean enough.

The smoking rooms are around back on the upper level, four in a row at the furthest end. Each one has an ashtray outside it and a notice below the room number that says *Smoking Room*. I think back to the list of criteria that the FBI field agents use. This place is good for multiple exits and vantage points, but it's pretty quiet. It'd be hard for the Feds to blend in here.

⌒

My second stop is the Missingdon Suites. Housed in a square, cream stucco building, this is a hotel rather than a motel, and looks in a league above Hampton Lodge. I park in the lot around back and stride round to the lobby. There are two well-groomed ladies behind the tall marble-clad counter, both wearing matching brown uniforms and orange neckerchiefs. The lobby's full of people checking out and the receptionists are busy with customers, allowing me to move unnoticed to the elevators. This place certainly fits the FBI's 'busy' requirement, and it's mid-range for sure.

Stepping inside the nearest one, I press the button for the eighth floor and wait for the doors to close. My own image stares back at me in the mirrored wall. I look neat enough, especially for someone who spent the night in their vehicle, but there are dark circles beneath my eyes, giving away my lack of sleep, and the mottled bruise on the side of my forehead has turned a darker grey.

On the eighth floor I step out. To the left of the elevators the external wall is floor-to-ceiling glass, giving a great view of the town and the landscape beyond: trees and lakes, grassland and orange groves. At eight storeys this must be one of the tallest buildings in the town; from this angle it certainly looks that way. But although the Feds need a good vantage point, I'm thinking this is too high for a fast getaway. I walk around the floor, passing wooden door after wooden door, lining the cream-walled and beige-carpeted hallway. There's a fire escape in the farthest corner, and the sign on the door says it's alarmed and for emergency use only. I shake my head. Depending on where their rooms are, they would have a minute or two to run to the nearest exit. Not ideal. I figure that if the FBI used this place they'd want a lower floor.

I check out the Korda Motel last, and from the moment I pull up outside I know it's not a goer. There's only one other car in the parking lot, and it's so quiet there might as well be tumbleweed drifting through the lobby. Even the older woman wearing reading glasses behind the counter seems surprised to see me. There's no way the Feds could blend in here. I smile to the woman and turn on my heel. As I do she returns to reading her romance novel.

Back in the Jeep I take a gulp of water. It's almost eleven-thirty, and check-in for Hampton Lodge opens in thirty minutes. I figure I should stake out the place until two o'clock, when check-in at the Missingdon Suites starts. If there's been no action at Hampton Lodge by then, I'll have to decide whether to stay or go.

As I fire up the Jeep's engine I hear my cellphone beep. Looking down, I see I've got a message from Dakota. My heart lurches as a wave of guilt crashes over me.

Momma. I miss you ☹ ☹ ☹ ☹ :-* :-* :-* :-*

15

THURSDAY, SEPTEMBER 20th, 12:03

I wait, parked up on the far side of the Hampton Lodge lot – reversed into the space, so I have a clear view of those coming and going. I message Dakota, tell her the job's going well, that I hope she's having fun with JT and that I love her. As I press send the guilt of separation twists in my stomach, mingling with sadness at the way I left things with JT. I know he's worried, but I have to do this for us, for Dakota; and I need him to believe that I'm capable of looking after myself ... of us.

Putting my cell back into my pocket, I force myself to focus on the job. It's getting hot inside the Jeep without the air conditioning, but this is the optimum vantage point. With the sun high and directly behind me, it'll be tricky for anyone glancing this way to see me hunkered down in the driver's seat.

But no one comes. Correction, no Feds come, although I count five other groups checking in: three couples and two family groups. It's a quarter of two and I need to decide: stay or go, watch or relocate.

I decide to change locations.

Making the short, eight-minute journey to the Missingdon Suites, I park up and head inside. There's no sense observing from the parking lot here as it's spread out around the building with no spaces out front. The only option is to wait inside. Lucky for me there's a seating area to the side of the lobby. Taking a newspaper from the table, I settle down in one of the big armchairs facing the entrance.

My cell rings. The number on the screen isn't one I recognise. 'This is Lori Anderson.'

The voice is packed with menace. 'You got North?'

Luciano Bonchese. Shit. 'I'm working on it.'

'You got less than twenty-four hours to get him away from the Feds.'

'I'm real clear on the time frame.'

'Best make it happen then or—'

I end the call. Don't need threats from the Old Man's son.

Moments later my cell buzzes; a message. It's from Luciano's number. I open it. Inhale sharply and bite my lip. It's a photo of JT taken through the front window of my apartment. He's in sweatpants and bare-chested, looking good, but that's not what's caused my reaction. The photo has been taken at medium range and there's something blurred in the foreground; it's dark, and rounded like a pipe. I stare at it, trying to make out what it is.

My breath catches in my throat as I realise: the picture was taken looking down the barrel of a gun.

I message back: *Stay away from my family. I'm doing the goddamn job.*

Luciano's reply is almost instant: *Then get it done. Tick tock.*

I pretend to read the paper for more than an hour. Force myself to stay focused on my task every time my mind starts to wonder towards thoughts of the photo of JT. I want to call him, tell him about the messages, but there's no point; I told him the mob were watching, that they had pictures of him and Dakota – it's old news. I just have get the job done. It's the only way.

Over the top of my paper I watch people check in; singles, couples and families. None of them look like Feds. None of them are Carlton North.

It's just gone three o'clock and there's been no sign of them. It doesn't feel right. Monroe said they'd arrive just after check-in started. It's then I realise I've been made. The receptionist with dark hair is staring at me, frowning. I look down fast, pretend to read the paper some more, but when I look up a minute later she's still got her gaze fixed on me. I watch as she moves over to her colleague and nods in my direction. Damn. Her blonde colleague is nodding, moving towards the phone on the counter. I can't stay here.

Getting up, I put the paper back on the table and stride across the lobby to the door. The receptionists don't call out or try to stop me, but I reckon if I go back, they'll challenge me for loitering or call security. I don't need that kind of hassle, especially when I'm trying to keep a low profile, so I keep walking.

I'm heading back towards the Jeep when my cell rings. Pulling it from my jacket pocket, I glance at the screen and see Monroe's name on the caller ID. I press answer. 'You got something for me?'

'Just wanted to check you'd found them.'

I frown. 'Not yet.'

'You didn't see them? Word is they checked into their accommodation twenty minutes ago.'

I think back on all the folks I've seen come and go in the past hour; twenty minutes ago the only people in the lobby where a frazzled looking couple with twin girls and a baby that'd vomited down the front of its sleep suit. Wherever the Feds and Carlton North are, it isn't the Missingdon Suites. 'Which place?'

'I don't know. I just know they're there now.'

Cussing under my breath, I break into a run.

I slow my speed to forty miles an hour before reaching the turn into the Hampton Lodge's parking lot. I can't afford to attract attention, for all I know the Feds have a lookout installed.

I reverse the Jeep into a space at the far side of the lot and wait for a moment, watching. The place looks pretty much how it did just over an hour ago, when I was last here. The only changes are that there are a few more vehicles in the lot, and a group of gawky teens are hanging around the vending machine on the corner of the building.

I saunter towards the Lodge, taking my time so I can scan the vehicles around me for occupants who could be a Fed lookout. There's nothing, no one. All the vehicles look empty. Then I notice a black Crown Victoria parked in the corner, closest to the back of the building and the trees behind. The car wasn't here before.

Memorising the number on the Florida Oranges licence plate, I glance inside as I pass. I see it's completely bare of clutter; no go cups, no sandwich wrappers, no discarded sweater or shades. It could be a federal vehicle for sure, but it could also belong to someone who's a fan of big, roomy cars. I need to know which.

Slowing my steps, I pull out my cell and text Monroe: *Florida licence 893 2QX. One of yours?*

His reply comes before I reach the automatic glass door into the lobby. It's short, to the point.

YES.

My pulse quickens. They're here. Now I have to find out precisely where.

16

The smart play is to get a room. I can't sit around in the parking lot for long without the FBI spotting me; even though they don't seem to have a lookout, they're likely to have some junior agent on regular patrol duty. And as the Old Man's instructions are that I go in alone, I'm going to need darkness plus a power blackout to have a hope in hell of busting out Carlton North. Sundown isn't for at least another four hours. Until then I need to blend in, like the Feds try to. I need a reason to be here, and the best excuse is to be on vacation. So that's the card I play.

It's a different guy taking afternoon shift on reception. This one's a little younger and a whole lot keener. He smiles, genuine and enthusiastic, as I enter the lobby. His voice has the slightly desperate tone of a sales assistant getting scored on customer service. 'Welcome, ma'am, how can I help you this afternoon?'

I fake a broad grin. Try on a nasal Boston accent to disguise my roots. 'I'm looking for a room.'

'Well, sure. How many nights would you like to stay?'

'One for definite, maybe a couple more.'

Up close the reception guy is even younger than I first thought – nearer eighteen than twenty and still plagued by pimples. He makes a show of checking the ancient computer on the desk, but I can see there are at least twenty keys still hanging on their hooks on the wall behind him. Looking back at me, he smiles. 'You're in luck, we have availability tonight.'

'Great.' I lean in a little closer and lower my voice. 'A little bird over at Joe's Diner said you have a few smoking rooms?'

He fidgets in his seat, looking uncomfortable. 'We do, but the thing is, most of them are booked.'

'Most of them?'

'Well, there's one left but I've been asked by management to hold it until the rest are booked out.'

I remember Monroe's words. How he'd said that the Feds would book three rooms in a row. This place only has four smoking rooms. I guess the FBI would prefer the fourth stays empty. But that's too bad. I want to be as close to the action as I can, and the room alongside theirs is the obvious choice.

Giving the guy a seductive smile, I drop my voice an octave and make it a little husky. 'But if it's free, couldn't I use it? Is it around back? I'd sure love a view of the forest. I just love trees, don't you?' I use the tip of my tongue to wet my lips. Lean closer so he gets a look-see down my top, and say suggestively, 'I can't wait to hike your trails.'

He blushes and holds my gaze a little longer than necessary, then nods. Turning to the wall behind him, he plucks key number forty-five from its hook and hands it to me. 'Up the stairs and along, fourth from the end.'

I smile and take the key. 'Appreciate it.'

Leaving the lobby, I fetch my go bag from the Jeep and head around the building to the back. The place is busier than it was earlier. Rock music comes from the room closest to the stairs. The smell of cooking spices and garlic wafts from the open window of the room a couple of doors along. I keep walking.

Up ahead, standing between the last room and the top of the metal fire escape, I spot two men – one shorter, heavy-set guy, the other taller and more athletic-looking.

Feds. That's my first instinct.

It's the way they hold themselves that alerts me; the slight rigidity in the spine, the bulge around their right ankles. The deep creases in the front of their pant legs as if they've just taken them out the packet, and the whiteness of their fresh-on T-shirts. They can't wear suits here – they'd stick out rather than blend in – so they've had to take a trip to the local clothes store and buy a different kind of uniform; average, nondescript. Forgettable.

But I can't forget them. Old Man Bonchese won't allow that. What I need to know is how many of them there are.

As I approach, the heavier of the two men moves towards the door for room forty-seven and pauses outside. He watches me stop at the door of the room two along from him. I give him a half-smile and fumble with my key in the lock. Use my Boston accent again: 'Jeez, these things are sticky, huh?'

He says nothing, but his expression tells me he's pissed that I'm staying so close. Pretending not to notice his scowl, I turn back to my door, make as if I've wrestled the lock open and step inside my room.

Throwing my go bag onto the bed, I take a look around. The room's nice enough. Clean, with the usual inoffensive décor of cream and fawn most places use these days. Aside from the bed it's got basic furnishings – a closet, a desk with a coffee-maker, an easy chair – but they don't interest me none. What does is the connecting door between my room and forty-six, next door. I stand stock-still and listen. I can hear movement, maybe in forty-six, maybe a little further over. But one thing's for sure: the walls in this place are paper thin.

Crossing the room to the window, I pull the heavy blackout drapes back as far as they go but keep the lace voiles drawn. The heavier of the two Feds is still outside room forty-seven, keeping watch. There's no sign of Carlton North.

I think on my next move. Chances are the Feds won't let North out of the room. That means I'm going to have to go in blind, hoping I'm right and that luck has my back. Sure, I could sit around here, waiting to see if I can spot him, but that doesn't seem a good use of time. Assuming I can get him free and clear of this place, we'll need an escape route. And on that I've gotten an idea.

Always be prepared; that's one of the rules of the trade that I learned from JT. *Use what you've got to get the job done*; that's a rule I added myself. This place isn't any of our home turf – not mine, not the Feds and not Carlton North's. I figure I can use the local terrain to my advantage.

Pulling the map I got from the rest stop out of my go bag, I look for the Silver Point Trail and Carter Lake. Like the guy in reception this morning said, neither are printed, but he's drawn the trail and the lake in pencil real neat so I can see how they link to the local roads and other trails. Opening the internet browser on my cell, I bring up the maps app. Using the 'find my location' search, I magnify the view to the maximum and search the surrounding area. There are plenty of hiking trails around Missingdon marked, but none that lead directly out the back of Hampton Lodge.

I wonder if the Feds know about the trail. Hope that they don't.

Judging by how the reception guy has drawn the Carter Lake, it looks like I can get to it by road. I remember him saying it was a good place for camping so I figure it must also be accessible with a vehicle. Leaving my go bag in the room, I grab my keys and head for the door.

The drive takes twenty minutes. The route takes me out of town a few miles before looping back into the forest. The road is narrower here, the blacktop new and starkly artificial against the green of the trees. It doesn't feel like I'm in Florida.

A few minutes later I see a wide expanse of water a little ways ahead. The light catches the surface, making it sparkle and shimmer. It's beautiful and, with the trees circled around it, makes for an unlikely oasis in this forest. Carter Lake, I assume. On my right I spot a wooden sign with a tent symbol carved into it. Pulling off the blacktop onto a dirt track, I follow the signs between the trees towards the lake. I think how much Dakota would love it here then immediately push the thought away. I miss my baby, but I can't think on her now; I have to stay focused.

The campsite is little more than a clearing in the trees. It's fifty yards or so from the lake and is empty. I'm not surprised. First, there's no restroom facilities here, so it's really only a site for tougher campers. Second, any serious camper will know that pitching a tent this close to water in Florida is as good as inviting a gator for dinner. But that doesn't effect me none. It's perfect for my needs.

Parking the Jeep at the far end of the clearing, where the trees are most dense, I grab my cell and a bottle of water, get out and lock up. According to the Silver Point Trail the reception guy drew, the start of the path should be a little ways south-east of this campsite. I can't spot any obvious trail, so, using the compass on my cellphone, I check my bearings and move in that direction.

The ground is dry beneath my boots. Old branches and leaves crack and rustle as I step on them, causing the birds singing in the canopy above to scare and fly away. Ignoring them, I keep my eyes on the ground, watching where I walk, vigilant for snakes. I check the compass; I'm walking south-east, but there's still no sign of the path.

Stopping, I check the map. The direction I'm going is correct according to the hand-drawn line, but I'm thinking it's not so accurate as I'd hoped. Retracing my steps back to the Jeep, I think about the roads I drove to get here, and find the spot on the map where I turned off the blacktop onto the dirt track. I keep my finger on the place – it's an inch higher and across from where the reception guy drew Carter Lake – and find Hampton Lodge with my gaze. Damn. By my reckoning the direction is more directly south than south-east. Folding the map, I check the compass reading on my cell and head in the new direction.

I find the path fast. It's narrow, already starting to get overgrown with creepers and lichen. Following it through the trees I march in the direction of Hampton Lodge. I check my watch. It's almost five. I want to get back before the sun starts setting so I can see every inch of the trail, commit it to memory, ready for later.

The hike is longer than I expected, the path snaking between the trees rather than taking a straight route. The sun beats down, the light blinding when it flares through the canopy. I stay alert to markers that I can use later: a gnarled fallen tree; a collection of grey boulders at the side of the path; what looks like an ancient rope swing hanging from a nearby branch. I see no one else.

It's hot and humid. The path has been on a gradual incline for at least a half-mile, and now there's a film of sweat over my skin, making my T-shirt stick to my body, damp and clingy. I halt for a moment and finish the last of my water. Looping my hair up into a bun to get some air to the back of my neck I start walking again, hoping that I'm getting close.

The terrain ascends sharply to a ridge. As I step up to the crest I see that the ground slopes gently away, down to the back of Hampton Lodge. Standing under the shade of the trees, I catch my breath. Take in the view. The door to room forty-seven is open; the taller Fed is framed in the doorway. On the upstairs walkway, a little ways along from my room, I can see another man standing at the top of the fire escape. His body shape is different to the heavier Fed I saw earlier. I wonder if he's a third Fed or someone different. There's only one way to find out.

Staying under the cover of the trees, I hustle down the slope towards the building. With the sun high above me, the canopy casts deep shadows on the ground. The man is staring back towards the parking lot, away from me. I move faster, aiming for an area just to the side of the fire escape. Stay real quiet. Get closer.

The tree line ends a few yards short of the building. Halting on the edge of the shadows, I watch the man at the top of the fire escape. He's a little shorter than the Fed in the doorway, but in his fitted black tee and black jeans I can see he's more muscular and athletic than either of the two Feds I've seen. His black hair is short and styled up at the front. He's wearing shades. He takes a long drag on his cigarette, pauses then exhales. As the smoke plumes around him, he turns and looks straight towards were I'm standing. Now I know for sure that it's him.

I've found Carlton North.

17

THURSDAY, SEPTEMBER 20th, 17:01

It's almost twenty-four hours since she left, and JT still hasn't heard from her. He picks the flowery dress out of the trashcan in the bedroom and stares at it. Lori said the Old Man made her wear it. Asshole. He's always enjoyed playing mind games, and his son Luciano is a vindictive son-of-a-bitch. JT hates that Lori's out there on a job for the pair of them, that they've forced her into doing it. It's a suicide mission, trying to bust Carlton North out from FBI custody.

The bell chimes and JT hears Dakota running along the hallway to the door. He hurries out of the bedroom. Calls out, 'Dakota, wait.'

Dakota skids to a halt in front of the door. Turns. 'Why, JT?'

He strides over to join her. 'Let me get it.'

She looks confused, but moves aside for him.

Standing outside on the mat is Dakota's little friend, Krista's youngest kid, from next door. She looks up at him. Her brown hair is coming loose from her braids, and there's a dirty smudge on her cheek. She bites her lip. Looks nervous.

He cracks a smile. 'Can I help you?'

'Dakota wasn't in school today.' The kid's voice is hesitant. 'Is she okay?'

'She's doing just fine.'

'So does she want to come to the mall with us?'

JT shakes his head. 'I'm sorry she can't today. Maybe next time.'

The kid blushes, already turning away. 'Okay.'

Closing the door, JT turns back to Dakota. She's standing with her hands on her hips. 'Why do I have to stay in? I'm not sick.'

'That's true, you're not. But for the next day or so I think we should stay put.'

'Why?'

JT doesn't want to tell her what's going on and worry her, not after everything she's been through already. He keeps his tone firm. 'Because I think it's best.'

She tilts her head to one side. 'What aren't you telling me? Are we in danger?'

Damn, thinks JT. She's real perceptive, just like her momma. 'It's just grown-up stuff is all,' he says, heading out of the hallway to the kitchen.

Dakota follows. 'But I'm nearly ten. I can handle it.'

He pours himself another cup of strong black coffee. He's not slept since Lori left last night – been too busy scanning the internet and the news channels for information. So far there's been nothing. His daughter might act tough, but his worries about Lori and his need to keep the three of them safe from the Miami Mob are his alone to bear. Sharing the burden with Dakota would be pure selfishness.

'I'm sorry sweetheart, this is between me and your mom.'

Dakota frowns. She leans back against the countertop and watches him closely as he drinks. He can tell she doesn't believe him. 'If it's just about you and momma, why can't I go to the mall?'

'Because it's almost dinner time.'

She glances at her watch. 'It's only five o'clock. Momma says it's too early for dinner before seven.'

He tries to keep his tone light-hearted. 'Maybe I say different.'

Dakota narrows her eyes. 'Momma will be mad.'

'Sure, could be that she will.'

Dakota holds his gaze for a long moment then smiles. 'Well, if she's going to be mad anyway, we could have ice cream.'

JT knows Lori doesn't allow too much of the sweet stuff, but this could be his opportunity to get Dakota on-side. He raises an eyebrow. 'Well you're quite the negotiator, aren't you?'

'Did it work?'

He laughs. 'You want mint choc chip or chocolate swirl?'

'Mint choc chip, please.' Dakota grins. 'Guess that I *am* a good negotiator.'

As JT fetches the ice cream, he thinks back to last night and how he'd tried to negotiate with Lori – persuade her not to take the job, or if she insisted on doing it, take him with her. He'd failed on both counts, and now she was out there somewhere alone, with no one protecting her six. The thought makes him sick to his stomach.

He passes Dakota the mint choc chip. Nods. 'You're a whole lot better at it than me, for sure.'

18

THURSDAY, SEPTEMBER 20th, 17:54

The moment I step out from the trees, the tall Fed moves fast. He lunges out from the doorway, grabs North and shoves him into the room. As I reach the bottom of the fire escape the Fed slams shut the door to room forty-seven. When I get to the top of the steps I see he's standing guard outside the room.

I smile and gesture back towards the trees. Use my fake Bostonian accent again: 'Amazing trails. You here for the hiking?'

The tall Fed looks at me, his expression neutral. Shakes his head. 'Not my thing.'

'Well, if you're planning a hike tomorrow be sure that you take a lot a water.' I fan myself. Pull my empty water bottle from my back pocket. 'It's humid in there, and I just wasn't prepared enough today.'

He's obviously reluctant to engage in conversation, but doesn't want to be rude. He glances at the bottle. 'It's important to stay hydrated.'

'For sure.' I keep my tone bright, carefree and unthreatening. Oftentimes it's easier as a woman to get a whole lot closer to your target. Both men and women tend to view a female as less of a threat. It's everyday sexism at work, and something I'm not sorry about using to my advantage. With my peripheral vision I scan the door behind him and its surroundings. 'I'll take two bottles tomorrow.'

Sensing I've pushed him to talk to me as long as he'll tolerate, I continue towards my room. As I walk past forty-seven I see that the blackout drapes are still drawn across the window, so there's no view of North or the other Fed inside. I wonder if there's just two Feds or if there are more in the room. If the Crown Victoria in the parking lot is the only vehicle they have, that limits their number to a maximum of four Feds plus North. Considering the distance they've come from Miami, chances are they wouldn't travel so bunched together, so my money is on there being three Feds, no doubt all male.

I remember another of the rules of bounty hunting that JT taught me years ago, back when I was a rookie and he was my mentor: *Don't make assumptions*. But in the field you sometimes have to take calculated risks; I've learned that from ten years in the business. I figure this is one of those times. I'll plan for three Feds, one North: three hostiles, and one whose allegiance is unknown. Because, even assuming North wants to escape and get back to the Miami Mob, as the Old Man has told me, there's nothing to say he'll believe that I'm taking him there. The last time we met I was a very different woman.

Sticking my key into the lock of room forty-five, I open the door and step inside. The room's cool, thanks to the air conditioning that I left cranked up to the max.

Monroe told me to be on the lookout for some kind of counter-surveillance. While I was talking to the taller Fed, I did a visual check and saw nothing unusual. But this is the FBI – their technology will be small and state-of-the-art, so it's likely I'd not notice any cameras or motion detectors they'd installed. I still have to operate as if they're there, though.

Grabbing another bottle of water from my go bag, I sit on the bed and take a long drink. I've got my escape route sorted; next I need to plan how to get North clear of the room. If I break in, guns blazing, it'll be two or three to one. I'll be outgunned and taken out. I need something smarter, more stealthy. I need to get them to come out of the room. Then I need to get Carlton North alone.

But there's something I have to do first. Pulling my cell from my pocket, I tap out a message to Luciano Bonchese, telling him I've found North and will be moving to break him free tonight.

His reply comes less than a minute later: *Address?*

I stare at the screen. Don't reply. I feel reluctant to tell him. I remember the sneer on his face as he told me to give him North's location as soon as I had it so he could send his boys to bust him out if I failed.

I flinch as my cell starts ringing in my hand. 'Yeah?'

'Give me the address.' Luciano sounds real pissed. 'You fail and I'll—'

'Just stop with the threats already. I'm doing what you asked, I've found North. Just give me a little time to break him free.'

'You're running out of time. He's due in court in the morning.'

'And I'll have him free before dawn.'

'So shoot me if I don't totally rely on the bitch who murdered my brother. I've got a back-up plan for when you screw up. The address. Now.'

I grip the cell tighter. Wish I could shoot him right now. Instead, I tell him my location and North's room number. Ending the call, I toss the handset onto the bed. I clench my fists. Feel grubby.

Screw up, my ass. One thing's for sure: I won't let myself fail.

I'll bust Carlton North out and stick it to Luciano Bonchese.

19

FRIDAY, SEPTEMBER 21st, 02:37

Deep night. No moon. Pitch-black outside.

I wait until it's almost three to make my move. This is the time of night that drags the longest if you're on sentry duty. It's when fatigue is most debilitating, it's when the lure of sleep makes you slow. In a quiet place like this, on a dark night like tonight, that lure can get real bad. Which is why people oftentimes make mistakes at this hour, even if they're FBI.

Moving to the window, I lift the edge of one of the blackout drapes and peer out onto the external walkway, illuminated by the fluorescent lights. It's empty. There's no one outside room forty-seven.

I turn back into my room. I've got my tools laid out on the bed. I'll get one chance at this. Blow it and I'm screwed. Scanning my equipment, I check everything's all set. Hairdryer and paper: check. Lock picks: check. Go bag packed: check. Concealed body armour on; gun and Taser in my holster; check, check, check.

I select the torch app on my cellphone and switch it on. Place the cell on the top of my go bag and drop the bag softly onto the carpet beside me. Taking my lock picks off the bed, I thread them into the lock of the connecting door between my room and room forty-six.

I'm ready.

Stripping two pillowcases from the pillows on the bed, I double them up and wrap them around the nozzle of the hairdryer, making a muffler. I plug the hairdresser into the socket on the wall between my room and forty-six and switch it onto the lowest setting. This is the risky bit. Will the dryer noise alert the Feds? It'll be an unfamiliar sound at this time of night.

Tilting the dryer upwards, I feed a folded piece of paper into the nozzle. There's a hiss and it spits flames as the paper catches fire. The acrid smell of burning fills my nostrils and the hairdryer gives a soft pop.

The power and lights go out. The air conditioning stops.

I hope my gamble's paid off. I hope, by making the socket fuse, I've caused a power outage that, if I'm right about the circuitry in this place, has cut the power to all the rooms in this block. I move fast to the window; peer out through the gap between the drape and the glass.

Blackout.

The fluorescent lights on the walkway have gone out. The moon is hidden behind the clouds.

Now, I hear raised voices – they're coming from a couple of rooms along. Shielded by the darkness, I watch as the door of forty-seven opens. The Feds are awake. I have to act fast.

Hotfooting it to the connecting door, I grab my go bag and use my lock picks to release the mechanism. I can hear voices on the walkway; recognise one as the taller of the two Feds.

Taking a deep breath, I twist the handle and step into room forty-six.

The first shot makes me jump. The second has me diving for cover. The window shatters, shards of glass cascading onto the floor a few yards from me. The rapid fire of an automatic weapon blasts into the building. But not into this room. The shots are ahead of me. I'm not the target. It's the Feds and Carlton North.

Who the hell is shooting?

I'm scrambling to my feet as the connecting door between this room and forty-seven opens. A dark-haired man in a leather jacket rushes through, pulling the door closed behind him.

It's Carlton North.

As he turns, our eyes meet. He tilts his head a fraction and I see recognition in his eyes, my old name on his lips.

Then the external door to room forty-seven crashes open and rapid fire rips through the room he's just fled. We're in the danger zone. Need to get out of here fast. The walls are thin and offer little protection from these bullets. We could get dead real easy from a stray.

I draw my gun. 'You want to live? Come with me.'

He nods. 'I'm with you. Go!'

We sprint through the connecting door, across my room and out the external door onto the walkway. To my right I see the broken, bullet-hole-ridden bodies of the two Feds sprawled on the floor outside forty-seven. The shooters must still be inside. It won't be long before they discover Carlton North's missing and the connecting doors are open. Then they'll come after us.

We need to move.

Too late.

There's a shout from one of the rooms. A crash as another door is kicked in. Turning to North, I gesture towards the safety railing. 'This way.'

In three strides I'm across the walkway. I vault the railing and drop down onto the dumpster below. Bending my knees to soften the impact, I jump from the dumpster onto the ground. North lands beside me.

'Head for the trees.' I say, pointing to the start of the Silver Point Trail. 'There's a path; follow it. I've got a vehicle up there.'

We sprint stride-for-stride towards the tree line.

We're almost there when the first shot ricochets off a tree to our left, sending the bark splintering in our faces. I yell at North to keep running then turn, raising my weapon. There's a figure on the walkway. I see a muzzle flash from their gun, and feel heat as the bullet just misses my ear. I aim and return fire.

The figure on the walkway jerks back from the impact then flops forwards onto the railing. Gravity takes them over the top, and they land with a bang on the dumpsters. They don't get up.

Then, in the gloom, I see movement in the doorway of my room.

I turn and sprint after North. Don't wait to see who it is.

We run over the ridge and through the trees, following the Silver Point Trail. My go bag bounces against my back with every stride, the single shoulder strap not designed for carrying at speed. I pay it no mind.

Focus on trying to make out the path in the dimness. The moon has reappeared from behind the veil of clouds, casting a pale light through the canopy. The undergrowth snags against my jeans. Gnarled tree roots try to trip us. North almost falls, but recovers well. I pump my arms harder, determined to stay close on his tail.

We reach the campsite clearing at Carter Lake breathless. Doubling over beside the Jeep, we catch our breath. The air tastes earthy, the humidity lingering through the night.

I grab a couple of bottles of water from my go bag and hand one to North. 'We should get on the road.'

As he drinks, I unlock the doors and sling my bag onto the back seat. When I turn back towards North he's looking at me funny. 'You okay?'

He nods, but the strange look remains. 'Long time, no see. Seems you've had a career change.'

'I've changed a lot of things.'

'Heard about that.' He smiles, but it looks fake – too toothy. 'I was sorry to hear about Tommy.'

I don't want to get into that now. I'm not sure how much North knows, whether he believes JT was behind Tommy's death or knows that I killed him. And I don't know how good friends they were. So I turn away and open the driver's door. Focus on getting him clear of Missingdon and back to Miami.

'We need to get going.'

'Yeah, about that...'

As I turn to climb into the Jeep, North lunges for me. His right arm garrottes my neck, his forearm pressing tight into the flesh. His left hand grips my waist, his fingers like claws digging into my hip. He snarls into my ear. 'Why'd you come here? Who sent you?'

'What the hell, North.' I'm gasping. Fighting for breath. Jabbing my elbows backwards into his body, trying to get free. 'I'm here to help you.'

'Helping them kill me, more like. What was your plan – they shoot up the FBI agents and you get my trust by "rescuing" me?'

I kick back. Feel my heel connect hard against his knee. 'No.'

He steps backwards, off balance. But his arm's still tight around my throat. 'Don't lie. I know how you people operate. I've seen all your—'

His words are cut short by a burst of gunfire. The undergrowth a few yards in front of us dances under a hail of bullets, grass and bracken fly into the air.

North releases me and we both dive for cover behind the Jeep.

I return fire in the direction I think the attack is coming from but I'm blind; I've got no eyes on the shooter. North, weaponless, steps away from me towards the trees.

'North, stay with—'

Another round of shots cuts into the ground on my right and riddles the Jeep's trunk with bullets. The rear tyres hiss, and I smell gasoline in the air. But this time I saw the muzzle flash. Raising my gun, I fire into the darkness.

When I turn back to look for North, he's already gone.

Goddamn.

I crouch behind the hood of the Jeep. Hear footsteps; dry branches cracking underfoot, unnervingly loud against the silence of the forest. I don't know if the noise is from North or the shooter. I hold fire, and wait for them to make the next move.

Waiting is a mistake.

I feel the bullet's hot bite before I hear the shot. It tears through my T-shirt and then through the flesh of my upper arm. The wound feels volcano hot. My left arm starts shaking but, with the adrenaline, I hardly feel the pain.

Raising my weapon, I get off another shot, but my aim's crooked; it goes wide. I pull the trigger again, but there's an empty click. I'm all out of ammo.

The shooter volleys back. The first shot ricochets off the Jeep's hood; the second and third spray straight up into the tree canopy.

That's when I glimpse him. In the light of the muzzle flash I see North standing behind the man with the gun. He bellows as North grabs him in a headlock. I see them struggle. Hear the crack as North breaks his neck.

Hot damn.

I run towards North. He's crouching beside the body of the man he's just killed.

As I stop beside him, North blinks up at me like he's coming out of a trance. Shakes his head. 'It's been a long while since I had to do something like this.'

'I thought you're...' Movement behind North draws my attention. I spot the glint of eyes in the moonlight. Eyes at human head height rather than an animal. Keeping my voice low, I look at North then move my gaze towards the movement. 'There's a second. I'm empty.'

North acts fast. He pulls the Glock from the hand of the dead guy and pivots round. His movement's smooth, practised. He squeezes the trigger. I hear a shout, a thud.

North's up and running towards the fallen man, gun trained on him, ready. I follow. There's no need for another shot. The bullet hit the guy straight between the eyes; near impossible, in this dark gloom.

I look at North. 'You've got crazy good aim for a number's man?' There's a question in my tone.

He grimaces. 'The numbers I dealt with weren't the kind you input into spreadsheets.'

My stomach flips. 'You're a killer?'

He holds my gaze. 'I'm more like a fixer.'

I shake my head. Old Man Bonchese hid the truth from me. He knew I'd assume North was his accountant. And he knew rescuing an accountant would give me the druthers a whole lot less than having to bust out his fixer. 'Goddamn. Why the hell am I surprised?'

'He didn't tell you?'

'Who?'

'Luciano. When he sent you here to kill me?'

I glare at him. Keep my tone steely. 'I'm real good at what I do. If I wanted you dead, I'd have done it already.'

He smiles. It makes him look like a shark wearing veneers. 'Yes ma'am.'

'And Luciano didn't send me. The Old Man did. He wanted you

back safe. Didn't want the Feds holding you and forcing you to testify.'

'I doubt that's the truth.' North kneels down beside the dead guy. 'This man, his name's Nico. He's one of Luciano's guys; inner circle – very loyal.'

I shake my head. It makes no sense. 'Luciano knew I was here, that I'd got things handled.'

'Sure he did.' North pulls down Nico's T-shirt. In the hollow below his collarbone there's a tattoo; a stylized double M with a serpent in an L-shape around the letters. 'This is Luciano's mark. He likes all his inner circle to have it.'

North stands and strides back to the body of the first shooter. Yanks down the man's shirt, revealing an identical tattoo. Then he reaches into pocket of the man's jacket, takes out his wallet and shows me the name on his driver's licence: Giovanni Ricci. 'These men are both Luciano's.'

I remember my last conversation with Luciano. 'Luciano said he was sending his men as back-up; if I failed then they'd bust you out. But why send them in first? Why deliberately sabotage the job the Old Man asked me to do?'

North says nothing. Just stares back at me.

Then it hits me.

Before the shooters started firing, North said to me, *I know how you people operate*. He wasn't captive; I've been played. Damn. 'You didn't want to be rescued, did you? You went to the FBI with information voluntarily.'

He nods. 'Man's got to get a conscience sometime.'

I look down at the body of the man he's just killed. 'Yup. I can see that.'

North drops the Glock onto the ground. 'This was self-defence. You point a gun at a man, you've got to know he might pull the trigger first. But what I've done for the Family, that's a different story.'

I hold his gaze. 'And how does the story end?'

'Honestly? Now, I'm not so sure.'

20

Bending down, I pick up the Glock that North dropped and point it at his chest. I need us to get away from these bodies fast, before the cops arrive at Hampton Lodge and start tracking us, so we don't have time for a long conversation. 'The Old Man tasked me with getting you free and bringing you home to him. I need to deliver.'

North raises his hands. 'Even if that's not what I want?'

'Afraid so.'

He shakes his head. 'You were such a sweet kid. What the hell happened to you, Jennifer?'

Sweet kids finish last, that's what I learned. Sweet kids get beat on ... and murdered. Sweet kids don't get respect. I glare at him. 'Don't ever call me that again. Jennifer died a long time ago. My name's Lori now.'

North holds my gaze. Waiting for more of an explanation.

I don't owe him anything, but he was kind to me once and that makes me want to oblige. 'Tommy killed my best friend, Sal, and didn't care a damn. Jennifer Ford, the victim I used to be, died that same night. I vowed I'd bring him to justice. Toughened up. Trained as a bounty hunter and changed my name – shortening my middle name to Lori and taking one of the most common family names in America: Anderson.'

North softens his voice. 'Look, I get that you were in a tight spot. I saw what your husband Tommy did to you, remember?'

I nod. Sure I remember. I remember every one of the black eyes, busted ribs and broken fingers. The shouting and the hatred, the guilt and the remorse.

'So I'm not judging you on that count. What I don't get is why you didn't just run. Why work for the Miami Mob?'

I narrow my eyes. 'I don't work for them.'

North raises an eyebrow. 'You sure about that? Because from this side of the gun it sure seems that way.'

'I'm not being paid for this. You and me, we're not the same.'

He shrugs and flashes that toothy smile of his. 'If you say so.'

I've no patience or time to debate for a moment longer. The sun is starting to rise, sending the pale light of dawn flickering and shimmering across the surface of the lake. I look across the clearing towards the Jeep. Gesture at it with the barrel of the Glock, and say, 'Enough talking. We need to get gone.'

⌢

Even in the half-light I can see that the Jeep's going nowhere fast. The bodywork's shot up, the smell of gas tells me the tank's most likely ruptured, and three of the tyres are blown into shreds.

'We need another set of wheels,' I say.

North makes a show of looking around the empty campsite. 'Not much choice around here.'

I scowl at him, already sick of his wisecracks. 'You don't say.'

Crouching down, I feel under the Jeep's belly, my fingers searching for holes in the tank. I use my good arm – my right. The left's throbbing like a bitch. My shoulder muscles are aching, the fingers of my left hand barely able to grip the side of the Jeep for stability. I try to act like I'm fine, thankful that the black tee I'm wearing is long-sleeved and that, in this light, it'll be hard for North to see that I'm bleeding. I don't want him knowing I'm shot. Don't want him sensing weakness.

My search doesn't find any ruptures in the lower half of the tank. The problem's higher up; my fingers feel the pockmarks in the bodywork a little ways below the fuel cap. Standing, I push my right hand against the Jeep's body and push. As the vehicle rocks, I hear the ripple of gas in the tank.

I turn back towards North. 'I think there's enough gas to get us out of here.'

'Yeah?' He gestures towards the shredded tyres. 'You got a few spares inside?'

'Don't need them.' I pull open the door to the back seat. 'We just need to put some distance between us and this place. Doesn't have to be pretty.'

'We'd be better sinking it in the lake.'

The Jeep was less than two months old. I'd written off the last one on a mountain road in West Virginia. Couldn't claim another write-off so soon; they'd never insure me again. 'Not on my watch.'

North shrugs. 'Suit yourself, but don't say I didn't warn you. This Jeep, it links you to the shooting. It's not just Luciano's men who died tonight. My FBI handlers were killed back at Hampton Lodge – good men, with wives and families.'

I hold his gaze. A good man is a good man whether he has a wife and family or not; plenty of assholes have both of those, and they're still assholes. 'I was in the room two along from yours. When the police investigate the crime scene they'll find me packed and shipped out. The ballistics report on the bullet in Luciano's man shot on the walkway will be a match for my gun. Like it or not, I'm tied to this already.'

'Hope you know what that means.'

'Means I need to be quick at getting you back to the Old Man. Which is why we need the Jeep and we have to move now.' Turning, I grab my jacket off the back seat. Grit my teeth to stop myself from wincing as I put it on. Don't quite get away with it.

He frowns. 'You're hurt?'

'It's nothing.'

North's voice is softer; his expression all concerned. 'Show me.'

I shake my head. Wave his concern away. 'There's no time, I've just tweaked it.'

His expression tells me he doesn't believe me.

Taking my Swiss Army knife from my jeans pocket, I walk around to the offside rear wheel and stab it hard. The impact jars through my body. Pain spikes in my left arm and I bite my lip, trying not to cry out. Exhaling hard, I put my knife back in my pocket and move around to the driver's door. Look at North. 'There, now at least the wheels are even.'

He stares back at me, raises his eyebrows but doesn't speak.

I climb up into the driver's seat and turn the key in the ignition. First there's nothing. Second time I press the gas harder and the engine rattles and coughs. Third time it catches.

Revving the engine, and hoping it'll stay alive, I lean across the seats and open the passenger side door. 'Come on, North, get in. It's time we got out of here.'

21

FRIDAY, SEPTEMBER 21st, 05:08

I coax the Jeep through the narrow country roads around the wild-life management area, away from Missingdon and towards the main highway. I figure Route 98 will be a better call than I-10. We have a good few miles to reach it, but oftentimes fewer vehicles mean fewer state troopers, and we need to stay off the grid for as long as we can.

Without tyres we feel every bump in the road a hundred times more than normal. The metal wheel rims scream like strangled cats against the blacktop; an ear-piercing, nerve-grating sound that makes the hairs on the back of my arms stand on end and puts my teeth on edge. But it's worth it. We're making progress – getting further from Missingdon, and the crime scenes, faster than we ever could have done on foot.

But still North looks pissed. 'The noise this thing's making, we may as well use a megaphone to announce where we are to the cops.'

'I thought you said you were with the Feds voluntarily. Why are you worried about the cops?'

He looks at me like I'm as dumb as a stump. I'm not, but I hold his gaze, playing the role. Waiting to hear his take on things.

'Dead bodies tend to change a situation.'

The Jeep's engine coughs and fades. I stamp on the gas pedal hard, forcing it back into life. 'You didn't kill the Feds.'

He stares at me though his shades, his expression unreadable. 'You seem very sure of that, but how'd you know? You weren't on the walkway or in my room; you didn't see who fired the shots.'

'I heard the two agents exit your room out onto the walkway and then the gunfire. I'm not some tadpole bounty hunter or rookie kid.

I know how to judge where a shooter's at by sound. The shots were fired from outside your room. A split-second later you bust through the connecting door. The lives of those two agents, they aren't on you.'

He looks away. 'I knew Luciano would do something.' His tone's bitter now. 'I told them two agents wouldn't be enough.'

'You didn't pull the trigger. Like I said, it's not on you.'

'I swore I'd never let that happen again. That I'd never have to do that.'

I tug at the wheel, limping the Jeep around a bend as if it's a mustang with a busted leg. 'What?'

North looks back at me. His jaw is rigid. There's a muscle pulsing in his neck. 'Watch good citizens die.'

'Not your call. Luciano's men—'

'The Old Man thinks I've turned.'

'That's not what he said to me. But based on what went down here tonight, yeah I reckon so.' I frown. 'You wanted to help the Feds, though, so he's right, isn't he?'

North exhales hard. Shakes his head. 'It's more complicated than that.'

The road's really rough in this section – the bumps stab through my left arm like a bitch. I grip the wheel tighter with my right. Grit my teeth. 'Yeah. Always is.'

'Anyways, it doesn't matter what the truth is. Luciano will have poisoned the Old Man against me. They're out for my blood now, both of them.'

I nod. Know that it's the truth. 'So they don't want you safe, they just want you silenced, huh?'

'That's about the sum of it.'

'I still have to take you back.'

'Yeah. I get that. I worked for the family my whole life. I know that there's no sense in running – I've seen what happens if you do. The only way to do this is head on.' He grabs the map from my go bag. Spreads it out over his side of the dash. 'We've got maybe twelve miles to go until we reach Route 98, not much more.'

The engine misfires and I shake my head. 'This thing's running on fumes. I don't think it'll get us that far.'

'Then we need to ditch it before we run out of gas.'

'Agreed.' Busted tyres and bullet holes are guaranteed to draw attention if we leave it here. I'd rather have the Jeep hidden out of the way than parked up at the side of the highway. 'I was thinking the same thing.'

I keep driving and about half a mile on I see a good spot; a knocked-about barn, near-on totally covered in creepers. The Jeep will be hidden from the road, so hopefully the cops won't find it, or at least it should take them a while. And it'll be a whole lot easier to fetch it once this is all over.

Taking my foot off the gas, I glance at North. 'I'm thinking here.'

He looks at the barn and nods. 'Good call. There's a truck stop a couple of miles up Route 98. We walk there, we can hitch a ride.'

Twisting the wheel, I steer the Jeep off the road and behind the abandoned barn. The tyreless wheels clunk over the rutted ground, shaking us about and sending hot spikes of pain shooting down my left arm. I clench my jaw and, clutching the wheel tighter with both hands, steer the vehicle into hiding.

I park it tight up against the barn on the passenger side, blocking North in. Opening my door, I climb out, then open the back and pick up my go bag. Slamming the back door shut, I peer through the front at North. 'You coming?'

'I guess so.' He scoots across the seats and jumps out of the Jeep. Taking his shades from the inside pocket of his leather jacket, he puts them on and gives me one of his smiles. 'Let's do this.'

Pocketing the keys to the Jeep, I lead us back out onto the side of the road. The sun is higher in the sky, its rays growing in strength, preparing for the scorching heat of the day. The air above the road ahead of us seems to warp and flex, an illusion from the hot air mingling with the colder, dew-damp ground. Before long I know that the blacktop will be hot as a griddle pan at a cookout.

I look across at North. I can't figure him out. He claims he's turned state witness voluntarily, yet when he was talking earlier it sounded like he's still loyal to Old Man Bonchese. There's something at play here that I'm not aware of; another game aside from Luciano's bloodlust and the Old Man's fake rescue mission.

North's moving purposefully, keeping time with my stride. Sensing I'm watching, he glances up and gives me a half-smile. With his shades shielding his eyes, it's impossible to interpret what he means by it.

I smile back, but I know it'll look a little forced. The man I knew all those years ago seemed like a genuine guy, but I didn't know then he was a mob man, a fixer for the Old Man himself. That knowledge changes things, makes me a whole lot more wary. North might be with me for now, and say he wants to face the Bonchese family head on, but I'm damn sure he'll make a break as soon as a better option comes along. And, the thing is, although I've got handcuffs in my go bag, I can't use them. If I cuff him to me it'll draw attention, and we can't have that. So, for now, I have to leave him be.

Doesn't mean that I'm not watching his every move.

22

FRIDAY, SEPTEMBER 21st, 05:54

Sirens. In the distance ... but getting louder.

North grabs my jacket and yanks me sideways, throwing us both into the undergrowth at the side of the road. 'Get down.'

His hand pressing in the centre of my back pins me flat.

'What the hell?' My left arm hurts like hell from falling onto it. Fire nettles sting my hands. Stones from the road edge dig into my legs. I push myself back up to my feet. I glare at North and point across the flat grassland towards the horizon. 'See the blue lights? The cops aren't on this road. We've a ways to go yet before we need to start diving into bushes.'

North mumbles an apology. The humidity's rising, and he looks a little sweaty beneath that leather jacket of his. We're nearly out of water and we've still got around eight miles to hike before we reach Route 98.

We keep walking. I don't let us slow, even though my head's starting to pound like there's a jackhammer bashing against it in time with each stride.

A mile later North stops. Breathing heavily, he steps across onto the grass at the side of the road and flops down. 'Let's take five?'

We can't afford the time; the cops must be looking for us by now. It seems the hot-shot fixer isn't as fit as he used to be. But he looks clammy, his face pale rather than red, as I'd have expected. 'You okay?'

He's silent a moment. Looks real earnest, like he's thinking on what to tell me, then says. 'I've got a heart problem, recently diagnosed. All this walking, the heat ... My chest's feeling tight.'

I pass him the last of the water. 'You got something you can take?'

He shakes his head. 'Left my medication in the room. It's okay. I'll be fine in a minute.'

'Hope so. I don't want to have to carry you.'

He laughs. Drains the last of the water and squashes the plastic bottle into a nugget. Puts it into his pocket. 'Okay, let's go.'

I look at him and raise an eyebrow. 'You going to die on me?'

He smiles. 'I'll try not to.'

That's when we hear a vehicle.

I look at North. He's still not looking great and I figure riding would be a whole lot better for him than walking. I gesture for him to get down low in the bushes. Then I run my fingers through my hair and step out onto the road with my thumb up.

I look back over my shoulder as a silver RAM 1500 appears around the bend. It's a new model, shiny, with a lone male driver. I fix my best smile to my face as he approaches.

He slows, braking to a halt beside me, and winds down the window. 'Looking for a ride, honey?'

I've hitched plenty before, and I know on instinct this isn't the type of man a girl should be getting into a truck with alone. He's a big guy with longish blond hair, few-days-old stubble, and he's looking at me like a mountain lion does a deer: real predatorily. But I think of North lying in the bushes and his dodgy heart and know taking this truck to Route 98 will be a whole lot better for him than hiking. 'Why that would be so kind of you.'

'Well, jump in, darling.'

I glance behind me at North. Then I open the truck's door and climb up into the truck. As I fasten my seatbelt, I see in my peripheral vision that North's crawling fast around to the back of the truck.

Widening my smile, I look at the driver. 'Sure appreciate this.'

'My pleasure,' he says, in a tone that tells me he thinks it will be. 'Love to help a damsel in distress.'

I force myself to keep smiling despite his sexist bullshit. As I do, North vaults up over the side of the tailgate and lands lightly onto the flatbed. To disguise the sound I clap my hands, faking delight. 'You're a real hero.'

The driver pulls away, setting off along the road at a fast lick. I try to ignore the way he keeps glancing across at my breasts.

'You from around here?' he asks. 'Haven't seen you before. I know I'd have remembered if I did.'

'I'm just visiting.'

He nods. Licks his lips. 'Where you hail from, then?'

I'm not a fan of all his questions. Wish he'd just shut up and stick to the driving, but know I need to act natural, not arouse suspicion. 'I'm on vacation, hiking, you know? Only I lost my bearings this morning.'

He grins. Looks down at my chest again. 'I think your bearings are just fine.'

Jeez, the nerve of this guy. Shaking my head, I gesture out through the windshield. 'So how far are you going?'

He puts his hand on my thigh. Winks. 'All the way, baby.'

'No, I don't think so.' I push his hand away. 'That's not what this is.'

'Oh, I think that's exactly what it is.' He laughs. Grips my leg harder, sliding his fingers upwards. 'Come on, baby, loosen up.'

I slap his fingers away. 'I said no. I'm not your damn baby.'

'You are if I say so.' He jerks the steering wheel hard right and brakes to a stop at the side of the road. 'I'm giving you a ride. Now you give me some sugar.'

I glare at him. Keep my breathing steady even though my heart's punching my ribs like a heavyweight champion. Reach for the door release. 'I'll walk from here.'

'No, baby, you're not leaving so soon.' He presses a button, and I hear a clunk.

I pull the door handle. It doesn't release.

He laughs, louder this time, and lunges for me. 'Quit fighting, you might enjoy it.'

I don't wait to see what happens next. Won't have some dick-for-brains guy thinking he can do what he wants with me – with any woman. I reach under my jacket, pull out my X2 Taser and fire it through his jeans and into his balls. 'Get the hell off me you fucking pervert.'

He jerks away from me, although that's due to the Taser rather than him suddenly getting a conscience. I keep firing, letting the volts pulse through his convulsing body until he's peed himself and is crying to his momma for it to stop.

Leaving the pin probes in his pants, I put my X2 back in my concealed holster, and lean over him to press the door unlock button.

He cringes away from me, and I shake my head. 'Learn that no means no.' I glance at his balls. 'You try that again with any woman and, next time, I'll shoot them off.'

Climbing down from the cab, I slam the door behind me. North raises his head above the side of the flatbed. 'What's—'

I gesture at him to get out. 'Quick. We're going.'

He jumps down and peers into the cab. Looks back at me and raises an eyebrow. 'What the hell happened to him?'

I sling my go bag over my shoulder, wincing as the movement jars my left arm. I frown at North. 'He tried taking something that wasn't for him.'

North's expression tells me that he understands my meaning. 'Damn, Lori, if you were in trouble you could've—'

'*I* wasn't in trouble. He got what was coming to him.'

'I see that.'

'So come on, we should move.'

North glances into the truck, at the driver who's still sprawled and shaking inside, then back at me. He raises his hand to his forehead in a mock salute. 'Whatever you say, boss.'

I head out at a run, and North follows. My go bag's banging against my back and my left arm feels hot and swollen beneath the sleeve of my jacket. I need to take a proper look at it, but first I need to get us out of the truck guy's sight. He's disabled for now, the volts having disrupted his muscle control and balance, but give him five minutes and he'll be charging down this road with a hair up his ass about getting bested by a girl. Sure, I could have taken his vehicle, but that seems like a bigger risk. In small-town places like this, folks tend to be all up in each other's business. I figure once word got out it wouldn't take long for them to find the truck, and I sure don't need any other kinds of mob on our tail right now.

We'll stay out of sight better on foot.

And we need to get off the road.

23

FRIDAY, SEPTEMBER 21st, 06:32

Half a mile away from where we left the truck, we hang a right into a patch of forest. The ground is overgrown, the footing rough and uneven. North's breathing is becoming more laboured. I drop our speed under the shade of the trees, but keep us marching. The sun's up and we're in full daylight now. Cops and Feds will be swarming around the crime scene back in Missingdon, and they'll have most likely found our trail up to Carter's Lake. 'It's not much further to Route 98 – maybe a couple of miles.'

North nods. 'I was trying not to ask if we were there yet.'

I smile. He's using humour to try and hide it, but he looks worried. With a heart condition and no medication, I know he can't keep going at this pace for long. He needs a break. We both do. Maybe we should find someplace to lie low for a while.

We hike through the trees and out into an orange grove that stretches as far as the horizon. Using the compass on my cellphone, I check our position against the map and keep us heading towards Route 98 and a rest stop that's marked as being a couple of miles from our current location.

Time passes. We stay off the road, and fate is kind to us; we don't see the guy in the truck again.

⌐

The rest stop is set a little ways back from Route 98, between the local road leading from the orange groves and the highway. There's a gas station and a rundown motel, and not a whole lot else. From the number of eighteen-wheelers parked up, it seems the place is popular with truckers.

I glance at North. He's trying hard not to show it but his breathing is definitely a struggle. He looks pale despite his tan, and his skin seems to have a strange, waxy texture. I can't get him his medication back, so, if we're going to make it to Miami without, he needs rest.

I catch his eye and nod towards the motel. 'We should take cover here for a while. I'll get us a room.'

North doesn't argue.

Having pulled on the Red Sox ball cap from my go bag and slipped on my shades, I push open the door to the motel. Before I step inside, I see North slump onto the bench seat out front, his head in his hands. Right now he doesn't look like a big mob fixer; he looks like a broken man.

The older lady behind the desk looks up at me over her small oval glasses. Her tone is lukewarm pleasant, but her expression is full-on suspicious. 'Good morning. Can I help you?'

'I'm looking for a room.'

She looks me up and down, taking in my raggedy appearance. 'We don't rent by the hour here.'

In truth an hourly rental would've suited me just fine, but I don't want her getting her panties all twisted. 'Well, good, because that sure isn't what I'm after. I need a room: one night, with twin beds. No connecting door to any other rooms.' I lower my voice. 'I had a bad experience like that one time.'

'One night, twin room, no problem.' Any embarrassment she might have felt about having insinuated my reason for needing a room was because I was a working girl she hides well with her firm tone and efficient manner. She takes a key from a hook behind the desk. 'Room six is vacant. That'll be fifty-eight bucks. Cash or card?'

Fifty-eight bucks is at least double what this place is worth, but North isn't going to make it much further without a break, so she kind of has me over a barrel.

'Cash,' I say, peeling three twenties from the roll in my go bag and handing them to her. 'Go ahead and keep the change.'

⌒

Room six is as basic as it gets: two beds, one closet, and a small bathroom with an even smaller shower, which has a load of black mould growing along the bottom edge of the tiles. It might smell a little musty, but it's enough for our needs, and it'll keep us out of the sun and off the roads. Right now, that's all that matters.

I fetch us a few bottles of water and a couple of sausage biscuits from the hot-food vending machine outside the room. As we eat, I switch on the television and flick through the channels until I find the local news station.

On screen there's a pretty blonde and an older, deeply tanned man, who are both wearing too much make-up. They're talking with barely contained excitement about a shoot-out in nearby Missingdon. From the look on their faces I'm guessing this is the most thrilling piece of news they've ever reported on air.

But it's not thrilling to me. I killed a man. Shot him and watched him drop off the walkway onto the dumpsters. My hands start to shake with the memory. I hate guns – only ever use one as a last resort. And it *was* a last resort: the man was firing at me. It was shoot or be shot.

That still doesn't make it right.

Clasping my hands together to stop them shaking, I wince as pain darts through my left arm. I try to focus on the news report. The banner scrolling along the bottom of the screen reads: *Four Dead in Missingdon Massacre*.

Four dead? That doesn't ring true. There were two Feds, the Miami Mob guy on the walkway, then Luciano's two men killed by North at Carter's Lake.

On screen the blonde is talking, I increase the volume.

'*...officers are on the scene, and we understand that our local police force are working side-by-side with the FBI to find the vigilantes responsible* *for this horrific night of violence.'* She looks down and puts her finger to her ear, obviously listening to something being fed to her, then looks straight back to camera. *'We've just had an update through to the studio about the victims who lost their lives in this sickening tragedy. They were Federal Agents John Jackson Junior and Otis Young, and Miami residents, Giovanni Ricci and Nico Moretti. We are unclear at this time about how they're connected, but we've been told the man injured during the attack has now been stabilised and is helping the investigators from his hospital bed...'*

Relief that I didn't kill the man on the walkway floods through me. Fear crashes into my chest fast behind it. I glance over at North. 'I shot the man on walkway.'

He grimaces. 'Not well enough.'

'If he's one of Luciano's men, he knows who we both are.'

'He won't help the Feds.'

'You sure about that?'

North looks thoughtful. 'The bigger problem is he'll be straight on the wire to tell Luciano what went down.'

'I need to call him, make him understand the situation.'

'Won't do no good. We killed two of his best men. Even if you take me to him, he won't forgive you that. It'd make him look weak. He won't be able to let that stand.'

I shake my head. Think of JT and Dakota, of the threats the Old Man and Luciano have made against them. Look back at North. 'I have to try.'

24

FRIDAY, SEPTEMBER 21st, 08:43

Luciano's cellphone rings once before he picks it up. He doesn't say his name, just waits for me to speak first.

North's in the bathroom, and I'd prefer he doesn't hear, so I get straight to business. 'I have North, but from the three men you had shooting at us I'm guessing that's not the way you wanted things to play out.'

There's a pause at the end of the line, then a single laugh with no happiness in it. 'An error.'

'The fact that North and me are still alive?'

'That North is.'

'Sure didn't feel that way. Anyways, you said you wanted him alive.'

'I don't believe I was that specific.'

I harden my tone. 'You and the Old Man sent me to do a job, and I'm damn well going to do it. I have North, I busted him out from the Feds and stopped him testifying this morning, and now I'm going to bring him back to Miami. So tell your dogs to back the hell off.'

'A bitch with an invalid lover and little kid back at home in her apartment isn't in any position to tell me what to do.'

I clench my fingers tighter around the cellphone. Can't let anything happen to Dakota and JT, just can't. They've already been through enough because of me. But I know Luciano will exploit any weakness. I make my tone hardball tough. 'She is if you want North back.'

'Well, you see, Lori, that's the thing.' He lets out another sinister laugh. 'I don't want him back. What I want is for you to kill him.'

'But that's not what we—'

'Do it, and send me proof within the next hour. Or I'll give the order to execute that cute kid and son-of-a-bitch lover of yours. And then I'll hunt you and North down like the vermin you are. Sixty minutes, Lori, so get busy. Tick tock.'

25

North comes out of the bathroom and I'm not fast enough on the draw to get my poker face on.

He stops in the doorway, frowning. 'You look like a dog that ate a hornet. What happened?'

'Luciano's not happy.'

'Don't say I didn't call it.'

'Wasn't hard to call,' I snap back, trying to buy time.

He shrugs and walks around the bed I'm sitting on to the one nearest the door. He puffs up the rather flaccid-looking pillows and flops onto it. 'So, what now?'

My mind's going bat-shit crazy. I need an answer. A plan. I think of the only person who can overrule Luciano's instruction, and I know what my next move has to be. 'What's the landline number at the Old Man's house?'

North raises his eyebrows. 'Why'd you want that?'

'I need to speak to him.'

'Not a good idea ringing the house, he doesn't like to—'

'I'm not much in the mood for caring whether he likes it or not, I need to speak to him. Now, you got the number or what?'

'Yeah, I know it.' North reels off a number.

I tap it into my cell and press call. My stomach flips as it connects.

It takes thirteen rings before it's answered. There's a load of rustling, then a woman with a strong Spanish accent says, 'Bonchese.'

'I need to speak with Giovanni Bonchese.'

'He's not here.'

On the television the news channel is showing footage of Hampton Lodge. The rooms we'd been in are closed off with crime-scene tape. 'It's important. I'm doing a job for him and—'

'No.' Her voice is panicked, her words fast. 'No business on this line, never.'

They held me hostage in that place, but they won't speak business on the telephone? Ridiculous. I raise my voice. 'Don't hang up, I have to speak with—'

'He's not here. Away. No contact. Try Monday.'

The call disconnects and I'm left staring at my cell.

'No joy?' North says. 'Don't say I didn't warn you.'

I swivel around to face him. 'Don't be such an asshole. I saved your sorry ass last night, so try to be a bit less of a dick, yeah?' It's difficult not to take out my stress on North.

'Maybe try listening to me, then.' North holds my gaze. 'Even if the Old Man had been there, they wouldn't have let you speak to him. I know that because I've lived and worked with the family for years. I know how they operate.'

'How did you know the Old Man wouldn't be there?'

'Because of the date. Every year he makes a sort of pilgrimage to the place his brother died – out in the wild country. He takes three days and goes alone, except for his two most trusted men. They all leave their cellphones behind. No business for the time they're away – it's one of the Old Man's rules.'

'You sure seem to know a lot about it.'

'Yeah.' He looks sad. 'Until this year, I was one of the men with him.'

'And Luciano?'

North shakes his head. 'No. He never went.'

Real interesting, but it doesn't help my immediate problem none. I check the time on my watch; it says 09:16. The clock's ticking down. Luciano wants North dead by a quarter of ten. I have less than half an hour.

I feel the pressure building in my chest. My throat's dry. Nausea whirls in my stomach. Without the Old Man to overrule Luciano's orders I'm screwed. I can't kill North; murdering someone in cold blood just doesn't sit right with me. But if I don't I'm condemning Dakota and JT to death from my lack of action. Whatever I do, somebody will die.

I gesture at North's bed. 'Rest, okay. I need to call home.'

⌒

Stepping outside, I close the door behind me. The area around the motel is quiet. There are a couple of cars parked up close, but no noise from the other rooms. At the far end of the building there's a maid's cart stationed in the open doorway of the last room. The maid is far enough away to be out of earshot, so I lean back on the wall and call JT.

As the call connects my stomach flips. I hope he'll answer. I didn't leave on good terms, and I know he doesn't approve of the job I'm doing. But, tough or not, I need to hear his voice right now. Sometimes even the most independent people need a little support.

He answers on the third ring. 'You okay?'

It's not the question I want. Not something I want to talk about. I'm injured, but until I can take a proper look I don't know how bad. I don't want to tell him that my arm feels on fire, and that I fear this job is more than I can handle, so I bite back the doubt and the worry, and say, 'I'm fine. How's Dakota?'

'She's good. Working on a math problem for me right now.'

It's gone nine; Dakota should be in class. Regular attendance is important, especially as she missed so much last year when she was sick in hospital. 'She's not in school?'

'I thought she'd best stay home given what's going on.'

He's right. 'Okay, good call.'

He lowers his voice. His words sound more urgent. 'What the hell happened, Lori? I saw online that there was a shooting in Missingdon and some Feds got killed. Is that where you are? Did you do that?'

'I was there.'

JT lets out a long whistle. 'Well, shit.'

'Luciano set me up. His men killed the Feds. They tried to kill me and North.'

'You're with North?'

'Yeah.' I think about what Luciano's told me to do. 'For now.'

'Then you need to think fast, Lori. His face is all over the news reports – they're saying he's a fugitive.'

Shit. 'The Jeep's busted up. We had to go a long way on foot and North's not in a good way. He can't travel further right now.'

'Then, much as I hate to say it, call that bastard Monroe. He's with the Bureau, he can help.'

If he chose to, Special Agent Alex Monroe could help, but it's always hard to tell which way he'll jump. 'I'll figure something out. But, look, Luciano has asked me to do something else, and I don't think I can. If I don't do it he says he's got people watching you and Dakota and he'll have them kill you.'

'I'll look after her, Lori, you know I always—'

'You're still injured, JT. I know you don't want to hear it, but what they'll come at you with, you're not fit enough yet to—'

'I'll take Dakota to my cabin.' JT's tone is firm, no nonsense.

I shake my head. Bite my lip. I know I have to get him to see reason and accept he's not ready yet to face up to the mob. I can't lose him and I cannot lose Dakota. He needs to get away from the apartment and out of Luciano's sights. I need them both safe. 'That's not going to work. They'll know about the cabin. You leave the apartment and they'll guess that you're headed there.'

He says nothing.

'Look, I've got another idea. Somewhere closer to home, and with someone who can help you both stay safe.'

He sounds distant, pissed. 'I'm listening.'

I know JT doesn't like accepting help, and he dislikes pity even more, but he needs to get over that. There's only one other person that I trust to do right and keep my daughter safe. I give JT their name and tell him how to find them and what to say when he does. 'Go now. Luciano's men will be coming for you any minute.'

'Yup.'

The distance seems to widen between us. I hate that I can't reach out and touch him; that he can't see from my expression that I'm asking him to do this because I love him. 'JT, I—'

'Take care of yourself, Lori.' His gravel-deep voice is gruff. 'Do what you need to do to protect our girl.'

I swallow down the words I'd been going to say, instead telling him I'll do everything I can to protect Dakota and asking him to do the same. As I speak, my throat contracts and I struggle to hide my emotion. I feel my eyes welling up, and shake my head, telling myself to get my head back in the game.

There's no room for error. No time to think on the tension between us.

We have to stay focused if we're going to get out of this alive.

⌒

Back in the room, North is stretched out on his bed, asleep or as near as damn it. I lock the door, put the chain across and walk over to my go bag. I glance again at North, checking his eyes are closed, then take out the small bottle of antiseptic and the roll of black duct tape and head for the bathroom.

Locking the bathroom door behind me, I put the tape and antiseptic down on the basin and take off my leather jacket. I gasp at the pain as it gets stuck on my left arm. Even though there's a tear in my usually fitted jacket, it's as tight as a tourniquet, but I have to get my arm free. I don't want to cut the sleeve. If I do, North will know that I'm injured, and I don't want that. He might seem happy enough to stick with me for now, but I don't know his endgame. And until I do, I need for him to think that he's in a worse way physically than I am.

Gritting my teeth, I grasp the bottom of the left sleeve and yank hard and fast. The pain is quick and brutal. I feel suddenly light-headed, dizzy. Dropping the jacket onto the floor, I hold tight to the edge of the basin with my right hand and take deep breaths through my mouth.

The left sleeve of my long-sleeved tee is crusted with dried blood and as tight around my forearm as the jacket. I can't face the pain of pulling it off, and I can afford to lose the sleeve, so taking hold of the fabric where it's been ripped by the bullet, I pull. It tears easily, peeling away from my upper arm like a second skin.

My bicep is painted dark with dried blood. Pulling off the jacket has reopened the wound; a thick trail of crimson snakes down over the mottled skin. Leaning over the basin, I wash away the blood, cleaning the injury. The cool water feels as if it's as cold as ice.

It's hard to get a proper view of the damage, so I use the mirror. As far as I can see the bullet scraped through the outside of my upper arm, leaving a track mark. Still, I need to be sure.

Clenching my jaw, I press my fingers against my skin, feeling around the wound and checking to see if I can locate a bullet lodged in my flesh. The arm is inflamed and swollen and the pain of pressing it brings tears to my eyes. It's so bad I think I might pass out. But I don't feel any foreign objects. If I'm lucky – and I hope to hell that I am – the wound is a through-and-through.

I take the bottle of antiseptic and pour the liquid into and over the wound. As it touches my raw flesh, the pain punches me in the chest and I bite back a stream of obscenities. Then I grab the duct tape and bind the wound together, hoping to stop any further bleeding.

It feels like I'm going to vomit.

I hold onto the basin. Inhale and exhale real deep. Eventually the sick sensation goes and I'm left with a pounding ache in my arm. I know I need medical attention; the wound needs proper cleaning and stitches for sure. Every minute without increases the risk of infection. But I can't go to an emergency room – they'd notify law enforcement the minute I give them my name, so for now the antiseptic and the duct tape is the best I can do.

Pulling my jacket back on, I check my watch: 09:31. Less than fifteen minutes until the time Luciano's given me to get North dead is up.

It's time to make my choice.

26

FRIDAY, SEPTEMBER 21st, 09:32

Kill or let my family die? That's no kind of choice. But the clock's counting down and Luciano will take any indecision on my part as a choice to sacrifice Dakota and JT, I'm certain of it. I think back to Wednesday morning, before everything turned about face, remember JT standing behind Dakota, his brow creased in concentration as he focused hard on twisting her strawberry-blonde hair into two raggedy-assed pigtails, and Dakota sitting on the stool, grinning like a Cheshire cat on a sugar high because he was helping her get ready for school.

It feels like there's a knife twisting in my belly. I can't let harm come to them.

Can't.

Shoving open the bathroom door I march back into the room. North's still lying on his bed, eyes closed, looking real pale beneath his tan.

Without opening his eyes he says, 'You call home okay?'

'Yeah.'

I check my watch: 09:34. I feel a tightening in my chest. I have to make a decision.

I recall first meeting North, before I knew he was a fixer and believed him to be a friend of Tommy's. He was kind to me at a time when there hadn't been many folks in my corner; he would have done more to help if I'd have let him. That still counts for something, I think; it has to.

'They know you're out here with me?' North says, eyes still closed.

'Yup.'

I think about my conversation with JT. How he promised to get out of the apartment and move Dakota to somewhere safer. He'll have to shake off the mob heavies watching them first; the guys that took the photo of him and Dakota down the barrel of a gun. Men so low on morals that they'd shoot a nine-year-old child dead as revenge for something her momma did ten years before.

I feel my lower lip quiver and bite it to make it still. Feel the ache in my left arm getting stronger. Hope JT has enough stamina to get free and clear. No matter the tension between us, I have faith in him. And I know for sure that he'll do anything to protect Dakota.

Do what you need to do to protect our girl – that's what he said to me. He will. And I will too, always have.

Deep breath. Steady hand. Do what needs to get done.

I stride around my bed to North's. Stop alongside it, facing him.

He opens his eyes. 'What's up?'

I shake my head. Stare at him real serious. 'No talking.'

North pushes himself up to a sitting position, putting more distance between us. He's frowning, his eyes searching mine for a clue to what's happening. 'I don't like the way you're looking at me. Lori, what are you...?'

I pull the Wesson Classic Bobtail from my shoulder holster and point it at North's head. 'I'm sorry, North, but this is the only way. I kill you or Luciano kills my family, and then they kill you and me afterwards anyway. I can't let my daughter die.'

For a moment I think North's going to attack me. But then he shuffles across the bed towards me. Leans in, pressing his head against the muzzle of the gun. 'Go on then.'

His reaction back-foots me. This man's a mob fixer; where's his fight, his will to live? I wonder if it's a bluff. 'Why offer to sacrifice yourself?'

He looks up at me. 'I've done a lot of bad shit in my time. Guess it's about time I do what's good and right. If killing me saves your kid, you best get it done.'

I say nothing.

'Sometimes things happen that you didn't cause but you feel responsible for, you know?'

I shake my head. 'Help me understand.'

'Luciano has a whole bunch of businesses he operates as a sideline. The Old Man conducts things the traditional way, honouring the old code. Luciano doesn't. This got the Old Man concerned, so he asked me to keep a watching eye on Luciano's practices.' North exhales hard. Glances away. 'I watched him shoot an eighty-four-year-old woman in the foot because she was behind on her rental payments in an apartment that was damp with mould and had cockroaches crawling across the kitchen floor. Saw him scald an six-year-old kid's hand in a pan of boiling water because the boy's meth-head mom had been skimming a few hundred bucks off the drugs money she made selling Luciano's crystal. I saw these things and I didn't intervene.'

I frown. Feel sick at the thought of an old women and a young child being mutilated by Luciano while North just stood there and watched. 'You did nothing?'

North looks back up at me. 'I didn't stop what Luciano did. And he got worse – brasher and bolder. Thought he was untouchable. The things he did couldn't be allowed to stand. He needed to be stopped and we – I – thought I could do it from the inside but ... it didn't go that way. So I went to the Feds and offered information about him.' He shakes his head. 'Like I said, I've done a lot of bad things in the name of the Bonchese family, but I've always had a code, a line that I won't cross. A man like Luciano, he has no code, no limit. He can't be allowed to take over from the Old Man.'

I stare at North. Keep the gun against his head. Think of Dakota and JT, and how we'd just gotten a fleeting taste of how it might be to live as a family.

I tighten my finger against the trigger.

It takes a real desperate kind of a woman to kill a penitent man.

27

FRIDAY, SEPTEMBER 21st, 09:35

Relationships, attachments – they're a weakness in this business. JT knows that; it's why he's always been careful. He's lived alone, been alone; kept distant from those who think they care about him. Always pushed them away when they got too close, too invested. Until now.

He looks across at Dakota sitting at the kitchen table, concentrating on her math problem. Her braids have fallen forwards over her shoulders, the tip of her tongue's poking out from her lips. Damn. It's attachments like her that make you vulnerable. But ever since he found out, just a few short months ago, that he has a daughter, he realised he wouldn't want things any other way.

If Lori believes Luciano Bonchese's people are watching the apartment he has no reason to doubt her. That means they need to get gone right now.

'Dakota?'

She looks up and grins. 'Yeah?'

'Your momma's going to be out of town a while.' He tries to inject some excitement into his voice. 'You want to have an adventure?'

Dakota tilts her head. 'What kind of adventure?'

'An overnight one.' He moves away from the counter, towards the door. 'The rest's a surprise. You ready?'

She frowns. Doesn't get up. 'Something's going on isn't it?'

'I just thought a trip would be fun.'

'Aren't we going to pack first? Mom always has us pack a bag each if we're going on a trip.'

He nods. He hasn't got a proper handle on this parenting thing yet, but Dakota's testing him, he knows that much. She's a smart kid and he won't be able to keep the truth from her for much longer. He'll go along with Dakota's thinking, but won't let it stall them long. Once they're free and clear he'll tell her what's really going on. 'Sure, pack your bag. We leave in five.'

⌒

JT's rucksack is already packed – serving as a temporary go bag – so he slings it over his shoulder, closes the blinds in the front window and locks the apartment door. He takes hold of Dakota's hand, and they head down the stairs to the parking lot.

'So did you fix the math problem?' he says.

Dakota starts to answer, chattering away about the type of problem and how fives are her favourite number. He keeps the conversation going, but beneath the brim of his Yankees ball cap, his focus is on the surrounding area – windows and rooftops especially. Anyplace the mob might use to site a sniper.

He sees nothing. But that don't mean they're not there, watching. They could be behind a drape in a high window, or too far back from the edge of a flat roof to spot easy from the ground. Rifle aimed at Dakota and him. JT walks faster.

'Do you think I'm right?' Dakota asks.

He hadn't heard what she'd said. Nods anyways. 'Sure.'

She slows her pace, and gives him some side eye. 'I don't think you were listening.'

He forces a laugh. 'Of course I was.'

Dakota halts. Pulling her hand from his, she puts her hands on her hips and sticks her chin out. 'What did I say then?'

They can't stop. They're easy targets for a sniper. He needs her to move. 'I'll tell you in the car.'

'No. Here.'

Damn, she's one stubborn child sometimes. That's what comes from having a dad like him and a mom like Lori, he guesses. Dakota was always going to be a person who knows her own mind. But he can do without the sass now, needs more compliance. Giving her a stern look, he opens the door and folds the driver's seat forward. 'The car, now.'

She looks pissed, then hurt. Biting her lip, she leaps into the back of the Mustang and scoots across the jump seats to the side opposite the driver's. He folds the driver's seat back and throws his rucksack over onto the passenger side. This parenting stuff is hard. He's missed nearly ten years of Dakota's life. Ten years of a daughter he never knew he had. He won't miss any more, and he won't let anything bad happen to her. Even if, sometimes, that means he has to act in ways she isn't going to like.

He climbs in. As he goes to pull the door shut, he hears an engine start up somewhere across the lot. Adrenaline fires into his blood. He takes care to act normal, doesn't look round. Doesn't want to alert them that he's onto them.

Over on the back seat, Dakota lets out a loud sigh.

JT tries not to let it get to him. Strange really, how he'll take a guy shooting at him less personally than a sigh from a nine-year-old girl.

As he pulls away from the parking lot, and out onto the highway he keeps checking the rearview mirror. He's fifty yards down the street when a brown sedan pulls out of the same lot and settles into the traffic, four cars behind.

Just as he suspected, they've got themselves a tail.

He cruises just under the speed limit, thinking on his next move. Takes Highway 27 out past Lake Louisa State Park. Needs to lose the tail before they turn onto I-4; if he let's them follow him that far, there's a chance they'll guess where they're heading. JT can't allow that.

The traffic gets more congested as they near the turn for Highway 192. The brown sedan is keeping three cars back. Problem is, a car like JT's – a dark-blue, 1968 Mustang – is always going to stick out in the crowd. It's not a car for a job like this, but it's all he's got. As they approach the next intersection, the sedan is forced to brake hard by an eighteen-wheeler changing lanes. As JT reaches the lights they start to change. This is his chance.

Flooring the accelerator, he speeds the Mustang through the lights and takes a left. The signal turns red. The sedan's stranded, blocked in by the eighteen-wheeler and a bunch more vehicles.

JT steps harder on the gas, making the most of his lead. Passes Wendy's, down Morning Star Drive, looping through the residential area. Keeps his gaze part on the road, part on the rearview. Waiting for a sign the tail's caught up with them. Watching to be sure that they haven't.

In this business you make your own luck. Seems he might have got lucky.

To be sure, he steers the Mustang a few blocks in one direction, looping back around, then going a couple of blocks in another. He takes his time checking and double-checking the brown sedan's lost them. Then he heads around to Ashtown Chase and back onto Highway 27, a couple of miles back behind the turn they just took off it.

JT settles the Mustang back into the stream of traffic, but he knows they're not done yet. He stays alert to the vehicles around him, watching for another tail, or the return of the sedan. You can't ever be too careful, especially with the mob. Especially when his daughter is in the car. He glances in the mirror at Dakota.

She's watching him, frowning. 'This isn't about us having an adventure, is it?'

JT swings the wheel, accelerating hard to overtake a slowpoke red SUV. He says nothing.

'It's because of the bad guys, isn't it?'

He doesn't meet her eye. Keeps his tone steady. 'What makes you say that?'

'Momma and me got followed before. She had to lose them. That's what you've been doing, right?'

He's not going to lie. 'Yep.'

Her voice is quieter when she asks, 'Will it be like it was before?'

Dakota's seen more than a kid ever should. A few months back she'd been snatched, and it'd taken all JT and Lori's smarts to get their girl back again ... but not before Dakota had watched men die and nearly died herself. JT looks over his shoulder at her. 'I won't let anyone harm you.'

'Okay.' She's silent a moment, her expression thoughtful. Then says, 'Maybe I should learn to shoot a gun.'

'You should not.'

'Girls can, though. Momma can. Did you teach her?'

'I did.'

'So you can teach me.'

'No.'

'Why?'

'Your momma wouldn't like it.'

Dakota lets out a big sigh. 'Guess I'll have to use my slingshot then.'

JT smiles. 'I guess you will.'

They fall into silence. He drives; Dakota plays some game on her cellphone.

After another eight miles with no sign of a tail he decides it's safe. Signalling right, he takes them out onto I-4, heading towards Tampa. He's memorised Lori's directions. He knows there's sense in taking Dakota to this place, recognises the options it'll give them should things get worse, but he's feeling tense nonetheless. He doesn't like the idea of involving someone else. But Lori trusts this guy, and JT trusts her, so he'll do it.

He takes the Mustang up to the speed limit and stays vigilant for vehicles that could be new tails. As long as they're in this car and on the highway, they're vulnerable.

The drive will take them another hour.

28

I hesitate before I press send. Luciano wanted a photograph of North's dead body, and that's what he's getting. I hope that it'll be enough: for JT and Dakota to get free and clear, and to give me enough time to get back to see the Old Man, explain what happened, and to try and make him listen to reason. It's not an easy call, but it's our best chance; our only option.

I stare at North's waxy skin; the way his dark eyes stare into nothingness; the crimson stain in the hairline just above his right temple and the scarlet liquid trickling down his forehead, underneath his ear and onto the grey carpet below. I feel sick, dizzy, and the photo seems to blur. I close my eyes, take a few full breaths, then open them again. They focus on the picture and I tap the screen, sending the image to Luciano.

It's done.

My legs suddenly feel wobbly, and I drop onto the bed. The sour taste of bile is in my mouth. My breathing's rapid and shallow. The ache in my left arm is turning into a throb. I ignore it. Keep staring at my cellphone, waiting for a reply from Luciano.

'Did it work?'

I turn towards the bathroom. North's standing in the doorway, scrubbing a wet flannel against his face.

'No reply yet.'

'Hope I didn't have to get covered in ketchup for nothing.'

It'd been all we could get in the few minutes left before the hour ran out. The only red sauce in the vending machine was ketchup so that's

what we watered down and used for blood. It was pretty amateur –
wouldn't be convincing in real life for sure, but on a photo, with a filter
that made North look even paler, by my reckoning it was just about
passable. 'You get cleaned up okay?'

'Mostly.' North disappears back into the bathroom.

My cellphone beeps. It's a message from Luciano: *Send me a video of
you shooting North's body again. Do that and I'll believe you.*

Heat flushes through me. We're screwed. 'Luciano wants me to
shoot a bullet into your body to prove you're dead.'

Cussing, North walks back into the room and sits on his bed.

'We need a way out of this.'

North looks thoughtful. 'I've got an idea. Tell Luciano you're bringing me back to the compound so he can prove to the Old Man I'm a
traitor and then execute me in front of him.'

'That could work. The Old Man does like an eye for an eye.' I cock
my head to one side. Blink twice to stop the room from spinning. The
throbbing in my left arm is getting worse. 'But why would you let me
take you back there willingly?'

He holds my gaze. 'I've got something on Luciano that the Old Man
will find interesting. I'm hopeful that, once we're back, I'll be able to
get him to see reason.'

'And me – my family?'

'You said the job the Old Man asked you to do was bust me out of
federal custody and bring me back to the compound. You'll have done
exactly what he asked of you – your job will be done.'

I think on it for a long moment, then nod. 'Okay.'

Dialling Luciano's number, I make the call. It goes straight to voicemail so I leave a message. Keep my tone no-nonsense as I lay out what
will happen. I don't ask permission; I don't apologise. It's not perfect,
and the gnawing fear growing in my belly is due to the fact that Dakota
and JT will still be targets until we arrive back at the compound and
speak to the Old Man, but it's the only plan I have for now.

I look back at North. 'It's done.'

He's frowning, staring at the television. 'Goddamn.'

I turn to look at the news channel. The sound's muted but I don't need to hear the commentary to realise that the faces on screen are mine and North's. They're hunting us both now. It's worse than JT said.

As I watch, our pictures disappear and a blond man in a dark suit takes their place. He's outside the Hampton Lodge crime scene, being interviewed by a reporter. On the screen the caption reads: *Special Agent Jackson Peters*.

Grabbing the remote, I unmute the sound.

'*...the fugitives at large are armed and extremely dangerous. If you see them, do not approach. Call us on the number on your screen and stay at a safe distance. I repeat: do not approach them.*'

Jackson Peters looks more like a movie star than an FBI agent. I'd guess he's in his mid-thirties. Tall, with short blond hair and the kind of smile that makes you want to trust him.

'*Our fugitives are Carlton North and Lori Anderson.*' Agent Jackson Peters looks straight at the camera. '*And rest assured that we will do everything in our power to bring them in.*'

Shit. Snatching my cellphone from the bed, I switch it off and take out the battery. If they've IDed me they'll be fast as flies on shit to get a trace on my cell. I look at North. 'You got a cell on you?'

'I left everything in the room at Hampton Lodge. There was no time after Luciano's men took out the lights.'

I decide not to go telling him that I overloaded a power socket and made the electrics cut out. 'So the FBI and cops have your cellphone?'

'Yeah. My wallet too.'

I can't use my credit cards now they're onto me. I've got a few hundred bucks in my go bag, but that's not going to get us far. I gaze at my disassembled cell. I can't contact JT on it, can't talk to Monroe that way either, and if Luciano tries to contact me he won't have any joy. From here on out me and North are off the grid and on our own.

'We need to get out of here. Hitch a ride with one of the truckers and get back to Miami.'

North's frown deepens. 'And how is that going to work, Lori? Our pictures will be on every news channel. We'll get recognised and sold out to the cops in no time.'

Standing up, I start packing my stuff back into my go bag. My head's banging. My heart's racing. It feels like there's a Taser firing electricity through my left arm. The room seems to whirl around me. Putting a hand on the bed to steady myself, I glare at North. 'So what do you suggest?'

As he starts speaking my legs buckle and everything fades to black.

29

FRIDAY, SEPTEMBER 21st, 11:09

I feel like I'm floating. My eyes are closed but colours dart across the inside of my eyelids like technicolour strobe lights; pink and blue and green. They move faster, dancing around each other, dazzling me. I feel like I'm about to be sick.

'Hey. You okay?'

My mouth's dry and my throat is sore. My voice comes out in a croak. 'North?'

'Right here.'

I blink open my eyes. The sunlight feels like needles stabbing into my retinas. My surroundings come into focus. I'm in a car, and North's driving. The highway ahead of us isn't one I recognise. 'Whose car is this?'

North shrugs.

We pass a turn. The sign says we're three miles from Woodville. 'Where the hell is Woodville?'

'About three miles away.'

'Don't be such a smartass.' I'm sweating and my left arm feels boiling hot and leaden. 'Where the hell are we going?'

'Tallahassee.'

I frown, feel groggy ... on go-slow. 'Tallahassee ... but...'

'We need to get you fixed up.'

I shake my head. The movement makes me feel like I'm going to vomit. 'I'm fine.'

'Yeah, sure looked that way when your eyes rolled back into your head and you keeled over.' He turns to look at me, a stern expression on his face. 'You should have told me you'd been shot.'

I grit my teeth. 'It's a through-and-through. I was dealing with it.'

'I saw that. You patched yourself up, but you've lost a lot of blood, and not had enough water. You need proper medical attention.'

The throbbing in my arm is intense. The pressure is growing and it feels like my flesh is going to burst clear out of my skin. But still I don't want to admit that North is right. Dakota and JT are at risk – I have to finish this job and get the Old Man to make Luciano call off his dogs.

'Tallahassee's the wrong way, we need to go to Miami, we can't—'

'We can't do anything until you've had medical help.'

Every bump in the road is making my stomach flip. It's true that I'm in no kind of state to face down the Old Man and Luciano, but I sure do hate it that North's talking sense. 'Why Tallahassee?'

'I've got a friend there who can help.'

'But Luciano...' My mind feels slower than molasses in winter. Black spots dance across my vision. Through the windshield the road ahead of us seems to tilt.

'The Old Man is on his pilgrimage into the wild country, so he's not at the house right now. You've got time to get right. Then we'll go back to Miami. Trust me, I've got this.'

Trust me, he says; but can I really? As my eyes start to close and I feel the blackness taking hold again, I think of Dakota and JT, and I hope to hell they're free and clear of the heavies Luciano had watching them.

30

FRIDAY, SEPTEMBER 21st, 11:10

JT pulls off the road at the sign that reads *Deep Blue Marina* – orange script against a bright-blue background; the smiling fish pointing towards the words looking just as Lori had described it. He steers the Mustang across the lot, looking for a place to park. He needs someplace he can tuck it in behind a bigger vehicle – something large enough to screen it from the road and any eyes scouting them out for Luciano.

There's not a whole lot of choice; the only half-decent spot is between a medium-sized RV and the high wire fence at the far corner. The RV has a dirty windshield and one of the tyres is almost flat. He's guessing it doesn't get taken out often, and right now that's a good thing. Less good is that it's been parked over the edge of the bay, cramping the space into which to squeeze the Mustang.

Pulling forwards, he sticks her into reverse and eases her backwards. It's tight, but they fit. Just. It makes getting out a bit of a drama. In the end the window is the best option.

Dakota giggles as she climbs free of the car. As JT pulls their rucksacks through the window and then winds it back up, she turns to him. 'Where are we?'

'Near Tampa.'

'Are we going to the beach?'

He shakes his head. 'Not exactly. We're visiting with a friend of your momma's.'

Dakota looks at him all suspicious. 'If a friend of Momma lives here, how come I've never been here before?'

'I don't know.' JT says, giving what he hopes is a reassuring smile. 'But you're getting to visit now.'

They walk across the gravel lot to the white security hut. JT's surprised that it's empty but also relieved. It means he won't have to sign the guest register and leave a record of their visit.

Continuing past the hut, they stride onto a wooden walkway flanked on both sides by boats. He can smell the salt on the air as the water laps at their sides. The marina seems to cater more for houseboat dwellers and Florida residents with smaller yachts; there are only a few big vacation boats, and none of the millionaire cruisers you see in the marinas around Miami.

Dakota frowns. 'Are we going on a boat?'

'Could be,' JT says.

Taking her hand, he follows the directions Lori gave him to the end of the jetty furthest from the marina entrance. He stops outside the houseboat with the gleaming green and gold livery. This is it, just as she described. He hopes her judgement of the boat's owner is as accurate.

Stepping onto the boat, JT raps twice on the door to the cabin then steps back onto the jetty and waits.

'Who lives here?' Dakota asks.

'Your momma's friend.'

'Who are—?'

The door of the cabin opens. An older guy, barefoot and wearing sun-faded jeans and a black tee, steps out onto the deck. JT appraises him a moment; he's fit and rugged with a deep tan and silver-streaked hair; he fits the description Lori gave.

'Are you Red?'

The man looks from JT to Dakota and back again. His tone is guarded. 'That depends on who's asking?'

'I'm James Tate – JT – and this is my daughter, Dakota. Lori said you're a person who can be trusted in a crisis.'

'Could be that I am. Where's Lori?'

JT gives a little shake of his head and glances towards Dakota. He doesn't want to get into specifics right now. 'Handling the crisis.'

Red nods. 'I understand that.' He glances along the walkway then looks back at JT and Dakota. 'Well, I guess you'd better both come on board.'

Holding his hand out to Dakota, Red helps her aboard. JT follows, watching how she's doing. The last time she was on a boat it nearly sank. He's amazed she doesn't seem fazed by getting onto one again. He guesses kids are just a whole lot more resilient than most adults give them credit for.

'Take a seat,' Red says, gesturing to the padded bench seats that run around the side of the deck. 'Can I fix the pair of you a drink? Coffee, sweet tea?' He looks at JT. 'A beer?'

Dakota glances at JT, seemingly overcome with shyness. JT answers for her. 'Coffee would be great. Dakota'll have an iced sweet tea if you've got it.'

'For sure,' Red says. 'Make yourselves at home, I'll just be a moment.'

As Red disappears back into the cabin, JT puts his hand on Dakota's shoulder. 'You okay?'

She looks up at him. Bites her lip. 'This man, he's one of the good guys?'

JT smiles. 'Your momma says he is, and she's known him a lot of years. Says we can trust him.'

Dakota smiles. 'Okay.' She looks out into the ocean and points towards the horizon. 'It looks like it goes on forever.'

'Not quite forever, but a long ways across the gulf to Mexico.'

'Cool,' Dakota says, her voice animated, her worry forgotten. 'My friend Alejandra's grandma moved here from Mexico.'

JT smiles. Tries to act normal. Doesn't want to let on to Dakota just how much danger they could be in, and the fact that if Lori can't finish the job she's on to the mob's satisfaction, they'll have to skip town and Dakota won't be seeing her friend ever again.

'Here we go.' Red steps back onto the deck, carrying a tray with two iced teas and a coffee. Setting the tray down on the bench seat, he hands the coffee to JT and one of the iced teas to Dakota. 'I thought you'd like a straw.'

She grins. 'Thank you, Mr Red.'

'You're welcome.' Sitting down on the bench seat opposite, Red takes a sip of his iced tea then looks at JT. 'So what kind of help is it you're looking for?'

JT appreciates the guy's directness. He's never one for small talk himself. 'We need a place to hide out until the job Lori's on is done.'

Red looks from JT to Dakota. Leaning forwards towards her, he smiles as he says, 'Honey, you want to go and explore inside the boat while I have a little chat with JT?'

Dakota looks unsure.

'It's okay,' JT says, giving her a reassuring smile. 'You go ahead.'

Red waits until Dakota has disappeared through the cabin door before speaking again. He takes another sip of iced tea, then rubs his hand across his face. 'You know what happened last time I helped Lori, right?'

'She said there was a bit of trouble.'

Red laughs, and shakes his head. 'That's one way to describe it. The Old Man's heavies beat on me pretty bad. Only left me breathing so I could deliver a message to Lori.'

JT frowns. He'd not pegged this guy as a coward. 'So you won't help us?'

'Didn't say that. What I'm saying is the Miami Mob know who I am and where I live. They know I'm connected to Lori too. You staying, that's fine with me – any family of Lori's is family of mine. But don't think for a moment that Luciano's men can't find you here.' Red glances towards the cabin. 'Or that they'll go easy on you or the kid if they find you.'

JT thinks on what the man's said. Appreciates his honesty. 'Lori says you'll help me protect Dakota.'

Red's expression gets real serious. He nods. 'That I will.'

'Then I think it's best we stay.'

Red smiles. 'Well, alrighty then. I'd best make space for you to sleep.'

As Red heads into the cabin, JT hopes he hasn't just made a big mistake. Two recently injured men and a nine-year-old child – if the mob find them, the odds will not be good. But there's something about the calmness and quiet confidence of this man, Red, that makes him believe he's a good person to stick with.

If the shit hits the fan, he seems the sort who'll fight for what's right, until the very end.

31

FRIDAY, SEPTEMBER 21st, 13:28

I wake to the sound of beeping. Opening my eyes, I see there's a heart-rate monitor attached to my finger, and the beeping is from the machine that's measuring each beat. There's an IV line running from a cannula in the back of my right hand to an electric IV pump. The liquid in the bag is clear, and there's no writing on it to tell me what's being pumped into me.

I'm alone, lying on what looks like a hospital gurney in the middle of a small, windowless room. Bare white walls surround me. The door directly ahead is shut.

Where the hell I am, and where the hell is North?

My head feels like it's full of cotton candy. My left arm throbs with a dull, continuous ache. My skin feels damp, clammy. It's hot in here. Too hot. Airless.

There's a cream blanket draped over me. I try to move my hand to push the blanket off, and that's when I realise: I'm trapped. A prisoner. Strapped onto the gurney.

'North?' My voice is more of a croak than a shout, but even I can hear the panic in it. 'North, where are you? What the hell's going on here?'

There's no reply. No one comes into the room, and I hear no movement outside.

In the car, just before I blacked out again, I remembered what North said: *Trust me*. Given my condition I hadn't really been given a choice.

Never trust no one. That had been one of JT's rules when I'd started training with him. I'd learned his rules by heart and followed them to the letter. Not trusting easy was a part of me now. But it hadn't helped me this time.

'North, show yourself,' I shout. 'Let me the hell off this gurney.'

Still nothing.

I thrash beneath the restraints. The movement sends needle-sharp pain jolting through my left arm and I gag, fighting the urge to vomit.

Looking around me, I search for something that will help me get free, but there's nothing. The room is bare aside from the monitor, the IV pump and the bed that I'm on. My leather jacket and go bag are gone.

Then I spot the camera; a tiny spycam mounted in the far corner of the ceiling, like a brown widow spider waiting to attack.

I glare at it. 'Stop watching me, and get your ass in here.'

I wait ten seconds. Twenty. Forty.

The door opens.

I frown. 'Who the hell are you?'

The woman has cropped platinum-blonde hair and a whole lot of dark eye make-up. She's petite, dressed in cut-off jeans and a blue plaid shirt over a grey tee. She's strikingly pretty, but that's not the thing I'm staring at most. Black against her pale skin tone, rising from beneath the neckline of her tee, up the side of her throat, and coiling its tail around her right ear, is a tattoo of a snake. 'I'm your guardian angel.'

'Yeah right, because they're real well known for being into bondage.'

'I'm here to look after you.'

'And I'm the head of the FBI. Where's North?'

She doesn't respond to my jibe. 'He's sleeping. You should be too.'

'That's kind of hard when I'm tied down.'

'It was for your own protection. You were disorientated and unstable when you arrived, I didn't want you trying to walk unaided and falling.'

I stare at her, not sure if I believe what she's selling. 'Forgive me if I'm a little sceptical. I've already been abducted and held hostage once this week; I'm not in the mood for it to be happening again. Tell me why I'm here.'

She signs. 'Look, North will be awake soon. Then you can ask him.'

I'm not waiting a moment longer. 'If I'm not a prisoner, untie me. Believe me, you don't want to get me pissed.'

'Alright, fine.' She steps closer to the gurney and pulls back the blanket. 'Just hold still, yeah, and don't get any stupid ideas.'

Stupid ideas are relative, but I nod anyways. She's not carrying a weapon and she's got to be a good few pounds lighter than me and about a foot shorter. I'm pretty sure I'll be able to take her out if it comes to hand-to-hand combat.

She pulls the blanket back and I see there are four leather straps tying me to the gurney. Slowly, keeping eye contact with me as she does it, she unbuckles each of the straps. As she's removing the final one from around my ankles, I yank out the IV line and hurl myself off the gurney. But my legs are weaker than I'd reckoned on and I stumble as I land.

'Lori, stop.'

I refuse to be kept captive a moment longer. Ignoring her, I sprint for the door.

She blocks my path but I don't stop. Hunkering down like a football player, I brace myself ready for impact.

Next moment I'm knocked off my feet. She pulls some kind of martial arts move, flipping me backwards and sending me slamming down onto the hardwood floor. I yell from the pain as my bad arm hits the ground. The noise is cut short as the impact knocks the air from my lungs. My head pounds, my vision is blurring, and I feel like I'm going to be sick.

She's looking down at me. 'You done?'

I cuss under my breath. I have no idea how she just handed me my ass. 'What are you, some kind of ninja?'

'Something like that.' She gives me a half-smile and holds out her hand. 'You ready to get back on the gurney?'

I don't want a replay, so I take her hand and let her help me up. I move across to the gurney and push myself onto it, legs dangling over the edge. I use my right hand to support my injured arm. The pain's real bad.

She shakes her head. 'You went and bust your stitches.'

Looking at my arm, I see there's a red stain spreading across the white bandage around my upper arm. I glance back at her. 'I think you kind of did that.'

'Maybe.' She fixes me with a hard stare. 'But you started it. Stay here. And don't try anything stupid.'

'No promises.'

She gives a small shake of her head and turns back to the door.

I stay sitting on the gurney as she leaves the room. The door clicks locked behind her, and I figure it must have an automatic-locking mechanism.

I wonder again where the hell I am. My watch has been taken off me, and I have no idea of the time. Suddenly it seems my world has shrunk down to this small, windowless room, and I sure don't like the way it feels.

I'm not left alone for long. She returns after a few minutes with a metal kidney dish containing purple-hued liquid and a tray of medical equipment. 'Lie down. I need you to be still for this.'

I stay sitting. Look at her real suspicious. 'Why should I trust you?'

She looks at me with a no-bullshit expression on her face. 'Because right now, Lori, I'm all you and North got.'

It's a fair point. I lie back onto the gurney. 'So where is he?'

'I told you before, he's sleeping.'

I shake my head even though it's hurting like a bitch. 'You're not one for conversation are you?'

'I'm going to need to concentrate.' She starts unwrapping the bandage from around my arm. 'I need you quiet and I need you to lie still. If you can't do that I'll have to knock you out.'

'Okay.' I stay still, watching as she finishes unwrapping the bandage and inspects the gunshot wound. Like she thought, the stitches are busted.

Picking up a syringe of clear liquid from the surgical tray, she sticks the needle into my arm and depresses the plunger. Within a few seconds the pain begins to subside.

She cleans off the blood with the purple-coloured liquid in the kidney dish then looks at me sternly. 'Hold still.'

'Yup.'

I watch as she stitches me up. Her brow is creased in concentration, the tip of her tongue poking out between her lips a fraction, just like Dakota's does when she's concentrating hard. Dakota, my baby girl; I hope that JT has gotten her away from my apartment and safely to Red's boat.

'There you go.'

Her voice pulls me out of my thoughts of Dakota and JT. I look at her handiwork – a line of neat, evenly spaced sutures. 'Nice job. So you're a ninja and a nurse?'

'I'm a physician actually.'

I gesture to her tattoo with my good arm. 'I've not seen so many docs inked like you before.'

'Maybe you didn't look close enough.'

'Could be.' I keep my tone friendly. Need to find out as much as I can about my situation so I can figure out how to get free. 'So how do you know North?'

'We've been friends a while.'

From the flush that blooms across her cheeks and neck as she says the word 'friends', I'm guessing that they're a little more than that. 'Is that why you're helping me?'

'I'm helping him. He says you're part of the deal.'

Maybe I can trust North after all. 'You got a name?'

She holds my gaze. Deciding whether to give up her name I guess. 'You can call me Carly.'

'Okay, Carly. So what happens next?'

She takes a second syringe from the tray and injects it into my arm. 'Now, Lori Anderson, wanted fugitive, you're going right back to sleep.'

32

FRIDAY, SEPTEMBER 21st, 14:03

The living area inside the houseboat is far roomier than JT would've guessed. Red's set up a space for him and Dakota to stash their things and pulled down the twin bunks for them to use. Dakota called the top bunk as hers. JT wasn't going to argue.

They eat lunch on deck – roast chicken and bacon subs from plates balanced on their knees. The sound track is an occasional splash as a fish breaks the surface. He smiles as Dakota quizzes Red about the boat and the marina, but his attention remains focused on the jetty and the parking lot way beyond. This isn't a holiday; it's a hideout. He can't afford to let his guard down.

Dakota finishes her sub, puts the plate on the deck and takes a sip of iced tea. Tilts her head to the side. 'What's the name of your boat, Mr Red?'

'What is this, an interrogation?' Red says, but he's smiling. 'Her name is *Liberty*.'

Dakota nods thoughtfully. 'Like the bell?'

'Indeed.'

A loud revving a ways behind them draws JT's attention. Turning, he scans the lines of boats bobbing at their moorings, trying to work out the source. He hears shouting, but can't make out the words. The revving gets louder, sounds like more than one engine.

He tenses his shoulders, adrenaline coursing through him. Ready to act.

'Look,' Dakota laughs, pointing a little to the left of where he's looking. 'That looks fun.'

Two jet skis race out from behind the line of boats towards the exit of the marina. Two girls in bikinis are driving, two young guys in board shorts are riding pillion. They're laughing and shrieking as they race, the boys yelling trash talk at each other.

Red shakes his head but he's smiling. 'They shouldn't be going that fast until they're out on the ocean.' Looks at JT. 'The fun of the young, huh?'

JT nods. Then exhales and rolls his shoulders, trying to release the tension. It's just kids. Not a threat.

'Do you have any jet skis, Mr Red?' Dakota asks.

Red shakes his head. 'I'm sorry, that I don't.'

'Maybe we can go fishing?'

'Maybe.' Red nods, but he isn't looking at Dakota now, his stare is fixed back along the jetty, towards the parking lot.

'Things okay?' JT asks.

'Not rightly sure.'

JT follows his gaze. There's a brown sedan in the parking lot that wasn't there a moment ago. The doors open and four big guys jump out. Red's jaw tightens. 'Goddammit. We need to move.'

The men are looking their way.

Red's sprinting to the helm before JT can ask if the boat's seaworthy.

Leaping up, JT gestures at Dakota to go into the cabin. 'Go inside, honey. Find a life preserver and put it on. Stay away from the windows.'

She stays put. Her lower lip's trembling. 'Why? What's happening? Is it—'

He glances back towards the lot. The men are running down the first walkway, heads moving side to side, looking from boat to boat, searching. JT knows exactly what they're looking for, and he'll be damned if they'll get it. He puts his hand on Dakota's shoulder and pushes her towards the cabin. 'We'll talk later.'

Her eyes fill with tears, but she does as she's told.

He hears the boat's engine tick over. The heavies are at the cross walk, turning onto their jetty.

'Cast us off,' Red yells from the helm. 'Now.'

JT hurries to the ropes tethering the boat to the mooring. Yanking them undone, he pulls the coils back onto the deck. 'Clear.'

The men are fifty yards away and closing.

Red opens up the throttle and the engines fire thunder loud. The boat's faster than JT expects, and as Red accelerates them away, he's knocked off his feet and onto his ass on the deck.

He braces himself for the gunfire that's inevitable.

But it doesn't come.

Twisting round, JT looks back at the shore, searching to see what's happened. On the end of the jetty four heavies are standing with guns in their hands, but not firing.

JT doesn't get why not.

33

I wake with a jolt to find North standing over me. 'What the hell are you doing?'

'Checking to see how you're doing.'

'Yeah, right.' I push myself up. My head's stopped pounding and the pain in my arm isn't so bad.

'You're looking better.'

'Than what?' I don't hide the anger in my voice. 'Being out cold? Drugged?'

He shakes his head. 'You gave me a scare, Lori. You collapsed. I didn't even know you'd been shot.'

I look around. There's no sign of Carly. 'You not knowing was kind of the point.'

He looks at me, his expression serious. 'No secrets from here on out.'

'Good luck with that.' There are always secrets. I'm not some naïve kid that a man can persuade otherwise. I swing my legs over the side of the gurney. 'So why are you pulling this shit and keeping me prisoner?'

'You're not a prisoner. I just needed to be sure you'd be fit enough for what happens next.'

'How nice that you're so concerned about my welfare,' I say, sarcasm thick in my tone. 'I thought you were the one with the fitness problem.'

'Carly got me some meds. I'm doing fine.'

Now he mentions it I realise that he's right; he does seem a whole lot better. His skin has lost the pale, waxy sheen, and the look of permanent exhaustion is gone.

'And I'm more than capable of travelling to Miami,' I say.

North shakes his head. 'That's not what happens next.'

'It sure is. We agreed. I told Luciano we're—'

'No. There's something we have to do first.'

I narrow my gaze. 'What's that?'

'Come and get something to eat and I'll tell you.'

I feel anxiety fizzing in my belly. I want to get on the road. I need to be doing something. And I'm not real happy about the change in dynamic between North and me. But, given the situation, I figure it's best to go along easy for now, get the layout of this place, then decide what my next move should be.

North's acting like we're on the same team, but I can't help thinking that for him hotfooting it away from here would be preferable to heading back into the mobsters' den with me. Nevertheless, I remove the cannula from my hand again, hop down from the gurney and follow him from the room. I'll check out my exits, and hear him out. Then I'll decide.

⌐

We're not in a medical facility. The room I was in is at the far end of a mezzanine level. The lower level is a large, achingly stylish, minimalist living space that stretches out towards a floor-to-ceiling wall of glass. Through this window I see the city of Tallahassee spreading below us into the distance. We're high, ten floors up at least. And there's no sign of a fire escape. Damn. That means there's only one way in and out of this apartment.

As we walk past the open door to the other room on the mezzanine, I see it's a huge bedroom rather than another clinical area. It contains a bed with jewel-coloured linen and a bunch of cushions. There are two doors off the bedroom – I assume they're a bathroom and a walk-in closet. Either that, or this place is a crash pad rather than a home.

As I follow North down the stairs, the smell of spices and herbs wafts up to greet us. Though I'm anxious to get back on the road, my stomach rumbles. I've no idea of the time, but the sun's position low over the city skyline suggests it must be late in the day, heading towards dusk. I haven't eaten since the sausage biscuit at the rest-stop motel. That could have been this morning or even yesterday; whenever it was, it feels like a lifetime ago.

Recessed into the space below the mezzanine is a sleek steel kitchen, kitted out like a professional chef's. 'Is Carly making food?' I ask North.

He shakes his head. 'I am.'

I raise an eyebrow.

'Sit.' He gestures towards the island unit. It's laid for dinner; three placements. 'I like to cook. It relaxes me. Helps me think.'

'Okay.' I hop up onto one of the stools at the island unit. 'What is this place?'

'It's kind of like a safe house. I pay Carly a retainer to keep a bunch of stuff here for me and to give me assistance if I come out this way to do a job.'

'She works for the Old Man?'

North shakes his head. 'She's independent. No mob ties.'

I cock my head to one side. For a moment my vision blurs. I blink, waiting for it to clear. 'So she's a gun for hire?'

'Not really; more like a private contractor. She's picky about who she'll partner up with. Those she does pay a premium for the privilege.'

I frown. 'If you had her on speed dial why didn't you just ditch me and run as soon as I passed out?'

'Not my style. You didn't pull the trigger when Luciano told you to, even though not doing so put your family at risk. I owe you for that. And we're both being chased by the same people. I figure there's strength in numbers.'

I stare at him. Wonder if he's talking truth or bullshit. 'So what I'm thinking is we need to get back to Miami.'

North turns to the stove and gives one of the simmering pans a stir. He shakes his head. 'There's no point. Like I said, the Old Man is away on his annual pilgrimage. His schedule is always the same. He won't be back at the compound until Sunday evening and we don't want to get there before he's back, I don't trust Luciano not to shoot us on sight.'

I hear a door open and close upstairs, and a moment later Carly comes down into the kitchen area. She nods at me, kisses North, then goes to the large fridge and takes out a bottle of wine. She glances at me. 'How's the arm?'

'Better.'

She pours the wine into our glasses. As she steps back to the fridge I turn to North again. 'So, what? You're saying we should hide out here for two days?' I think of JT and Dakota, of the threat they're under for as long as I don't take North back to the Old Man and Luciano. 'I can't wait that long. I need to—'

'I know what you need, Lori, and you won't get it from Luciano. Whatever deal you think you've made, I know how he operates, how he thinks. Even if the Old Man lets you go, Luciano will never allow the fact that you killed Tommy to go unpunished. You'll never be free, and neither will your family.'

His words hit me hard. Blinking, I pick up my wine glass and take a mouthful to disguise the emotion I'm feeling. The wine's good – dry and fresh, and goes down easy. As I drink I scan the room for the exit. At the far end there's a large door reinforced on the inside with highly polished steel and a keypad. Damn. I'm guessing getting out of this place will be a whole lot more complicated than just turning a key.

I figure I should hear North out. 'So what are you saying?'

'I'm saying that I've got another way to make this right, but I need to be able to trust you.'

'I'm listening.'

'That wasn't what I asked.'

I hold his gaze. 'But it's my answer. I'd find it a whole lot easier to trust you if you gave me back my weapons.'

North glances towards Carly. She nods, and the expression on her face makes me wonder exactly what the dynamic is between them.

'All your stuff is ready for you whenever you want it.' He ladles Thai red curry into our bowls and puts a dish of steaming rice in the middle of the island unit. 'Eat.'

I take a mouthful, and it's good. Real good. 'Alright, tell me what the other way is.'

'The trial I was due to give evidence at was a homicide. It's on the public record; easy to check. A young guy, barely twenty, was up for killing an accountant. The case was a slam dunk: the kid's prints were on the knife used to stab the victim; the man's blood was on the kid's clothes, which the cops found stuffed in the back of his closet. There was an eyewitness who put the kid at the scene.'

I frown. Not sure what this has to do with me. 'Like you said, sounds a sure thing.'

'Yeah, except the kid didn't do it; he was the patsy.'

'Okay. So how does this link to our situation?'

'The accountant was the Old Man's finance guy. His firm oversaw all the Miami Mob's income and expenditure – he knew everything about the family business and he was loyal to the Old Man. It was his loyalty that got him killed.'

I shake my head. 'I'm not following you, how can—?'

'Luciano killed the accountant. He'd uncovered that Luciano had been stealing from his father for years – at least ten, maybe longer. He'd been clever, hidden behind things that looked legitimate, but in the last year he'd gotten more sloppy. That's when the accountant found something that looked strange and started tracing it back. Once he did that the whole trail unravelled like a ball of yarn.'

'So Luciano silenced him and the kid was taking the fall.'

'Yeah. And I'm sure Luciano told the kid he'd be paid well for it. But the truth is they'd have gotten to him in prison. He'd have been dead within the first month.'

'So you stepped in.'

'I went to the Feds and told them I'd testify against Luciano.'

I shake my head. It doesn't stack up right. 'Why would the Feds believe you?'

'They're desperate for something on the family. I just needed to steer them towards Luciano, it was easy enough.'

'But why not fix it yourself? Why involve law enforcement? Aren't you the law when it comes to the family?'

North rubs his hand across his chin. 'He's the Old Man's son. I could have ended him myself, but the Old Man wouldn't have stood for it. I wanted him to see his son had gone bad, but for that he'd need to see hard evidence. I had to have proof; I had to get copies of the accountant's files. But they'd been seized by the Feds.'

What he'd done hits me. 'Jeez, you played the goddamn FBI?'

'I got what I needed without them knowing, and they got the truth about the homicide. It was a fair deal.'

I let out a long whistle. 'You've sure got some balls. And I see all this is useful to you getting back into favour with the Old Man, but how does it help me?'

'The proof I have of what Luciano stole means the Old Man will believe me when I say I didn't go rogue. He'll understand I did what I did to protect him. I'm his number two – he'll listen to me when I tell him that your debt is paid.'

What he says is starting to make sense, but there's a flaw to his plan. 'What if the Old Man doesn't believe you? Spreadsheets and documents can be faked. It'll be your word against Luciano's, and you're the one who's been spending time with the Feds.'

North takes a mouthful of curry and chews slowly. He nods. 'There's something else that will help. I've kept it safe for a good few years; thought it might be a useful lifeline one of these days. Looks like that day could be here.'

'So get it.'

'We'll get it tomorrow. First thing.'

I raise an eyebrow. Sure don't like the way North thinks he can call the shots here. '*We* will?'

'It's inside the First Fourth Bank vault in downtown Tallahassee.'

34

FRIDAY, SEPTEMBER 21st, 22:56

The couch is more comfortable than it looks and a whole lot nicer than the gurney, but I can't get to sleep. North wouldn't tell me what it is that he needs to get from the First Fourth vault, but the way he talked about it gives me a horrible feeling that whatever it is, it has something to do with me. There was something in his expression as he spoke – something I've only seen once before, all those years back when he'd found me after Tommy had been beating on me. Now my mind is whirling at double speed. What the hell does he have inside that bank vault?

I look up towards the mezzanine. North and Carly are in the bedroom together, so I guess I know what their relationship is now. But Carly herself is an enigma. It bothers me, not knowing more about her.

Getting up, I walk barefoot across the room to the far wall. Behind a concealed door that blends so perfectly into the slightly textured wall you'd never find it if you weren't looking, I visit the downstairs bathroom. It's as minimalist as the rest of the place: stylish, with white fixtures and chrome fittings, and real expensive for sure.

Back in the open living space, I close the door behind me and stare back at the wall. The bathroom takes about half the length of the room – down to the corner with the reinforced entrance door. I wonder what's behind the rest of the wall space. Another room? Storage? Like an earworm that won't quit playing, I can't shake the question from my mind.

I can't help but investigate. Feeling along the wall, I look for another recessed button like the one that opens the bathroom door when slight pressure is applied. I walk the length of the wall, step by step, my fingers feeling, testing every inch.

I'm a half-yard from the corner near the kitchen when I find it. I press the button and a recessed door opens with a soft pop. Slowly, not wanting to wake Carly and North upstairs, I pull open the door.

What the hell? I sure don't know what I'd been expecting to find, but it wasn't this: metal lockers – three rows of five – built into the hidden space. Each locker door is fastened with a heavy-duty padlock, and bears a nameplate. Of the fifteen lockers, eleven of them have names. The middle locker of the middle row says *North*.

Who the hell is Carly? She seems to live here, but what kind of woman keeps her guest bedroom as a pop-up medical facility and has a mini locker-room behind a hidden door? I walk along the line of lockers. They have family names only so there's no way to tell if the people they belong to are male or female. I glance up towards the bedroom. Eleven people, one bedroom. I wonder if Carly shares her bed with all of them. I smile to myself. Fair play to her if she does.

Closing the door, I head back to the couch. I sit down and reach to check my go bag is still where I put it. It is. At least now I have it back; my weapons and my gear. Knowing where they are makes me feel more confident, because, although we might be safe here a while, lying low, we're still a long way from being free and clear.

On the wall-mounted flat-screen television, I watch the local news channels cycle through their stories. We're still news, but have been relegated to third place now; beatings and robbery taking the top spots – more violence every day. It makes me feel fearful for the world I've brought my daughter into, and makes me more determined to protect her.

I clench my fists, fighting the urge to put my cellphone back together and call JT. I hate the not knowing how he is. Not knowing whether he got Dakota safe, and where they are now. Hate that this job is pulling us apart.

A change in the news update catches my eye. The footage has changed from the crime scene to the outside of the rest-stop motel

North and me stayed at. The reporter is talking. Beside her is the FBI agent in charge of the search for us. I turn up the volume.

'...*sightings of the two fugitives, Lori Anderson and Carlton North, were made at this motel earlier today. I'm joined now by FBI Special Agent Jackson Peters. Agent Peters, what do we know about the fugitives and how long will it be before you find them?*'

Jackson Peters' expression fails to conceal his irritation at the question he's been asked. '*I want to assure the public that we are doing everything in our power to find these fugitives. FBI and local law enforcement are working around the clock. We have a confirmed sighting of our fugitives getting into a black Range Rover outside this motel earlier today. We've set up roadblocks on all the main highways. So, rest assured, we're closing the net.*'

As the reporter hands back to the studio I mute the sound. Roadblocks? That sure doesn't sound good.

Once we've got into the bank vault, how the hell are we going to get back to Miami?

35

SATURDAY, SEPTEMBER 22nd, 07:43

I don't sleep well. Dreams of being chased, of Dakota slipping through my grasp into water, of JT getting shot, haunt me. I wake with my heart pounding, hot with sweat, and the blanket North gave me twisted and knotted around me like a straitjacket.

Wrestling free, I stand and walk across to the kitchen for a glass of water. I lean back against the island unit and gaze out of the huge window at the Tallahassee skyline. The sun is up and there's a whisper of mist across the tops and around the sides of the buildings, like they've been wrapped in cotton wool.

I take another sip of water. I'm done with inaction. My arm feels a damn sight better, and North's back on his meds. As far as I'm concerned that's as good as we're going to get, so we need to get gone. If North insists we need what's at the bank, we'll give it a go this morning but, whatever happens, I'm getting us back on the road before noon. In this life nothing comes to the people who wait. You want something done, you've got to get right on at it yourself.

'North,' I yell up the stairs. 'You up?'

The bedroom door opens and Carly appears. She's wearing a faded Aerosmith tee, denim shorts and fluffy boot slippers, and carrying a wicker basket with what looks like laundry.

She comes down the stairs and puts the basket down in front of me. 'These clothes should fit. There's hair dye in there, scissors too.' She passes me a photo. 'You're going to need to look like this to get into the bank.'

The woman in the picture has a sleek brunette bob and green eyes.

There's something about her that seems strangely familiar, although I'm pretty certain we've never met. One thing is for sure; she looks nothing like me. 'What the hell do you—?'

Carly holds up her hand, already turning to go back upstairs. 'North will explain. We leave in one hour.'

I clench my fists as she disappears back into the bedroom and mutter under my breath, 'Is that right? Since when is he the one calling the damn shots?'

Slamming my glass down onto the island unit, I bound up the stairs two at a time. Shoving open the bedroom door, I see North still in bed, his hair tousled, his face crumpled from sleep. Carly looks at me, then exits into the bathroom.

'I'm done with you keeping me in the dark.' I brandish the photograph at North. 'What's with the game of dress-up? Tell me the whole truth or I'm not doing a thing.'

'What I need is in a safety deposit box. The bank needs both account holders present to validate the access.'

'You want me to help you break into a bank?'

'The account is mine. It's just not in the name you know me by.'

I hold up the picture. 'And this woman?'

He keeps staring at my face, doesn't look at the photo. 'It's in her fake name too.'

'Won't she be pissed you've opened the box without her?'

'No.'

'You went to all the trouble of setting up a deposit box together. How are you so sure?'

He exhales hard and looks away. 'Because she's dead.' There's a muscle pulsing in his neck, and a look of anguish on his face.

I wonder who killed her; hope it wasn't him. 'You want to talk about it?'

He glances towards the bathroom. Shakes his head. 'No.'

'Okay, then.' I look at the photo. Whatever North isn't saying about his relationship with this woman, it's obvious they were more than just friends. 'So I change my appearance; then what?'

'We go to First Fourth Bank and get my stuff.'

'You know our picture is all over the news channels. There's road-blocks set up on all the major roads.'

'They're not looking for us in Tallahassee though; the FBI will be thinking that we're heading back to Miami. We're okay downtown.'

He's right, but that doesn't help us for after. 'Okay, so assuming we get to First Fourth, we're just going to walk into the bank? You think it'll be that easy?'

'Easy? No. Possible? Yes.' He holds my gaze. 'We're only going to get one shot at convincing the Old Man that we're on the level. Stands to reason we should have all the ammunition with us when we do.'

I nod. It's a risk going into the bank for sure, but the Old Man needs to believe what North tells him. I need the price on my and my family's heads lifted. And, right now, our plan is the only way I can broker safety for the ones I love.

36

SATURDAY, SEPTEMBER 22nd, 09:03

Glossy brown bob, green contact lenses, dark eye make-up. Navy pant suit, high heels and a designer purse. This woman I'm staring at in the mirror sure doesn't look a thing like me, but according to the ID North's handed me, and the anguished look on his face as he turned away, she looks enough like Nicole Bendrois to be passable.

Bendrois: I remember that name. Last night, in the concealed area I discovered, it was written on the nameplate of the locker next to North's. I wonder if the ID came from the locker; perhaps North knew the combination for the lock. It feels real strange to be dressed up like his dead friend.

Carly drives. Her hair's hidden in an orange and pink scarf and huge oval shades swamp her face like a cartoon Jackie O. Beside her, North looks different too. His dark hair is highlighted with greys, and his stubble has been replaced with a very realistic fake beard. He's still wearing his leather jacket, but over smart pants rather than jeans, and he wears black brogues and a lavender polo shirt. Before we left Carly swapped the Florida licence plates on the Range Rover to Chicago ones, added two lamps to the front rig, and a *Go Bulls!* sticker to the rear fender. It seems we've all had a makeover.

First Fourth sits on a corner towards the edge of downtown. It's a new building, all pale brick and fancy landscaping, with little hedges and flowers around the outside, and it has its own parking lot, meaning we can get close to the entrance. Carly pulls into a space opposite the glass doors and kills the engine.

North turns in his seat. 'You ready?'

I know the plan. It's solid. It's time to test if it works.

I nod. Put my hand on the door release. 'Yeah. Let's get this done.'

Carly waits in the car as North and me walk across the lot to the bank. The morning sun is high overhead and I feel hot and out-of-place in the smart pant suit and towering heels. I wish I was back in my faded jeans and leather jacket, and that I had my weapon with me. But this isn't a job where a Taser would be an advantage. This is a game of chance, and bluffing is the only hand we've been dealt.

The entrance foyer to the bank is a big, open-plan space with offices along one side and teller windows along the other. To our right is a waiting area of red sofas, and on the back wall is a heavy door with a keypad. I notice the security camera facing directly at the door and guess that's the way to the vault.

There's a greeter a little ways inside, who smiles as we approach her. I glance back towards the door we just came through. The two muscled-up security guys either side of it are showing no hint of a smile.

'Bradley Knox and Nicole Bendrois to see your personal securities manager,' says North.

The greeter's smile widens. 'Of course. Welcome, Mr Knox.' She looks towards me. 'Ms Bendrois. Can I take some ID?'

North passes her his fake driving licence. I do the same with Nicole Bendrois'.

The greeter takes a look at them both then taps something on the tablet she's holding. She hands the IDs back to North. 'Can I ask which type of account you hold?'

'We have the joint Premier Executive Securities Service.' He glances at me. Takes my hand. 'And we'd like to access our deposit box.'

'No problem, Mr Knox. Please take a seat in the waiting area. Your account manager will prepare the paperwork and be out in a moment.'

We sit facing each other on a pair of matching couches. The left sleeve of my jacket is tighter, the bandage around my upper arm adding extra bulk, and my eyes feel dry and itchy from the unfamiliar contact lenses, but I try to keep relaxed. Don't want to draw suspicion. I glance casually around the bank. Three of the glass-walled offices are occupied, and there are four tellers behind the counters. Along with the greeter and the security guys, that makes ten employees within ten yards of us. There's no obvious fire exit marked, meaning that, if this goes bad, the only way for us to get out is back through the main entrance. Ten against two, and two of the ten with weapons. I'd say that puts the odds at about thirty/seventy in their favour.

'You good?' North asks.

'Sure.' I notice he doesn't give me eye contact, instead keeping his gaze just past my right ear. I figure it has something to do with the way I look, or more specifically *who* I look like.

'Mr Knox, Ms Bendrois?'

We both look up to see a bald guy with a neat beard and horn-rimmed glasses smiling down at us.

'I'm Jonathan Decker, the account manager on duty today for our Premier Executive clients. If you'd like to come through to the office.'

Standing, we follow Decker across the open-plan area to the office in the far corner. He shuts the glass door behind us and gestures towards two chairs on one side of the table, while he steps around to sit on the swivel chair opposite. 'So you'd like to open your security box today?'

'That's right,' North says. 'My wife and I have some items we'd like to remove.'

Wife? That's news to me. I try to keep the surprise from my face. Resist the urge to look down at my left hand, where my ring finger is awful bare for a married woman, and look at North's instead. He's wearing a ring I hadn't noticed before.

'No problem, Mr Knox, Ms Bendrois. As you know, we need to go through the usual security checks, and then I'll take you through to the secure area.'

'Thank you,' I say. 'We sure appreciate it.'

'Do you have your key with you?'

North reaches into his pocket and removes a wallet. It's not his real one – that was left in the room at Hampton Lodge when we fled. This one belongs to Bradley Knox. There are bank cards, his driver's licence, some bank notes and a small fold of coupons inside, along with a silver card the size of a bank card, but without any writing on it. Removing it from the wallet, he hands it to Jonathan Decker.

Decker holds it above the QR scanner on his iPad and waits for the hourglass symbol to come onto the screen before handing the card back to North. We wait, and I hold my breath. Then the hourglass disappears and on the screen appears two pictures: one of Bradley Knox and one of Nicole Bendrois.

With an expression of intense concentration on his face, Decker looks from the pictures, to each of us, and back again. Then he smiles. 'Thank you. If you could confirm for me your account number?'

'PEX5406-K758-0034-874H.'

Decker nods. 'Good. Almost there, just a couple of security confirmation questions. 'Ms Bendrois, your city of birth please?'

Shit. I have no idea. I think back to the conversations we had on the way over but there's nothing; North revealed little about the woman whose identity I've taken other than that she's dead, and that's hardly going to help me.

My mouth goes dry. Sweat trickles down my spine. Decker is staring at me expectantly. I glance down at the screen of his tablet, and the image of the real Nicole Bendrois. Clench my jaw. Think. I need to speak, say something.

Then it comes to me. I know who the picture of Nicole Bendrois reminded me of and why. It's her eyes, the piercing stare. She has the same unwavering expression as Luciano Bonchese.

I meet Decker's gaze. 'Miami.'

He taps my answer into the tablet. The screen flashes green and he smiles. 'Thank you, Ms Bendrois.'

I can feel North staring at me, but I don't turn to face him. We've got to keep focused on getting into his deposit box, collecting the evidence he needs to convince the Old Man around to our side, and get gone.

The vault doesn't look how they do in the movies. It's smaller for one thing, more like a big safe rather than a room, as far as I can tell. But we don't get to see inside. Decker leads us the opposite way along a short corridor in the secure area and into a room whose walls are lined with small metal lockers that house safety deposit boxes.

'Take as long as you want.' Decker hands North the keycard and steps out of the room, closing the door behind him.

I look at North. 'You know which one it is?'

He nods, still not making eye contact. 'Yeah. I've been here a few times.'

With the real Nicole Bendrois I guess. I stay where I am as North walks across to the far corner of the room. There's a solemnness about him, and as he presses the keycard against the sensor on a locker door at eye height I hear him sigh. There's a clunk as the door unlocks. North opens it, takes out the deposit box and carries it across to the table in the centre of the room.

Taking the empty messenger bag from over his shoulder, he unbuckles the straps and puts it onto the table beside the box. He stares at the box for a long moment. His shoulders are tense, his jaw rigid. It looks like he's having to psych himself up to get this done.

I step closer as he opens the box.

Inside are two buff envelopes, an iPad, a cellphone and a charger that fits them both. North lifts everything out and puts it into the messenger bag. 'I'm not coming back.'

'Okay.' I watch him put the deposit box back into its slot and lock the door, then pick up the bag and lift the strap back over his head. 'Ready?'

He nods.

If Decker is surprised that we're ready to go so quickly he doesn't let on. He escorts us back along the corridor and out through the secure door into the public banking area. He tries to make polite conversation, but North is quiet and unresponsive. I smile and try to lighten the mood, keep the act going, knowing that we can't afford to arouse any kind of suspicion.

When we step back outside into the sun I'm relieved, but that doesn't last long. Carly isn't parked up where we left her. I scan the parking lot, but there's no sign of her.

I turn to North. 'Where's Carly? Did you plan that she'd meet us someplace else?'

He looks dazed, confused. 'We didn't—'

There's a squeal of tyres on the blacktop, and the Range Rover swings around the corner into the lot. It brakes to a halt beside us and the passenger window buzzes down.

'Quick,' yells Carly. 'Get in.'

North stares at her. It's like he's having a delayed reaction.

I move towards the vehicle. 'What's—?'

'We need to move ... now.' Her usually calm voice has an undertone of panic. 'We've got a big fucking problem.'

37

SATURDAY, SEPTEMBER 22nd, 10:51

We've hardly shut the doors before Carly guns the engine and pulls back onto the highway. The seatbelt sensors are beeping and I'm thrown sideways across the backseat as she accelerates hard to beat a red light, and then hangs a sharp right. 'What the—?'

'We've got a tail. I noticed them while I was parked up, waiting for you. They're in a silver Ford, two guys in the front, maybe more in the back, but the windows are tinted.'

North glances around. Frowns. 'You sure?'

'Yeah, I'm sure.' Carly sounds irritated by him questioning her. 'I pulled out of the parking lot and took a loop round the block. They followed. They looked like mob types.'

Damn. It looks like Luciano could have sent more men, but how the hell did they find us? 'Does Luciano know about your place?'

Carly looks at me in the rearview mirror, her expression implying I'm some kind of dumbass. 'Isn't the whole point of a safe house that it's a secret?'

North doesn't comment. He's scanning the road, glancing in the mirror. 'I don't see any tail.'

Carly takes a left. As we swing around the corner, I catch a glimpse of a silver Ford turning onto the street we've just left. 'I do.'

North cusses.

I catch Carly's eye in the mirror. 'Can you lose them?'

'No doubt.' She steps hard on the gas.

I hang on as she zigzags the Range Rover through the back streets. The buildings fly by fast. Every now and then, just before we turn into another street, I see a flash of silver and know we're still being followed. There's no question now: the silver Ford is after us.

I look at North. 'We need to get out of Tallahassee. Now.'

'Agreed.'

Carly yanks the wheel and slides the Range Rover around a tight bend, then tucks it tight behind a large dumpster and skids to a halt. 'We get shot of the guys following us, then you can take this car.'

'Won't do us no good,' I say. 'The Feds have set up roadblocks on all the main highways between here and Miami. We need an alternative. I'm thinking the train.'

North says nothing. He's staring down at the messenger bag.

'Could work,' Carly says. 'I'll take you to the train station.'

I think about my go bag. My Taser and gun are in it, and my purse with my real identity, but there's nothing I couldn't do without for a little while. 'We should go straight there.'

North turns in his seat. Shakes his head. 'We can't just leave; our stuff's at Carly's.'

I'm confused. He's got the contents of the safety deposit box in his messenger bag, and that's all we really need. He arrived with nothing. What can be so important that he'd risk us dawdling in a place Luciano's guys are searching for us. 'Why? Can't you get whatever it is later?'

'No. This is important.' North's voice has a note of anguish. He turns to Carly. 'There's something I need from her locker.'

Carly purses her lips, but nods in agreement.

'You'll have to be fast, then. Straight in and out. If Luciano's men have been following us, chances are they do know where we're heading.'

⌐

Having shaken off the silver Ford, Carly takes us back to her place the long way, using a bunch of double-backs just to be sure they haven't picked up our trail again. We park in the ground-floor lot and take the elevator to the fourteenth floor. Everything's quiet. It feels too easy.

Stepping out of the elevator, we move along the hallway to the end door, which I know leads to Carly's loft. That's when we see it. The electronic keypad beside the door has been pulled away from the wall at an angle and a jumble of wires have spilled out behind. The door is slightly ajar, and there's a hole in just below the handle.

'They've drilled out my fucking lock,' Carly says. 'Bastards.'

I put my finger to my lips. We need to stay quiet. If this is Luciano's men, I'm thinking there's a good chance they're still inside.

We move fast to the door. Carly draws her weapon, a Glock, and uses her toe to nudge the door wider. It swings open, giving us a view of the bottom half of the living space.

Nothing. No people. No mess.

Carly enters first; North and me follow. I keep my breathing steady. Stay alert. Aside from the door to the concealed locker area being ajar, nothing looks any different to how we left it. They haven't tossed the place.

As Carly steps silently up the stairs to the mezzanine, I stop outside the door to the locker area. On the ground there's a white photograph album. Reaching down, I pick it up and see that it's empty; all the pictures have been ripped from the pages. Putting the album down, I grasp the door and open it wider.

I gasp. Behind me, North makes a noise like a wounded animal; anger and pain expressed in one sound.

North and Nicole's lockers hang open, a bullet hole in each where the lock should be. Across the floor of the room, hundreds of photographs have been torn into shreds and scattered like mismatched confetti. Kneeling down, I pick up one that's almost intact. In it a dark-haired man in a dinner jacket and a brunette woman in a gorgeous white-lace wedding dress gaze lovingly into each other's eyes. I scan the photo fragments across the floor; a wedding ceremony on the beach, exchanging rings, cutting the cake, having their first dance. These pictures aren't from a fake wedding – they're not about creating cover IDs and aliases. They're real. The emotion between the husband and wife is real, that's obvious. The couple is Carlton North and Nicole Bendrois.

I turn to North. See the anguish on his face and the quiver in his lower lip. Silently I pass the almost complete picture to him. He takes it, saying nothing.

'Don't zone out on me, North. We *have* to move.'

That's when the shooting starts.

It comes from upstairs. I scoot around North and out into the open plan. There's another burst of gunfire, and I hear Carly yell, 'Run!'

I do as she says. Hustle back into the locker room. North's staring into Nicole's empty locker, catatonic. I grab his hand and pull him with me. Fetch my boots and go bag from beside the couch then hustle out of the apartment and back down the corridor. The elevator's still on this level. I jump inside, dragging North in with me, and press the button for the ground floor. The gunfire is getting louder, closer. I hold my breath until the doors close.

'Snap out of it, North,' I say. 'I need you with me.'

His voice sounds weak, his words more like a question. 'I'm here.'

'No, you're not. And you're going to get us killed.' I put my hands on his shoulders. Fight the urge to give him a shake. 'We don't have long. I know you're hurting, but right now you have to get your head in the game. If you don't, the people back there will catch us. You don't want that, do you?'

He clenches his fists. 'No.'

'Good.' I glance up at the floor counter. Three more levels to go.

I grab my Taser from my go bag and hand North my gun. 'Then start playing to win, okay?'

38

They're in lying wait, just like I figured they would be. Two armed heavies, blocking our path. I see them when I angle my head to see around the edge of the elevator and scan the foyer.

The uniformed concierge is slumped forwards over the desk, unmoving, a red stain spreading out from the gaping wound in his back.

I stab my finger back against the elevator button, keeping the doors open. The heavies are looking restless. They've got their guns drawn, and the closest one is starting to move this way. We don't have long. Someone must have heard all these gunshots and called 911. Cops could arrive at any time.

'Lori, it's—'

'Listen.' Stuffing the Taser back into my go bag, I turn to North. 'You'll need to cover me. Let me get close enough for hand-to-hand, then act.'

He frowns, but I can't explain more. One of the heavies is striding this way. If he gets much closer he'll see North.

'I'm coming out,' I shout. 'Don't shoot. I'm unarmed and alone.'

The guy stops where he is, gun trained on the elevator.

I raise my hands and move out into the foyer, heading one step at a time towards the closest heavy.

The guy furthest from me cusses loudly.

His colleague's mouth opens, slack-jawed. Shock written all over his face. 'Who the hell are—?'

'Lori Anderson,' I say.

'Lori Anderson?' He says my name like he doesn't believe it. Still staring, a mixture of shock and fear on his face, he takes another pace towards me. He's skinny with a ratty mullet and the yellow-hued teeth of a heavy smoker. His voice has a nasal whine to it. 'Where's North?'

I glare at the rat guy, walking towards him, keeping his shaved-headed, heavily inked mate in my peripheral vision. 'Bleeding out upstairs.'

A smile flickers across rat man's lips. He glances towards the other guy then back to me. 'Just got ourselves a little bitch to handle.'

Smug asshole. Underestimating me because I'm a woman – that's a real big mistake. I take another step closer. 'You going to take me back to your boss?'

'Luciano isn't interested in seeing your sorry ass again.'

Rat-face is too dumb to realise he's just confirmed two things for me: that Luciano is behind this attack, and that he's out to kill me and North. North was right – getting the Old Man on our side is our only hope. But first, we've got to get out of this trap.

I take another step closer to the rat. Tilt my head a little, looking coy. Bat my lashes. 'Are you sure we can't work something out?'

He raises his brows and beckons me forwards. 'Yeah, yeah, come to Daddy.'

I move closer, smile real seductive. He's just a couple of yards away now.

Rat-face looks over at his mate again, smirking. 'No reason why we can't have a little party first before...'

Two more steps and I'm square in front of him.

He looks me up and down. 'Bitch, you can suck—'

I smack my fist into his smirking rat face. As he doubles over, I bring my knee up and slam it between his legs. It's not as effective as a one-two punch, but I can't use my left arm with any power so it's the best I can do. It's good enough. Groaning, he flops onto his hands and knees. Down but not finished ... yet.

Out the corner of my eye I see Ink guy moving this way, raising his weapon. There's movement behind me, from the elevator, as North steps out and angles the gun, firing a shot at Ink guy, covering me.

It goes wide. Ink guy's still coming for me.

I need to act fast.

Lifting my heeled pump, I stamp down hard. The spike heel stabs into the side of Rat-face's head. Blood and a few teeth spray out of his mouth, and he goes down again. Doesn't move. Good.

Ink guy starts firing. Bullets cut into the stone floor to my right. I dive behind the Rat's spread-eagled body. Keep myself pressed close to the ground.

North moves further from the elevator, gun firing; one shot, two shots. Ink guy falls, flailing backwards, his aim unfocused as he lets off a shot. As he turns I see that his left eye is gone – there's just a ragged bullet hole in its place. He's dead before he hits the floor.

'Come on,' North shouts, running towards the exit.

He doesn't need to tell me twice. I'm already on my feet and sprinting, as best I can in heels, behind him.

⌒

We hurtle along the sidewalk. Each time my heels hit the ground the jolt vibrates through my body. I vow to swap back to my boots as soon as we're clear. North's got the gun concealed in the back of his pants. The Taser is in my go bag. We look like two smart dressed folks in a hurry, and that could work to our advantage.

I hear the distant sound of sirens getting closer.

'Wait,' I yell to North.

Stepping off the curb, I throw my good arm up to hail a cab; the first I've seen with its light on. We need to put distance between us and Carly's place. I feel bad that we don't know what happened to her, that we didn't help her, but we can't go back. We just can't.

The cab stops and we jump in. I smile at the driver and try to act like I haven't just almost had my ass shot off. 'Can you get us to the train station? Fast as you can, please. We're running late.'

39

SATURDAY, SEPTEMBER 22nd, 12:44

There's no direct train from Tallahassee to Miami. The closest stop on the line is Jacksonville, but there's no trains leaving Tallahassee going there either. So we're stuck, trapped without a ride and with no idea if it was Carly or the mob guys who got shot in the apartment.

'We could take a Greyhound...' North says.

We're standing opposite the bus depot, figuring it's easier to hide in a crowd. There's a line for the pretzel stand a few yards away, and plenty of folks hurrying around us, some with luggage, some without. All of them seem to know how to get to where they're heading.

I shake my head. Keep my gaze along the street, looking out for the silver Ford that was following us before. 'The route takes us back through Missingdon, we can't risk it. If there are roadblocks still in place they'll be around there for sure.'

'So what? How do we get back across state?'

Unzipping my go bag, I flick through the roll of dollars, working out how much I've got left. 'We take a cab to Jacksonville.'

North looks unconvinced. 'And what about the road blocks?'

'We hope they haven't fixed them that close to the state line in Georgia. They're expecting us to head back to Miami, not go east.'

'True.' He nods. Looks thoughtful. 'Could work.'

'So let's get it done.'

I start walking towards the taxi rank a few hundred yards up the street. North falls in step beside me. Neither of us speak, our thoughts on the chaos left behind in Carly's apartment building and the chaos we're no doubt heading towards in Miami. We have our new identities, sure, and look different enough to fool a casual observer, but with Luciano's men and the Feds on our tail, I don't fancy our chances of making it to Miami without another problem.

⌒

The cab ride takes more than two hours and almost a couple of hundred bucks. North falls asleep about a half-hour into it. I don't. I keep watching the road, scanning the vehicles around us for the silver Ford. Mindful that Luciano seems hell-bent on stopping me and North making it back to Miami.

As we get into Jacksonville I nudge North awake.

He flinches, his right hand reaching for his weapon.

'Steady. It's just me.'

He blinks. Relaxes. 'We there?'

'Almost.' Looking ahead, I notice the driver eyeballing North kind of strange and hope to hell we've not been made. He's been a silent driver, and for that I've been grateful, but his fondness for texting while driving has made me a little anxious.

The driver clears his throat. 'Whereabouts you want me to take you?' He sounds tense.

I meet his gaze and give him what I hope is a friendly smile. 'Be a doll and drop us at the trailer park on New Kings Road would you?'

He looks away, back to the road. 'No problem.'

North doesn't say anything about the changed location. While he was sleeping I checked out the local area. The trailer park is a short walk from the station, but if Luciano's men or the FBI get to the driver later, at least he can't tell them for sure that we got on a train.

Aside from the trailer park the area is real industrial. The places along the streets are transportation depots, food-processing warehouses and courier services. I pay the driver and we get out. There's no sidewalk here, just a strip of yellowing grass along the edge of the highway. As the cab pulls back into the traffic, I sling my go bag over my shoulder and wince.

North looks concerned. 'Arm hurting?'

'It's fine. I could do with some water is all.'

He nods, and we walk along the dusty grass towards the turning for Clifford Lane. Taking a left onto it, we follow the road along, past the vast parking lot, and freight storage area opposite, and along to the station.

While North goes to check the train schedule, I go get us some tickets. Ignoring the counter service, I head straight to one of the automated ticket machines. It takes a while to feed the bills into the machine, but it's a whole lot less risky than getting up close with a ticket teller.

It costs a little under a hundred and fifty bucks for the pair of tickets. I pick up a couple of bottles of water and ham and cheese subs from the vending machine nearby, and put the lot into my carryall. My roll of dollars is a damn sight slimmer than it was a couple of days ago.

I shiver. Get the feeling that I'm being watched.

Glancing around, I check whether there's anyone who has eyes on me, but see no one. I can't shake the feeling, but there's nothing to be done about it.

Crossing the concourse, I join up with North. 'You got any cash on you?'

'Some; maybe two hundred bucks.'

That's something at least. 'Good, because I'm running low and we've still got a load of miles to cover.'

He looks real concerned. Both of us know there's no guarantee we're going to have enough cash to get us where we need be. 'The next train is in ten minutes,' he says. 'Takes a little under nine hours to get to Miami.'

Right now nine hours feels like a lifetime.

We start up the steps to cross over the line to the platform. Halfway up, as we move around the twist, I halt abruptly. My breath catches in my throat and I shoot my arm out to make North stop.

He turns, confused. 'What the—?'

'Look.' I nod down, across the tracks, towards the platform. 'Feds. No doubt.'

There are at least three of them, spaced out along the platform. Dark suits, shades. All of them wearing the same look of intense concentration. At the furthest end, taller than the rest, his movie-star looks making him stand up from the crowd, I spot the lead agent who was interviewed on the news channel: Jackson Peters.

In that moment I know for sure that they're here for us.

Damn my misplaced confidence in our disguises. Different as we look, sitting in a car for two hours is a long time and gives a person plenty of chances to study their passengers. The damn driver and his texts; he must have been tipping off the Feds, texting the number the news channels were broadcasting. Trying to be the hero. Nearly two hundred bucks that ride cost, and he still sold us out.

We can't get onto the platform to catch the train. We can't stay here. Every which way, we're screwed.

40

We backtrack down the steps. My mind is whirring, thinking on what our next move should be. It makes no kind of sense that Special Agent Peters would put all his resources into waiting on the platform, yet if they're in the foyer, as I figure they will be, I don't get why they didn't grab us when we walked in.

'The cab driver must have ratted us out,' North says. 'We need another plan.'

'Yeah, no shit. But what?'

'Get a car, hope we can skirt the roadblocks?'

It might be our only shot, but it sure as hell is risky. We'd have to switch up our vehicles regularly to stand any kind of chance. 'Steal something? I guess it could work.'

North shakes his head. 'A rental is lower risk.'

True. But we'd be leaving a paper trail – names and photos on file in the rental office. Just because Jackson Peters knew where we'd be, it doesn't mean he knew our fake names; we didn't tell the driver them. 'You think our IDs will work?'

'They're legit. Proper legends. Social security, banking records, the whole nine yards.'

'Good.' I'm impressed. I make my decision. 'So we take a rental then.'

North keeps his focus on the concourse ahead. 'Agreed.'

As we reach the bottom of the steps, I scan the people around us, alert for anyone who could be an agent. My heartbeat's banging like a screen door in a hurricane.

'Nice hair.' A voice murmurs from behind us. 'Get in here, it's a camera blind spot.'

I recognise the Kentucky drawl. Turn in the direction of the voice.

He's skulking in the shadow of the stairwell. 'Monroe, what the—?'

'Get in here now.' There's stress in his tone and his body language. 'We don't have long.'

Still confused, I gesture at North to follow, and we move towards Monroe. 'How are you even here?'

'Got myself onto Peters' detail, didn't I.'

As I face Monroe, North stands with his back to me, still scanning the concourse for Feds. We're sitting ducks here. We need to get gone.

'Why?' I hiss at Monroe.

Monroe takes hold of my arm, trying to pull me further away from North. His voice is an urgent whisper. '*You* need to come with me now.'

I dig my heels in. Refuse to budge. 'And North?'

Monroe gives a small shake of his head. 'I can't work miracles. Jackson needs his trophy.'

'That's too bad, because right now, we come as a pair.'

'Don't try pushing me, Lori. It isn't going to happen.'

'I hate to break up your reunion or whatever this is.' North turns to face us, his expression grim. 'But there's a bunch of Feds out there looking for us, so we need to move.'

Monroe bristles. 'Yeah, I know. I'm one of them.'

'You're what?' North looks from Monroe to me. Clenching his fists, he steps closer to Monroe. Looks all set to punch him. 'What the hell is this?'

I put my hands out towards North as if quieting an anxious mustang. 'It's okay, North. Calm down.'

Monroe scowls at North. 'You should give yourself up.'

I turn on him. 'You want North to wave a white flag, but you'll take me out of here?'

'It's nothing personal,' Monroe to North. He looks back at me. 'I just have to protect my asset.'

So that's what I am to him now: an asset. He needs me to make his plans to take down the Chicago mobsters work, and he's too invested in this long game to let Jackson Peters get a bite at me. 'Like I said, you get both of us, or neither.'

Monroe shakes his head. 'Jackson won't give up. He needs something – one of you. And that needs to be North.'

North looks real twitchy.

I hold Monroe's gaze. Saying nothing.

'Goddamn you're stubborn.' Monroe looks pissed. He blows out hard. Checks his watch. 'Okay. So look, there's a freight train pulling out on the other line in two minutes. If you're sticking together, you should be on it. That's the best I can do.'

'Where's it heading?' North asks.

'Port Miami.' Monroe speaks through gritted teeth. His jaw is tight and there's anger in his eyes. 'Jackson reckons that's the direction you're heading in anyways. Is he right?'

'Best you don't know,' I say.

'You're making a mistake.' Monroe steps closer to me. 'Remember I'm a friend, Lori. And you've not got many who can help you right now.'

I think of the bodies left in my wake since Special Agent Alex Monroe became my *friend*. And the fact he's willing to sell out another agent's case for a win on his own. He's not about justice. He just plays that card when it suits his own needs. One thing's for sure, if he is a friend, I'm real glad I don't have no others like him.

⌒

Leaving Monroe spitting feathers, we duck off the concourse through the emergency exit near the stairs and hurry away from the main platforms, towards the freight line. It's quieter away from the main station building, but I know we're likely being caught by CCTV cameras. I just hope no one is paying the freight side of business too much attention right now.

Alert for anyone looking like a Fed, we skirt the low-rise building around the freight area and head towards the loading bay. I stay quiet, keeping on my toes to prevent my high heels from knocking on the ground. The red and yellow freight train, its engines already running, is in the siding just as Monroe said it would be. There are a few small cargo carriages behind the engine, then the rest of the train is made up of shipping containers. I spot a few people on the loading ramp; guys in fluorescent tabards, hauling boxes into the first cargo carriage.

I gesture to the rear of the train. 'We need to get around back. Find somewhere to get inside without them seeing.'

'Agreed.'

Staying low, eyes on the loading guys, we use the stacks of now-empty crates and wooden pallets on the platform to shield us as we run closer to the train. When the men are inside the carriage we hotfoot towards the train.

As we reach the end of one of the cargo carriages, I hear doors being pulled shut higher up the train. Bolts are being pushed home. Our two minutes must be up. The train is ready to leave.

I look at North. 'You ready to do this?'

He answers by leaping up onto the back of the carriage and sliding open one of the doors a few feet. He peers inside before turning back to me and holding out his hand. 'It's clear.'

I pass him my go bag, and jump up into the carriage beside him.

As he slides the door closed behind me, the train begins to move off. I stand braced for shouting, for the Feds to stop the train and start searching. But it doesn't happen, there's no shouting and we keep moving.

As the train picks up speed, I feel my heart rate begin to steady. Closing my eyes, I sink down until I'm sitting on the floor. It'll take us near on nine hours to reach Port Miami.

For now, at least, we're on our way.

41

It's been almost an hour, but I still can't breath easy. I've changed out of the pant suit and back into my own clothes, relieved to swap spike heels for cowboy boots, but when I searched in my go bag for the anti-biotics Carly gave me, I realised, in the rush of our escape, I'd left them on the kitchen countertop. My arm's sore, but it doesn't feel too bad right now. Without antibiotics I don't know how long that'll last.

The noise of the wheels against the tracks seem much louder in the no-frills, no-comforts carriage. Stacks of crates tower around us, while the rest of the carriage is filled with pallets of machinery that jingles and knocks with the movement of the train.

That Monroe knows where we are doesn't make me feel too great. He's helped us, sure, but he's out for himself. If something changes, and a better deal for him is to sell us out, I have no doubt that he'll do it in a heartbeat. I can't fail, though. JT and Dakota are depending on me making this right, getting the price off our heads.

As well as Monroe, there's something more eating at me, and I need to discuss it with North.

'I think we're heading towards a problem.'

'Guessed that, because you got a face on you.'

I frown. 'A face?'

'Like a cougar that tried taking a bite out a porcupine.'

I narrow my eyes. Feel pissed at North. I've saved his ass more than once in the last couple of days, and I could do with less of his lip. 'Is that right?'

'For sure.'

Damn. At times the man is insufferable. 'Look, I don't think we should go as far as Port Miami. If Special Agent Peters got tipped off we were heading to Miami by train, once he realises we aren't on the passenger service it's only a short leap for him to figure out we might have skipped over to the haulage track. We got a head start for now but, even if he doesn't try to stop us en route, I figure he'll have men waiting in Miami.'

North looks grim as he thinks on what I've said. We pass over a set of points, and the door, loose on its flip catch, rattles harder.

He nods his head. 'Yeah. It makes sense. Jackson Peters is obviously far from stupid. Even though he doesn't know how we're travelling, he's guessed where we're heading. He'll have agents waiting to apprehend us in all the transport hubs in Miami, no question.'

Standing, I step over to the nearest stack of crates. The shipping notices on them give their destinations: Fort Pierce, Fort Lauderdale, Miami, Port Miami. 'So we get off a few stops before Port Miami, get a rental vehicle and make our way to the compound from there.'

North says nothing as he gets up and joins me by the crates. He looks over the shipping documents. 'We should get off at Fort Lauderdale and head to the wild country. That's where the Old Man is.'

'But I thought you said we needed to go to the compound?'

North shakes his head. 'The way things are going we'll never get close. You said it yourself: the Feds are anticipating that's our move. With Luciano hell-bent on getting to us, too, we'll stand no chance of getting in, even if Peters doesn't catch us first.'

'So how do we find the Old Man?'

'I know where he'll be.'

'And then what?'

North pats the messenger bag with the contents of the safety-deposit box inside. 'I show him my insurance policy.'

It makes sense – trying to get to the Old Man before he gets home to his Miami compound. But I feel a gnawing dread at the thought of which 'wild country' North means. So I ask him the question. 'Where is this wild country the Old Man takes his pilgrimage to?'

North doesn't miss a beat. 'Everglades City.'

Despite the humidity, I feel a chill up my spine and shiver. Memories whirl in my mind: Dakota screaming; JT out cold; a sinking boat; a rifle butt jabbed into my ribs; blood in the water as gators feast on human bodies.

The last time I visited the Everglades I damn near died.

42

SATURDAY, SEPTEMBER 22nd, 16:29

They've had more than twenty-four trouble free hours at sea, but they still have to be vigilant. JT checks his cellphone again, but there's no signal. Red has said they're too far from shore. JT hates it. He hasn't spoken to Lori in a day and a half. He knows she's tough, at the top of her game, but he wishes he knew how she was doing. When they last spoke he got the feeling she was keeping something from him about the situation with North.

Up at the helm, Red's showing Dakota how to steer the boat. She's grinning, laughing, her long strawberry-blonde hair loose and whipping around her face in the sea breeze. She's caught the sun from being out here on the ocean – more freckles now dust her nose and her arms. He wonders if she always gets freckles in the summer. Regrets he doesn't know the answer. There's still so much to catch up on; the first nine years of her life. He wishes he hadn't missed it all.

He knows he shouldn't blame Lori for not telling him she was pregnant, not after how things ended between them all those years back. He'd pushed her away, hurt her, blaming her for what happened when they apprehended her husband, even though he knew she'd had no choice. He was too stubborn to reach out and make things right. The truth is, he was worried he'd gotten in too deep with her. Back then, emotional detachment and a pure job focus were more important to him. Now he's not so sure. Dakota laughs and JT smiles again. He's happy they've got this time together at least.

The roar of an engine jerks him from his thoughts. Turning, he squints into the distance and sees there's a white speedboat approaching them fast. It's not showing any signs of changing course.

'Looks like trouble,' JT shouts to Red, pointing at the craft.

Red puts his hand up to shield his eyes and looks out across the sea. 'This is a long way from shore for a boat like that.'

JT's got a bad feeling. He needs to limit the risk to his daughter. Leaping to his feet, he gestures to Dakota. 'Follow the drill.'

She moves fast this time; now she knows that they're in danger. He's explained the situation to her, and she knows that if the bad men find them it will get ugly. She's brave, and he's proud of that. Smart too, like her momma. She'll go into the cabin, get her life preserver, then open the safe-space closet and crawl inside. She's safest from bullets there. She knows to stay hidden until JT or Red come tell her they're free and clear.

Be prepared, always; that's one of JT's rules. He's never had to plan contingency moves with a child, but what he said seemed to stick. Seems now they'll put their preparedness to the test.

He glances back towards the speedboat. It's gaining on them. He turns to Red. 'This thing go any faster?'

'Nope, she's at top speed. We can't outrun them.'

'I'll get the weapons.'

Red pulls a keychain from the pocket of his blue board shorts and throws it across to JT. 'Pull the cushion off the middle bench seat.'

JT catches the keychain, and does as Red says, yanking the cushion away and lifting a lid to reveal the under-seat storage. Inside is a metal lockbox. Using the only key on the keychain, he unlocks it and removes a rifle and a handgun.

He hurries over to Red at the helm. Holds up the guns. 'This all you got?'

Red nods. 'I don't usually have need for firearms. I'll take the rifle. It's old, but serviceable.' He looks back across the ocean towards the speedboat. 'There's ammo in the lockbox. Get us loaded.'

JT follows his gaze. The boat's maybe a couple of thousand yards away and showing no signs of slowing. At this distance he can't tell how many people are on board. Grabbing the bullets, he loads the two weapons.

At the helm, Red's still gunning the engine, steering the *Liberty* away from the path of the speedboat. The water's choppier, the bumps as they breach each wave more jarring. Struggling to keep his balance, JT scoots across the deck and round to Red. Hands him the rifle and a box of ammo. 'You're ready to go.'

'Won't be long now.'

JT turns. The speedboat is fifty yards and closing. There are four big men on board – the heavies from the marina. They've all got guns, and they're pointed at the *Liberty*. Next minute, they open fire.

'Get down,' JT dives for cover as Red leaps behind a bulkhead.

Bullets splinter the green wooden livery where JT was standing. He raises his gun and shoots; hits one guy in the chest and another in the shoulder.

But they're still coming, accelerating fast.

Red's firing the rifle, not hitting any of them. Damn. JT shoots again, but the heavies are wise to him now, ducked down behind the windshield. He shatters the glass with one shot, then peppers a line of holes in the hull. Dives for cover as the heavies return fire. Reloads.

'Give it up,' shouts one of the mob guys.

JT doesn't answer. Won't surrender to men like that. Fires a couple more shots then ducks for shelter as they come back at him hard and fast. Bullets hit the boat and ping into the water around them.

The *Liberty* lurches right. JT glances over at Red and sees he's steering the boat around, taking it around the speedboat. He doesn't know why. 'What are you—?'

'Keep them occupied.' Red says. It's an order. His focus remains on the speedboat.

JT squints over the side. Three heavies are still standing in the speedboat; they've only taken one down. He cusses. This isn't working. He needs to think of something more.

Raising his gun, he fires until he's out of bullets. Reloads again.

The *Liberty* is now level with the back of the speedboat. Red turns, hands off the wheel, and fires the rifle at the back of the boat. JT doesn't get what he's doing – all the heavies are in the front.

Two shots later he understands.

The explosion is loud and dramatic. Flames plume into the air. The heat is hot as hellfire. The heavies yell as the speedboat fractures, the backend incinerated from the explosion. The front sinking fast.

Red guns the *Liberty*'s engine, speeding them away. JT can see three of the heavies in the water, floundering. Drowning but not dead, yet. He stares at them, thinking.

'You want me to keep going?'

Red's voice pulls JT from his thoughts. Only two of the men are still shouting from the water. Miles from anywhere out here in the ocean they won't last long. The sharks will have them if their injuries don't. JT thinks of Dakota. He can't go back and rescue men like that; mob men who'd put a bullet in a child if ordered to. Nope. He just can't.

'Yup. Keep going,' JT says, standing and walking over to Red. He pats the older guy on the back. 'Great work back there. I thought they had us.'

Red nods. 'Couldn't let them get to the little one.' His expression's still serious-looking, but there's relief in his tone. 'Boat like that, chances were the fuel tanks would be on the back. Out this far they had to be carrying plenty of gas.'

'Appreciate it.'

'I don't need appreciation. Lori's helped me from a tight spot often enough, least I can do is help keep her baby girl safe.'

JT nods and takes the rifle, packing it and the handgun back into the lockbox with the remaining bullets. He locks up, puts the seating back to normal and straightens up.

Looking out towards the wreck of the speedboat he sees fins cutting through the debris around the men. Keeps watching as the sharks clean up. Clenches his jaw as the men's shouts are silenced. Finally, the last man disappears beneath the water and doesn't resurface.

With a rueful shake of his head, JT goes into the cabin to tell Dakota it's safe.

43

SATURDAY, SEPTEMBER 22nd, 16:32

I sure don't want to go back to the Everglades. I turn away from North, thinking about what he told me before; how every year on the same date the Old Man makes a three-day pilgrimage to the site where his brother died. How he only takes his two most trusted men. That he turns off all communication.

I cuss out loud, the sound immediately lost in the rattle of the door, the thundering of the wheels on the rails, the sound of air whistling through the gaps in the carriages vents. Try as I might, I can't deny the sense in North's thinking. If we can get to Everglades City we've got a better chance of having the Old Man hear us out than in a temper-fuelled reunion, with Luciano and the Feds snapping at our heels.

I look back to North. Nod once. 'Alright, I'm in. But I want to know exactly how you're planning to turn the Old Man against Luciano. You said you have something on him; I need to know what.'

'I wondered when you'd get around to asking me about that,' North says.

'Didn't seem the right time when the bullets where flying.'

He tilts his head to the side and studies me for a beat. 'You've sure changed a lot since I met you ten years ago. It's since you hooked up with that bounty hunter I'm guessing.'

I frown at him. 'Women change all the time, what makes you think it's due to a man? Don't you think a girl can grow all of her own accord?'

North raises his eyebrows, surprised by the comeback. 'I didn't mean that. I just ... Do you ever consider running away from danger instead of towards it?'

'A lot of times.'

North makes a show of looking around the carriage. 'Yet here we are.'

I frown. Don't get his meaning. 'And just what are you saying?'

'You've been bounty hunting a while, Lori. And I've heard you're real good. Hell, these last couple of days I've *seen* that you're good. But although you claim you don't like the violence and all, you're still in the game.' He squints at me, like he's trying to puzzle something out. 'Way I see it, you wouldn't keep playing the game if you didn't like the taste of blood.'

'I like the taste of justice, not blood.'

'Sometimes they're the same thing.'

I shake my head. 'No. You're wrong.'

'What about your husband, Tommy?' North's words are said without judgement but are damning enough in themselves. 'You fired on him until the gun was empty, and he was the man you said you'd love and cherish.'

I clench my jaw. Remember how Tommy had knocked the idealistic love from me punch by punch. 'I guess I hadn't figured on him cherishing me with his fists.'

'I'm not saying you were wrong, Lori. I'm just checking I got the facts straight. You shot him, then you and your boyfriend dumped him in a shallow grave. It was a bloody kind of justice.'

'Wasn't meant to go down that way.'

'You tracked him to that lodge. The pair of you worked as a team, had the front and rear exits covered. You could have—'

'He got the drop on JT inside the lodge. When I blocked his exit, Tommy came at me, went to draw his weapon. He meant to kill me. I had no choice but to—'

'I know.'

'How the hell could you possibly know? It was just the three of us. There were no witnesses.'

'And yet the Old Man found out who killed Tommy.'

I stare at North, not speaking, as the parts of the jigsaw that have never fit together right suddenly slot into place. 'It was ... You were there?'

'Kind of.'

'Meaning what? Why are you so interested in knowing if you've got the facts right about something that happened ten years ago?'

He says nothing.

I let the silence hang between us; there is only the noise of the wheels on the rails and the rattling of the carriage. I'm determined to wait it out until he answers my question.

Finally North shakes his head. 'I had the place rigged with cameras. I was close by, in an old duck hide in the woods, a little ways back from the lake. I saw the whole thing play out, first on camera, then when your man dragged Tommy's body through the trees to bury him.'

I cuss again. Scoot across the floor, away from North. '*You* told the Old Man it was me. You bastard.'

'Lori, I...' He looks guilty, like a dog that's been caught thieving, and steps after me, trying to coax me back. 'I needed leverage over Luciano, something important that would get the Old Man over more to my way of thinking.'

I put my hands up, warning him away. I need more distance between us than the freight carriage can provide. 'No! You stay away.' My voice is louder now, my fury at him makes it feel like I'm spitting fire with every word. 'My *family*, my *child*, is in danger because of you. I should have let Luciano's men kill you back in Missingdon. You deserved it.'

'And there it is.' He gives a rueful shrug, and a smug little smile.

I glare at him. 'What?'

'You want my blood now.'

'I...' I start to argue, then stop. It's true. Right now I want revenge rather than justice. But I don't Taser him, or pull a gun. Instead I say through gritted teeth. 'I'm. Not. Like. You.'

North holds my gaze a long moment, and I think he's going to argue. Then he drops his eyes and says, 'I know.'

'Then what is this, some kind of messed-up confessional?'

'You needed to know it was me. You've saved my hide a few times now. Didn't feel right you not knowing the truth.'

'Yeah. And I did save you.' I step back towards him. Put my hands on my hips and look him straight in the eye. 'So, seeing as you're the asshole who got me into this situation with the Old Man, I'm real keen to hear your grand plan for getting me out.'

North picks up his messenger bag and unbuckles the fastener. Pulling out the iPad he switches it on. 'I sent the copies of the spreadsheets and accounts that the FBI had seized from the files of the accountant Luciano killed to my email. They show all the money Luciano has stolen from the Old Man.'

'You said even with hard evidence it mightn't be enough for the Old Man, that he might not believe it was Luciano and there's a risk he'll talk his way out.'

'True, but if he checks his accounts against the files he'll know someone's been stealing from him.'

'What's to say Luciano won't try putting the blame on you?'

North gestures to the iPad. 'That's why I needed this. I didn't go rogue – I'm still loyal to the Old Man. I'd been watching Luciano for a long time, even when I first met you I was aware he was doing something underhand.'

'That's over ten years ago.'

'Yes, it is.' Emotion clouds his expression, but it's difficult to tell what he's thinking. 'What I'm about to show you will force the Old Man to believe me when I say I was protecting him, that I've always been protecting him. It's taken a long time to piece everything together, but I've got it all now. I was his number two. Even if he decides to end me himself, he does things the old way – he'll listen to what I have to say first.' North taps the iPad. 'And when he sees this, he'll realise you have no debt to pay.'

I frown, not understanding North's meaning. Whatever he has on the tablet, I still killed Tommy. 'Tommy was still like a son to him though.'

'Yeah, like a carbon copy of his lying, cheating, murderous son who wants to kill his own father and take over the family business.'

'What?' I stare at North. 'Show me.'

He presses the iPad's screen and turns it around to face me.

I gasp as I recognise the interior of the lodge by the lake out by Big Mo's Fishing Shack. It's the place JT and me tracked my husband Tommy down in months after he'd skipped town after Sal's murder. 'What is this?'

'Just keep watching. You'll see.'

The picture quality is grainy but passable. It's in black and white rather than colour, but there's audio too. The date in the bottom corner of the screen puts the time at a few days before the day I killed Tommy.

The camera is fixed above what must be a mirror or a painting on the wall in the wooden-clad open living space of the cabin. There's a blanket-covered couch, a small kitchen table with two chairs and a line of kitchen units with a two-ring stove and oven beneath. At first the room is empty. A few seconds later the door opens and two figures enter.

I inhale sharply as I recognise Tommy. Unshaven, with a dark sweater and jacket over his usual cargo pants, and his hair a little longer than the norm, he looks more unkempt than was usually the case, but it's unmistakably him. As he closes the door I get a proper look at the man behind him. 'Shit.'

Wearing a ball cap, jeans and a heavy jacket over a sweater, he's younger and leaner, for sure, but it's definitely him – Luciano Bonchese.

I turn to North. 'What is this?'

'Tommy and Luciano were very close. They truly were like brothers, in a way he and I never were. Keep watching.'

I do as he says, even though my I feel breathless from the shock of seeing Tommy again. My knees are shaking.

Tommy closes the door. *'It's done. Now you need to make my problem go away.'*

'It's in hand.' Luciano strides over to the refrigerator and grabs a beer from the icebox. *'Just sit tight a few more days and you'll be clear.'*

Tommy does that thing where he runs his hand through his hair but keeps it on his head a while longer than necessary. Usually means he's suspicious. *'How though? There's warrants out on me, and I heard that fucker bounty hunter ain't giving up.'*

Luciano grabs a second beer and passes it to Tommy. *'Details, bro. Don't worry about them. I've got your back.'*

Tommy seems pacified. He twists the cap off the beer and knocks his bottle against Luciano's. *'Just promise me, when we take the Old Man down, I'll be the one to end North.'*

Luciano laughs. Raises his beer in a salute. *'He's all yours, bro.'*

I watch as they swig their beers, grab a bag of chips, and then flop down at the kitchen table. With them hunched over the table, it's harder to hear the conversation. The audio has become muffled and patchy, but from the snippets I do hear I get a feel for the wretched plan they've hatched.

I wrap my arms around myself. Swallow hard. It seems, even now, even after beating on me and killing my best friend, that my long-dead husband is able to shock me bad.

Looking back at North I say, 'They were going to kill the Old Man and all the men loyal to him?'

'Yup. Complete takeover,' North says. 'They'd been planning it a while.'

I rub my brow. 'They were ready to act. Why didn't it happen?'

'You and JT took out Tommy before it could. Luciano didn't have the guts to do it alone, without his lieutenant. A few months later, that's when he started upping the violence and diversifying away from the business the Old Man wanted him to do. It's also when the money started disappearing.'

I gesture towards the video on the screen. 'Did you tell the Old Man about any of this?'

'No. Like I said, it's been my insurance. I told Luciano about the video instead, showed him a short clip, just so he knew for sure that I was telling the truth.' North looks rueful. 'That's why Luciano's always hated me. He knew I'd stashed the footage somewhere, and he knew that I had a back-up plan – that there was someone else who knew about it and had access, so that they'd be able to get it to the Old Man if Luciano ever tried to end me.'

North minimises the video, scrolls down through the videos on the menu, and plays another. In this conversation Luciano and Tommy are agreeing dates for executing the Old Man.

The video fades to black, but I can't look away. Can't get my head round what I've just seen, and what it means. 'This is messed up.'

'Yeah.' North softens his voice. 'But it means when you killed Tommy you took out an enemy of the Old Man, not a loyal son, like he's always thought. You did him a favour and, if he stands true to his eye-for-an-eye approach, you deserve to walk free whatever he chooses should happen to me.'

I don't know what to say. North could have told the Old Man this before. It would have stopped JT and Dakota ever being in danger. I think of all the things we've been through in the past few months, in the past few years. North could have prevented most of it. It brings me up short like a slap to the face. However well we get on, and however much we need each other to get Luciano off our backs and the Old Man to change his mind, I have to remember a very important fact: North is still a mob guy.

North takes my hesitation for remorse over Tommy. He puts a hand on my good arm. 'Don't regret it. You did what you had to.'

I nod. 'But I was wrong to kill him. He should have had a trial. Faced justice. A bullet was too damn good for a man like him.'

'It's all the same in the end. Fast or slow. Dead is dead.'

'Yup.' I think of Sal. How she'd just gotten engaged the week Tommy shot her. She had her whole life ahead of her. 'Ten years ago, a few weeks after the last time I saw you, Tommy killed my best friend, Sal, because she tried to protect me from him and his fists. He shot her in cold blood. Wasn't even sorry.' I remember Sal bleeding out on my kitchen floor. How I begged her to stay with me as I tried to stem the blood. 'That she was with me in my home, in his way, was my fault, and I can't ever change it. I feel the guilt of what happened every minute of every day. It never gets easier.'

North looks away.

The carriage rattles and creaks.

His voice is low, guilt ridden, as he mutters. 'I know how that feels.'

44

SATURDAY, SEPTEMBER 22nd, 16:47

JT opens the closet serving as a hideout and finds Dakota wearing her life preserver and curled up among Red's deck shoes. Her face is pale, her eyes more watery than usual, but there's a determined expression on her face and her fist is outstretched towards him, the blade of the pocketknife he gave her glinting in the light.

She drops her hand and folds the blade away when she sees him. 'Is it over?'

'It is.' He gives her a reassuring smile and holds out his hand. 'You can come out now.'

Dakota slides her hand into his and he helps her to her feet. JT squeezes her fingers and pulls her into a bear hug. 'Were you scared?'

'No. I knew you and Mr Red would protect me.'

JT hugs her tighter. He'd rather die than have anything bad happen again to his daughter. 'I'll always keep you safe.'

As they step back out onto the deck JT hears the engine splutter. The boat slows for a moment, then the engine revs and they pick up speed. But a few seconds later the engine misfires.

Dakota flinches.

JT looks across at Red. 'Something wrong?'

Red's frowning. He listens to the engine as it splutters again. 'It don't sound right. Come take the wheel for me and I'll have a look.'

JT does as he asks, hoping it's nothing serious. Sure, right now the sea is calm and there's no immediate danger, but getting stranded out here would be bad. The mob are still after them, and when the speedboat doesn't return chances are they'll send more heavies to find them.

As he keeps the wheel steady, he watches Dakota. She's standing at the back of the boat, looking out towards the wreckage of the mobsters' boat. He knows she would have heard the explosion and the gunfire, and she's seen the damage on the deck from bullets that have bitten into the *Liberty*. Chances are she heard the screams of the men overboard too. He tenses his jaw, angry that he's allowed that to happen. She's just a child; she shouldn't have to experience this.

'JT?' Red's voice pulls him from his thoughts.

'Things okay?'

Red shakes his head. 'We got ourselves a problem. Most of the damage we took is cosmetic, and the fuel tank seems okay, but the fuel line's damaged. It's leaking fuel and not feeding the engine the way it should.'

'Can you fix it?'

'Depends.'

JT waits for more, but as Red speaks the engine misfires again.

'JT, look!' Dakota's voice is higher in pitch than usual.

Turning, he looks towards her and in the direction she's pointing. He swallows hard. Three fins are cutting through the foam in the wake of the boat and that tells him one thing; the sharks are still hungry.

That's the moment the engine cuts out.

45

SATURDAY, SEPTEMBER 22nd, 19:46

I jerk awake, heart racing. For a moment I'm disorientated by my surroundings; the stacks of crates and pallets of machinery are shrouded in gloom. But the creaking, rattling noises of the freight train travelling along the track continue the same, and I remember where I am and why.

I glance across the carriage. North is sitting leant up against a stack of crates. He hasn't noticed I'm awake. His focus is on the partly torn photograph he's holding. From its shape, I recognise it as the one I picked off the floor of the locker room back at Carly's place; him and Nicole Bendrois, on their wedding day. His cheeks are damp with tears.

My body aches and my neck's crooked from lying at an awkward angle on the floor. I straighten up. Rub the back of my neck, trying to ignore the film of sweat and dust that's formed across my skin. 'Who was she really?'

North flinches at the sound of my voice. He wipes his hand across his face then looks towards me but doesn't speak.

'You made me turn myself into a copy of her for that bank visit. Don't you think I should know the truth?'

'The truth isn't always best.'

I hold his gaze. 'In my experience secrets are a whole lot more toxic.'

'Not than this truth.' He looks back at the photo. His eyes are still watery, his expression grim. 'Her real name was Gabriella Bonchese. The Old Man and his wife, Juliette, had three children: two girls and a boy. Gabriella was his youngest daughter, and she was my wife.'

Damn. My intuition was right. The heavies back in the foyer of

Carly's building had been shocked by my appearance because I looked like a passable fake of Luciano's dead sister.

'How did she die?'

North doesn't speak for a few minutes. When he starts, there's a tremble to his voice. 'We waited a long time before we got married. She always said, if it ain't broke why fix it, and we'd been together since high school. I was the one who wanted to be married.' He puts his head in his heads. 'I should have left things the way they were.'

I let him be for a little while. Let the movement of the train rock us side to side, and the clacking of the rails distract from the pain of the conversation. Then I ask, 'Why?'

North rubs his fingers between his brows as if trying to order his thoughts, then pinches the bridge of his nose. 'It was a small wedding. Very private. The Old Man didn't want his rivals to know his attack dog had a wife, a weakness. He didn't want her to be any more of a target than she was already for being his daughter.' North hangs his head. 'He didn't realise she was more at risk from within the family than from outside.'

I frown. 'What do you mean?'

'Luciano loved his younger sister.' The anger in North's tone makes it as hard as granite. 'He couldn't stand that we were together.'

'Surely if he loved her, he'd have wanted her happy. I know he didn't like you much but—'

'You're not getting my meaning.' North fixes me with a hard stare. 'Luciano *loved* Gabriella. And because he felt that way, he thought she should belong to him ... and only him. The jealousy, the possessiveness, it'd been going on for years, since we were all teens.'

My stomach flips as I get what he's implying. 'He wanted to sleep with his own sister?'

North's jaw is clenched, his tone venomous. 'He did more than *want* it. He forced her once. It was back when we were teenagers. We'd all had a few drinks from a bottle of liquor stolen from the Old Man's cabinet. Luciano made sure Gabriella had more than the rest of us. Then, when she started feeling ill, carried her up to her room, saying he'd put her to bed. Except he didn't. He raped her.'

I stare at North, sickened by what he's telling me.

'I found her afterwards. She wouldn't let me tell the Old Man. So I helped her as best I could. Then I went after Luciano and damn near beat him to death.'

'But you stayed with the family?'

'We were thirteen. My Dad had died – the Bonchese family was the only one I had. And, even if I'd wanted to go, I could never have left Gabriella.'

I keep my voice soft. 'What happened to her?'

He pauses. Swallows deeply. 'She was gunned down in downtown Miami the day after we returned from honeymoon four months ago. It was my fault. I killed her.'

I shift away from him, not understanding. 'How? Why?'

'Because I was stupid.' The tremor in his voice is more obvious now, guilt replacing the anger. 'I didn't want there to be any secrets between us, not once we were married. So I showed her the video of Luciano and Tommy.' He shakes his head. 'I should have known she'd want to tell the Old Man. She gave Luciano twenty-four hours to leave the family compound but...'

My jaw goes slack. 'Luciano killed her?'

'I don't have any proof he did it. But it was him who gave me these and told me I never deserved her in the first place. Said she should have been his, so he took her away.' North opens the brown envelope that he'd taken from the safety-deposit box and removes a set of photographs, He hands them to me without looking at them.

I inhale real sharp. The first picture is of Gabriella Bonchese walking along a crowded sidewalk. The next picture shows the moment the shots hit her; she's falling backwards, the people around her scrambling for safety. The third shows her lying on the sidewalk in a pool of blood. Her eyes are open but unfocused. Dead.

I look back at North. 'How did they—?'

'Witnesses say the shooter was on the back of a motorbike. They pulled up, shot her and then left. The driver took pictures on his cellphone.'

'I'm so sorry.' The words seem worthless.

'I went to the Feds. If he was willing to kill his own sister, I realised that footage I had of him and Tommy wasn't going to stop him coming for me, and then the Old Man. I needed irrefutable proof of what Luciano had done. The Old Man needed to see, and believe, the deep dirty truth about his son.' Anger blazes in North's eyes, but there's uncertainty in his expression too. 'And I needed an eye for an eye.'

An eye for an eye. I realise North means to kill Luciano to avenge Gabriella's death. Right now, with the pictures in my hand, I don't have the desire to prevent it. 'You think there's a chance the Old Man won't listen to you?'

North rubs his hand across the stubble on his jaw. 'He won't want to hear what I've got to tell him. He's already lost a daughter. It'd be easier for him to pretend it's not true. How it plays out...? There's no guarantees.'

46

SATURDAY, SEPTEMBER 22nd, 21:04

As the freight train pulls into the siding at Fort Lauderdale we're all set to get gone. We jump down from the rear door as soon as the train stops and move along the tracks, away from the loading platform. It's dark, and that helps us move unseen. By the time we reach the road, it feels like I haven't taken a breath in minutes.

It's mainly freight parking and cargo storage around us, so there's nothing to do but hike. We've not eaten in hours, and our water ran out a long while back. I look at North. I can't remember when he last took his medication, but I know he needs a meal to take it with.

'We should find a diner. Take a quick comfort break before we move on.'

He nods in agreement, and we keep walking. The streets aren't real busy at this time, and although we keep a look out for Feds and Luciano's heavies, we see no sign that we're being tailed.

A little ways further towards downtown we find a drugstore and I tell North I'm going inside. He comes with me, following me through the aisles as I locate antiseptic lotion and supplies to dress the wound in my arm. I glance towards the medication dispensary. They'll have antibiotics back there, but without a physician's script there's no way I can get any. So I head towards the counter. I see a display of disposable cellphones. It's been twenty-four hours since I last spoke to JT. I need to check he and Dakota got out safe, and I figure a burner is the safest way to do that. I pick one up and add it to the items in my basket along with a couple of bottles of water and some candy bars. North raises his eyebrows but says nothing.

The teenager on the register hardly glances my way as she rings up my purchases. North stays a little ways away, pretending to browse the magazines near the door. I notice the camera fixed high in the wall, focused down on the register, and I hope to hell that our disguises hold.

'That'll be eighty-seven bucks and sixteen cents.' The teller looks at me with the glazed stare of someone going through the motions for money.

Her lack of interest is to my advantage. I pass her ninety bucks and tell her to keep the change, wanting to be out of the store as quick as I can.

Back on the street, we head further towards downtown. After a couple of minutes walk we spot an Olive Garden restaurant half a block up. North keeps glancing at me, his expression tense.

The next time he does it, I meet his gaze. 'You got something eating at you?'

He gestures to my go bag. 'The cellphone. You planning on using it?'

What kind of dumbass question is that? 'For sure.'

North exhales loudly. Shakes his head.

In truth I'm fighting the urge to use the cellphone right away. I'm desperate to make sure my family is safe, but I can't risk calling until North and me are on our way out of Fort Lauderdale. It's a stretch to think the Feds could be bugging JT's cell, but I can't rule it out entirely. They want North, their prized asset, back, and given his testimony could put away a member of the Bonchese crime family, and Monroe said Special Agent Jackson Peters is an ambitious kind of a guy, it stands to reason they may look to wiretap any phones they think could give them a lead. From the haunted expression on North's face I can tell he's thinking the same.

'Look,' I say, 'I'm leaving it till we're on our way out of town, okay? But then I'm calling. I have to know that my family is safe.'

'I get that.' North's voice is measured. 'Just wait until we have our transport sorted out, yeah?'

'Deal.'

⌒

We eat dinner at the Olive Garden. The soup, salad and breadsticks filling us up before our main meals have even arrived. We get them boxed to go, then head back into the night. We ask around, looking for somewhere we can get a rental car, but it seems there's no place open at this time.

The further we walk, the tenser I feel. The wound in my arm is itchy and uncomfortable. I wonder if it's my imagination or if I'm feeling hotter than usual. For a moment I worry the fever is returning. Hope the wound isn't getting re-infected. Then I push the thoughts to the back of my mind. We need to get out of this place. I need to call JT.

I look across at North striding beside me. 'We can't wait until morning, we need to get on the road now.'

'Agreed.' North looks grim-faced. 'The Old Man will be in the wild country until tomorrow lunchtime, but we'll need to find him, and persuade him. He doesn't change his schedule for anything.'

'So what are you suggesting? That cab driver was the most likely person who alerted Jackson Peters to us in Jacksonville. We can't risk another long cab ride where someone can watch us.'

North flicks his glance towards the line of parked-up vehicles alongside a fancy new apartment block, his gaze fixing on a red sedan – an older model than the rest. 'I was thinking more of borrowing something.'

⌒

North's speedy with the hot wire.

As soon as the engine's running I step on the gas and manoeuvre us away from the apartment block and out onto the street. As I drive, North investigates what's of use in the car. He finds a plug-in navigator in the glove compartment. Getting it out, North switches it on and searches through for the closest car-rental shops who do out-of-hours opening times. He sticks the navigator onto the dash with the sucker.

'There's a place near Wynwood. Twenty-three miles,' he says. 'We should be there before they close at eleven.'

'Good work.' I reckon a place near Wynwood, a few miles from Miami Airport, figures it can cash in on picking up vacationers who'd rather travel a ways from the airport to pick up a rental at a cheaper rate.

He smiles. 'Well, thank you, ma'am.'

I press the accelerator harder, speeding right up to the limit as I follow the directions of the tinny-voiced navigator. Hope we can make it to our destination without getting pulled over.

We make it twenty-two miles before I see the blue lights in the rearview.

47

SATURDAY, SEPTEMBER 22nd, 22:41

Blue lights. Getting closer.

Adrenaline fizzes through my veins. Pulling evasive manoeuvres isn't easy in a place you've never been through before, but I can't let them catch us.

I look at North. 'I'm under the speed limit. Surely the car can't have been reported stolen already.'

He turns, looking over his shoulder, watching the road and the blue lights. 'We can't stop.'

'Tell me something I don't know.' I can't drive us straight up to the rental place, not if the cops are following.

The navigator is jabbering away about taking a right at the junction. It's making me crazy. 'Shut that damn thing up, would you?'

North snatches it from the dash and presses a few buttons. 'Take a left at the next junction. A right down the side alley. Get ready to run.'

I do as he says. Make a smooth left, trying not to look suspicious. The blue lights are closer, but not on us yet, and there's no siren. Could be they're not after us.

As soon as we're on the next road I swing the sedan right down the side alley. The suspension creaks, tyres bumping over potholes. A few hundred yards in, I stamp on the brakes and we jump out and start running.

Out of the corner of my eye, I notice North has the car's navigator in his hand.

'Why are you taking that? We know where the rental place is.'

'So when the cops find the car, they can't see we searched for a rental place.'

I nod. It's good thinking, no question.

We hurry through the streets. It's near on ten minutes before eleven. If we get there too late we'll have to wait until seven tomorrow to get a car.

I can't let that happen.

⌐

We reach the rental office with two minutes to spare. The bleary-eyed guy behind the counter looks up when the bell over the door goes. He seems surprised to see people wanting a vehicle at this time of night. 'I was just closing.'

I keep walking towards the counter. 'Sign on the door says you're open.'

The guy gives a shrug and sighs loudly. 'Yeah, welcome to my world,' he mutters under his breath.

North rests his elbows on the counter and eyeballs the guy. 'We're looking for something mid-range, compact.'

'I can do that,' the guy says. His tone sounds like there's nothing he'd like to do less. He taps a few keys on the computer beside him. 'I've got a Jetta available. If you want something else you'll have to come back tomorrow after tonight's returns have been valeted.'

'The Jetta is fine.'

'Alrighty then.' He taps a few more keys. Looks back at me, then North. 'You got ID?'

As North reaches into his jacket pocket for his wallet, I put my go bag on the floor, unzip it and take out the wallet with Nicole Bendrois' drivers' licence. As I straighten up, the images on the television screen in the corner of the waiting area catch my eye. I inhale hard.

The banner across the bottom of the screen screams: *FBI Agent Killers Heading to Miami.*

On camera a female reporter is interviewing Special Agent Jackson Peters. They're on location somewhere; it looks like a train station, but it's not Jacksonville or Fort Lauderdale. The television's sound is muted, so I read the subtitles as they appear.

'*So are you any closer to catching these murderers?*' the reporter asks. Jackson Peters keeps his expression neutral. '*We're on their trail.*'

'*But you haven't caught up with them yet; why not?*'

Peters frowns. It looks like he's trying hard to keep his cool. '*We have reason to believe the fugitives are heading to Miami, most likely by rail, and we're prepared. I can't go into details, but we are poised to take them into custody.*'

As the camera moves away from Peters to focus solely on the reporter, I catch a glimpse of a sign a little ways behind them – Port Miami.

'Ma'am, your ID please?' The rental guy's voice pulls me back to the room.

Flustered, my mind still thinking on Jackson Peters, I hand over the driver's licence. 'Sorry, here it is.'

The guy looks at me for a beat longer than necessary, then takes the ID and studies it real careful. He holds up both of our IDs. 'I just need to scan these into the system.'

As he turns away, heading out back, into the office behind the counter, I look at North. 'You think he—?'

'Not here.' North's voice is firm. 'Wait till we're in the car.'

I nod. Gesture towards the television. 'Check it out.'

As North watches the news looping on a cycle – a kidnapping in Fort Myers, a stabbing in Ocala, then back to Jackson Peters – I wonder how Peters knew we'd likely be at Port Miami. Did he guess we jumped on the freight train when we didn't board the passenger one at Jacksonville, or did Monroe see an opportunity and tell him our plan? I hate not knowing.

I tap my fingers against the counter. What the hell is keeping the rental guy so long? It's ten past eleven now – past closing time. Surely he should be hurrying to get us processed. I glance over my shoulder through the glass shop front, looking for anyone waiting outside or vehicles parked up watching us. I can't see nothing; the glare from the lights inside reflect back from the glass, obscuring my view of the street outside. I feel a twist in my gut and hope I'm just getting paranoid.

'Ms Bendrois?'

My throat feeling suddenly dry, I turn back around. Knowing they'll be cameras on the counter, I keep my face angled down. Sure, the rental guy has a copy of Nicole Bendrois' ID, but that picture truly is her rather than me, so there's less chance of my real identity being spotted from it.

'Thank you, ma'am.' The guy hands Nicole's ID back to me, but holds onto North's, and stays watching him real close for a long moment.

My breath catches in my throat. Has he figured out who North is?

North frowns. 'Everything okay?'

The guy lets out a sigh. Shakes his head. 'Well, the thing is, our computer search has turned up a problem.'

I pick my go bag off the floor, ready to run. Catch North's eye and flick my gaze to the door.

North doesn't move. He narrows his eyes at the rental guy. 'What's that?'

'The points on your licence? You've got more than we allow.'

Trying not to let my relief show too obviously, I smile at the guy. 'It doesn't matter none. I'll drive.'

'Yes, ma'am. That's what I was going to suggest.'

Fifteen minutes later I've signed the paperwork in Nicole Bendrois' name, paid cash for two days' rental, and we've taken possession of a VW Jetta. It's a whole lot smaller than the vehicles I'm used to and makes me feel like I'm driving with my elbows squished in, but it runs okay and we're heading along out of Wynwood in the direction of Everglades City. With every mile we travel away from Miami, I breathe a little easier.

It's near on eleven-thirty when I finally get to power up the cellphone I bought at the drugstore and call JT's number. My heart thumps in my chest and I'm gutted when it goes straight to voicemail. I dial Dakota's cell but it diverts to voicemail too. Panic grips me. Fear that something bad has happened to my family.

In the passenger seat, North swallows his medication and follows it up with a candy bar and a swig of one of the water bottles. He raises an eyebrow. 'You okay?'

I drop the cellphone onto my lap. Stare out at the highway. 'They're not answering.'

'It's late. They could be sleeping.'

Dakota maybe, but not JT. He wouldn't have switched his cell off; he'd keep it on, waiting for me to call.

I shake my head. 'Something's not right. He'd answer. He always answers.'

'You can try again in the morning.'

'I want to speak to them *now*.' My tone is harsher than I intended.

Grabbing the cell, I try Red's number. It goes to voicemail, the same as JT's and Dakota's. I end the call and fear twists in my stomach.

The last time Red stopped answering his cellphone the Miami Mob had damn near beaten him to death. My stomach lurches, and I taste bile.

I got a real nasty feeling about this.

48

I follow Highway 41 out of town. My eyes are sore from the coloured contact lenses I'm wearing and the effort of concentrating on the dark road. I'm feeling hotter by the minute and my left arm is stiff and tender beneath my jacket. It's a bad sign. I know that if I want to avoid another infection I need to act fast.

'You okay?' North sounds real concerned. 'Your cheeks are flushed.'

'I left my antibiotics back at Carly's place. I need some more.'

He nods, looking thoughtful. 'Pull a U-turn.'

'What?'

'We passed a place, maybe a half mile back in that small town. We can get some there.'

I wipe the sweat from my forehead. 'They won't serve me without a script.'

North smiles. 'I was thinking more that we'd self-serve.'

The drugstore stands alongside a small grocery store on the edge of a cluster of homes that are too few to really call a town. I drive past, casing out the location. All the lights are off. The street is deserted. If we're busting into someplace, this is as good a shot as any.

I swing the car around and drive back along the street, parking up a couple of hundred yards from the drugstore. Cutting the lights, I undo my seatbelt and reach for my go bag on the back seat. 'I've got lock picks in my carryall.'

'Let me have them.'

Taking them out, I turn back to North. My breathing is a little laboured from the effort. 'Why?'

There's a concerned expression on his face. 'Because you're not in any state to get this done.'

He's right, though it pains me to admit it. I'm burning up and feeling weak. I need the antibiotics, but if I go inside with North I risk jeopardising the mission. Damn. Frustrated, I nod. 'Okay.'

North takes the picks and climbs out of the car. I switch the engine back on, keeping the Jetta idling as I wait for him to return.

Minutes pass. I hate waiting. Sweat runs down my face. I keep looking in the rearview mirror, watching for North to emerge from the drugstore. A streetlamp flickers. A stray food wrapper wafts along the sidewalk like a modern-day tumbleweed. The street stays ghost-town quiet. No vehicles pass.

Ten minutes later, and there's still no sign of North. I feel the tension tighten in my belly. This isn't good. He should have been done by now. What the hell is keeping him?

Movement on the street catches my eye. A few hundred yards ahead there's a person on the opposite sidewalk walking this way. It's hard to tell if they're male or female at this distance. But whoever they are, they're getting closer.

My breath catches in my chest. I look back in the rearview; still no sign of North. I put my hand on the door handle, thinking on whether to go help him.

An ear-splitting wail pierces through the silence. In the mirror I see a red light flashing on the front of the drug store. Goddamn it. North's tripped an alarm. Next moment I see him hurtle around the corner of the building onto the sidewalk and sprint towards the Jetta.

I put the gear into drive. Look forwards. The figure on the opposite side of the street is closer now. It's a man but he's still too far away to make out his features. I hope to hell he doesn't manage to get a good look at our faces.

North yanks open the car door and throws himself inside. 'Go!'

He doesn't have to tell me twice. Flooring the gas, I shoot the Jetta onto the highway and accelerate out of town. As we pass the pedestrian on the sidewalk we keep our heads turned away.

'Did you get them?' I ask North.

'Yeah.' He passes me a pack of antibiotics. I recognise the name – they're the same ones Carly gave me. 'Should last a while.'

'Thanks.'

'The door wasn't alarmed. It was the dispensary that was. I thought I'd disabled it. Trying to do it took a while.'

I press a couple of tablets into my palm and swallow them down with a gulp of water. I shake my head. 'Like I said, thanks.'

We drive on in silence, both knowing that the alarm and the eyewitness could bring trouble our way. If they got a look at the licence plate and the cops trace it back to the rental shop, they'll have our fake IDs. If they find the car we stole from near the station and left by the rental shop, then connect the two, it'll give them a picture of our movements.

Damn.

I hope local law enforcement don't figure out the connection fast. And, when they do, I hope it takes a long while for that information to reach Special Agent Jackson Peters.

Otherwise the FBI will be on our tail before dawn.

⌒

I keep driving. Forty minutes later, at Carnestown, I make a left turn onto the country road towards Everglades City. I'm already feeling better – my temperature has dropped and the sweating has stopped. I feel more alert too, which is a good thing because the terrain out here is way different from the urban sprawl of Miami. Swamps and scrubland borders the road, and there are no streetlights to guide our path, just the beams of the Jetta's headlights and a faint dusting of stars above.

A couple of miles along the road I have to brake hard before manoeuvring around a gator that's making its way along the side of the blacktop. Its eyes glint yellow as it turns to watch us pass, and I shudder.

Despite feeling better physically my unease has been growing stronger with every minute along the journey; my fear for the safety of JT, Dakota and Red mingling with the memories of the last time I came to the Everglades. Men died that night; me and my family almost died with them. I swore then that I'd never return to this godforsaken place – this wild country – yet just a few months later here I am.

Beside me, in the passenger seat, North stirs in his sleep. He's been dozing for the past hour and I've seen no sense in waking him. The road has been pretty clear, and there's been no sign of cops or Miami Mobsters on our tail.

'We're almost there,' I say.

North blinks awake. Rubs his face with his hands and peers through the windshield. 'Yeah?'

As if on cue a sign appears at the side of the road. There's a picture of a bird and a fish against the backdrop of a sunset over water. The words read: *Welcome to Everglades City. Established 1924 Florida.*

I glance at the clock on the dash. It's real late. In a place where we've done no recon, and I've got no sense of the geography, trying to get to the Old Man could be a risky strategy.

I look at North. 'So you know the Old Man's routine on this annual pilgrimage of his. What's the plan?'

'He always stays at a villa on Lake Placid. The community's gated. We won't be able to get in there now without drawing attention to ourselves.'

Keeping my foot easy on the gas, I glance out at the dark landscape around us. The road is built up higher than the land, making a causeway that crosses the swamps. Moonlight reflects off the water all around us. I know what's likely to be lurking beneath it. I shudder again. 'So what are you suggesting?'

'How much cash you got left?'

'Maybe a hundred bucks and change.'

'Keep going along Collier. There's a place we can stay until it's daylight.'

I drive along Collier, and a few minutes later North directs me to a place called the City Motel. It's small with a neon sign out front saying

Vacancies. We park the Jetta in the rear parking lot and I get out and head to the wooden-clad building with a sign saying *Office* above the door.

The door's locked, but there's a light on inside. I move around the building, trying to see whether I can spot anyone inside. I see a neat counter with information pamphlets, and a coffee maker with go cups on a table to the side, but no signs of life. Damn.

I move back to the door. That's when I notice the buzzer and a weathered sign instructing late arrivals to press long and firm. Figuring that's what we are, I do as it says and wait. No one comes.

I'm looking back towards the car and North, wondering on my next move, when the door clicks unlocked. I flinch at the sound, and snap around to face the door.

An older woman with her hair in curlers and a long fluffy housecoat wrapped around her, opens the door. 'What'd you want?'

I give her my most winning smile. 'We're looking for a room.'

'We got them, but we close at ten.' She makes a show of looking at her watch. 'You're four hours late and counting.'

'I'm sorry, ma'am, but we sure would appreciate a room. We've been driving a long time and my friend told us your motel is the best place to stay here in Everglades City. She said your rooms are neat as pins and the beds are real comfy.'

She narrows her eyes, deciding whether to let me in, then nods, seemingly pacified by my compliment. 'Fine then, come in here and I'll get you set up.'

⌐

Our room is number eleven, in the middle of the back line of rooms in the horseshoe-shaped one-storey cinderblock building that makes up the majority of the motel. It's basic but clean, and there's enough space for me not to feel like our twin beds are virtually next to each other.

North flops down onto the nearest bed. He takes a gulp of water, finishing the bottle he's been working on. 'We should rest,' he says. 'There's no guarantee how things will turn out later.'

'Sure.' Ain't that the truth.

I drop my go bag onto the other bed. My body aches, and the throbbing in my left arm around the site of my bullet wound has got steadily worse over the past few hours. Peeling off my leather jacket, I take the supplies I got from the drugstore back in Fort Lauderdale from my bag and head to the bathroom.

After locking the door, I remove the bandage from around my arm, then slowly peel back the dressing from the wound. It hurts like a bitch and isn't pretty, but there are no signs of infection and for that I am thankful. The antibiotics must have caught it just in time. Undoing the top of the bottle with my right hand, I angle myself over the washbasin and pour the antiseptic lotion over the wound. I cuss under my breath, gritting my teeth as the antiseptic stings my raw flesh. It's near on forty-eight hours since I last took a look at it in a motel mirror, and hurt as it does, it looks and feels a whole lot better than before.

Patting the skin around the wound dry with a cotton-wool pad, I attach a new sterile dressing over the wound. Although the dressing's self-adhesive, I double-up with an extra length of bandage wrapped and tied around the dressing.

I remove the green contact lenses and splash water over my face. As I freshen up, I try to swallow down the nerves that are building inside me about facing the Old Man tomorrow.

It's only as I turn to leave that I catch a look at my face in the mirror. The fluorescent lighting is unflattering for sure, but that's not what makes me do a double-take. Sure, the bobbed brunette hair stops me looking like myself, but it's not the change alone that unsettles me.

It's because I look like the Old Man's dead daughter. And that causes another level of concern about seeing him tomorrow.

The Old Man is big on respect. Old school, like North says. My family's lives rely on the Old Man listening to North and me and I sure as hell don't want the way I look to give him any excuse not to hear us out. Will he think I'm disrespecting his daughter's memory by being dressed up this way?

We've come too far: been shot at, ridden a freight train, stolen a car, rented another and covered well over five hundred miles today. I've no idea if Carly made it out of her apartment alive, or if Luciano's men managed to get our plans out of her. What I do know is that, given the damning evidence North has against him, Luciano won't rest until he's silenced us, and that Special Agent Jackson Peters will work just as hard to get the pair of us into custody.

The plan has to work. I can't fail my family.

Back in the room, North's lying on his bed, fully clothed and snoring. Taking off my boots, I step across to the other bed and sit down. I know it's late, near on three o'clock in the morning now, but I can't sleep without giving JT's cellphone another try.

I hold my breath as the call connects, then breathe out fast when his recorded voicemail message starts to play. I bite my lip as I listen to the gravelly rasp of his voice and wish that I knew where he is, how he and Dakota are doing.

When the message ends, I hang up and try Red's cell. It goes straight to voicemail too. Ending the call, I plug the cell in to charge and lie back on the bed.

I try to swallow down the fear that something real bad has happened. Try reassuring myself with the fact that JT and Red are resourceful and experienced, and that they're honourable guys who'll fight to the death to keep my baby safe.

It doesn't work. Sleep doesn't come easy.

When it does take me, my dreams are filled with an eternal loop of gunshots, blood and slow-motion images of gators taking a victim for a death roll. Frantic, heart racing, I try to help them, but I never get there in time. The gators thrash beneath the water until the surface is coloured with crimson.

In every loop, the victim is JT.

49

SUNDAY, SEPTEMBER 23rd, 06:12

I toss and turn, sleeping fitfully until I wake with the dawn, the small chink of light blazing through the gap in the drapes enough to rouse me. I roll over and see that North's still asleep on top of the other bed.

The tension builds in my chest as I unplug my cellphone and dial JT's number. As before, it goes straight to voicemail. So does Red's. And so does Dakota's. I clench my jaw, fighting back tears. Know that I need to focus on what we have to do today, but it's real hard when it feels as if my heart's going to burst out through my ribs.

Unable to lie still, I get up, pick some fresh jeans, a black tee and underwear from my go bag, and pad quietly across to the bathroom. The shower is weak and lukewarm, but still feels good. It's a little tricky washing with my left arm out of the cubicle, but I manage.

Plugging in the hairdryer, I dry off my hair and style it as best I can the way Gabriella used to do hers. I don't have any contact lens solution, and didn't pack the holder the green contacts came in, so I rinse them off and put them back in, then do my face while thinking on our next moves: find the Old Man. Get him to listen to North and view the evidence against Luciano and Tommy. Then get him to take the price off me and my family's heads.

Going back into the bedroom, I'm surprised to find North awake and watching the small television mounted on the wall opposite the beds. He hands me a mug of coffee and gestures to the screen, his expression grim. 'That FBI agent is causing all kinds of shit.'

I turn to the television and my stomach flips as I read the banner scrolling along the bottom of the screen: *Breaking News: FBI Stakeout Mob Compound.*

Above the banner the picture shows a helicopter view of a high-walled, gated compound. Acres of land separate the buildings from the wall and the civilisation outside it. In the middle of the compound there's a large ranch-house-style building, surrounded by barns or warehouses. Beyond the buildings I see a field with a herd of horses and then, as the chopper starts to turn away, a glimpse of the ocean.

Shit. 'The Old Man's place.'

'Yeah.' North sounds pissed. A blonde reporter in a pink pant suit appears on camera. It looks like she's standing a little ways from the compound; the outer wall is just visible in the distance behind her. North turns up the volume as she starts to speak.

'At first light FBI agents set up roadblocks around the residence of the infamous Bonchese family, home to businessman, and alleged head of the Miami Mob, Giovanni Bonchese. We believe these precautions are being taken because the suspects from a shooting in Missingdon, Florida, where two FBI agents were killed and one critically injured, are believed to be heading to the residence. The FBI and local law enforcement are working together and caution the public not to approach the fugitives but to call the emergency hotline – number on your screen below – if they see them.'

Our pictures flash up onto the screen, along with the phone-in number.

'At least they've not updated our descriptions to how we look now.'

I assumed that the cab driver who took us from Tallahassee to Jacksonville had called the hotline, but if that had been the case he would have given them updated descriptions. 'That's strange, isn't it? Why not?'

North shrugs. 'Beats me. At least we know their game because of the news.'

I'm not so sure. 'If the driver didn't call it in, that means Jackson Peters, or one of his team, guessed that we'd take that route back, probably using the same reasoning as us – that we couldn't travel by road. They thought the easiest alternative would be train, and Jacksonville was the closest station to Missingdon for a straight run-through to Miami, so they set up that ambush on the platform.'

'Could be. But at least that means they've not connected us to the drugstore last night, or figured out that we were heading out of Miami.'

He's right. North doesn't seem at all fussed, but I sure as hell am. If he predicted our move back in Jacksonville, it makes me far more worried about Special Agent Peters. He's career minded, according to Monroe, obviously smart, and he's got into our heads, pre-empted our move. That makes him a whole lot more dangerous.

We're back in the Jetta by seven o'clock and heading along Collier towards the villa complex at Lake Placid. As it comes up on our left I slow our speed and do a drive-past.

North frowns. 'I don't see any vehicles outside the villa he always rents.'

'Any chance he'd have picked somewhere else this time? He knows you're on the run and that you're aware of his movements here, so he could well have changed things up as a precaution.'

'He always stays in the same villa at the same place. Has done for fifty or so years. He has an annual booking for the same dates. He's a creature of habit, and he's too arrogant to believe anyone would get to him.' North looks back at the villa. 'God knows, I tried to talk him into changing his routine often enough, but he never listened.'

I brake to a halt. 'Then what next?'

'We should check out the villa just in case.'

It takes some sweet talking from North for the security guy at the rental villa's entrance to let us in. But luck is with us, and eventually the combination of him recognising North from the previous year, and me acting as Gabriella Bonchese and talking about paying my daddy a surprise visit, and how mad he'll be if I get turned away, does the trick.

As the guard raises the barrier, he shouts across at us. 'Not sure they're there. The car left a little while ago.'

I fake a smile to the guard and drive through the gateway. Soon as we're inside I glance at North. 'You think we missed them?'

'The Old Man visits the spot his brother dies each morning. He lights a candle, and sits there in a silent vigil until noon. If they're not here, I know where to go to find him.'

We crawl the Jetta along the private road to villa twenty-three and park on the driveway.

As we get out, I look at North. 'You ready to do this?'

He nods. He's clutching the messenger bag with the iPad from the safety deposit box real tight. 'Let's get it done.'

We step up onto the front porch, and I press the bell. The chimes are loud, easy to hear outside. But no one comes to the door.

I try again. Still nothing.

North cusses. Moving around the porch, he peers in through the front window. 'Can't see no one.'

We move around back. Try looking in through the doors onto the small yard that runs down to the lake. I see a fancy kitchen, but no signs of life. 'Looks like they're gone.'

'They could be. Oftentimes we'd drive straight back after the Sunday vigil. Could be they packed up before heading out.'

Once they head back to Miami we're screwed. With Luciano's men and Special Agent Jackson Peters on the lookout for us, we'd stand no kind of a chance in getting close enough to the Old Man to talk sense.

I stride back towards the car. Look over my shoulder at North. 'Come on then. We need to find them before they leave town.'

50

SUNDAY, SEPTEMBER 23rd, 08:01

North directs me to a place on the other side of Everglades City. The journey takes less than five minutes and, in the daylight, I realise, although it's called a city, this place is little more than a small town on a patch of firm ground surrounded by lake and swamp.

We park up in a lot and walk over to a squat wooden building painted yellow, perched where the ground meets the water. Over the door is a big hand-painted sign: *Jack's Hire*.

North gestures to the building. 'This is the place the Old Man always gets his rental craft.'

I scan the lot. 'You see his car?'

North takes a moment, looking around, then shakes his head. 'Nothing stands out, but there's a bunch of Florida plates. Could be his is one of these, or maybe he parked someplace else.'

I narrow my gaze. 'You said he was a creature of habit. He usually park here?'

'Oftentimes, yes.'

My gut tells me North's lying, but there's no way to prove it and, seeing as we both want to find the Old Man, what would be the point? 'So what does he rent?'

Rather than answering, North heads straight inside.

The man behind the desk is wearing a flamboyant Hawaiian shirt and has an even more flamboyant mullet. His skin is baked deep tan and looks like aged leather. He smiles as we approach. 'You folks looking to get out into the wild country?'

My stomach twists at the thought.

North raises a hand in hello. 'We need a couple of kayaks for the day. You got any?'

The mullet guy whistles. 'Well, they sure are popular this weekend, but I got a couple just returned you can take. I'll need them back by five though.' He winks at me. 'Got a load more pre-books arriving in the a.m.'

'That suits us just fine,' I say, the tremble in my voice betraying how I'm feeling about getting out onto the water. 'How much?'

'Eighty bucks.' Mullet guy looks at North real expectant. 'And your names for the register.'

As North takes the money from his wallet, I step up to the counter. 'You want me to sign?'

'Sure ma'am.' The mullet guy takes a battered journal from beneath the counter and opens it to the page marked with a ribbon. 'Names, car registration, and cellphone number.'

'Sure thing.' Taking the pen, I fill out our fake names – Nicole Bendrois and Bradley Knox – print the registration of the Jetta, and make up a bullshit cellphone number. I smile real sweet, softening the lie with a little sugar, and pass back the ledger. 'Here you go.'

North hands over the cash, and I see from what's left in his wallet that we're running low on funds. If this doesn't work – if we can't find the Old Man – we're going to be in trouble.

Mullet guy pockets the cash and moves out from behind the counter. He gestures for us to follow him outside to a long rack of green and yellow kayaks lining the side of the building.

He hands us an oar each. 'Numbers three and four are yours. Enjoy.'

As the mullet guy walks back inside his shop, I look out at the airboats bobbing against their moorings in the water a few yards away from us. Turning to North I say, 'Couldn't we take one of those?'

He shakes his head. 'Won't fit where we need to go. The mangroves are too tight.'

There are few things that scare me, but I shudder at the thought of getting in one of these little plastic boats and paddling out into the swamp. A couple inches of fibreglass don't seem near on enough to shield me from the gators that make this place their home.

North squints at me, sensing my uncertainty. 'If I'm going to find the Old Man this is the only way. I'm going whether you're coming or not.'

Gritting my teeth, I think of everything I'm staking on this conversation with the Old Man. My baby girl and JT are depending on me. I haven't come this far to give it up now.

Striding to the rack, I pull number three, a bright-green kayak, from its stand and stare at North real defiant. 'I'll be damned if I'm letting you go alone.'

51

This place smells like death.

As we paddle across the lake the sun's beating on our backs, and the water sparkles like gold in the bottom of a prospector's pan. There's no gold below the surface of this water, though. What lies beneath is a whole lot more dangerous.

North doesn't seem to care. He guides his yellow kayak through the water in front of me, heading for a narrow channel on the other side. I call out to him. 'You know where we need to go?'

'Sure.' He points towards the smaller waterway. 'This'll take us deeper in, towards the Ten Thousand Islands. I know the route to where the Old Man's gone, I've done this a lot of times.'

I should feel reassured by North's confidence, but I don't. As we reach the offshoot, and I use my oar to make the turn into it, I see the waterway gets narrower the further from the main drag we go. Pretty soon it's just a couple of yards wide, and hell knows how many deep. A black vulture squawks overhead and I flinch, hoping that it isn't some kind of omen.

Tightening my grip on the oar, I keep paddling.

North leads me through the mangrove labyrinth. The trees crowd over us, casting dusky shadows across the water. In the damp crook of tree roots I see the occasional white bloom of orchids, the kind that only grow in places like this, far from civilisation.

Another half-hour and the gully widens into an oval pool surrounded by gnarled mangroves. In the centre of the pool, North stops paddling and rests his oar straight across the hull of the kayak. He glances back at me. 'You got water left?'

I throw him a bottle. 'We nearly there?'

'Another half-hour and we will be. Take a few minutes break, what comes next is the hard part.'

I sure hate the sound of that. My shoulders are aching from the paddling, and my left arm is starting to throb again around the site of my gunshot wound. 'This is one godforsaken place.'

'Some people think it's beautiful.'

I glance around me. There's a natural beauty to the twisted mangrove roots and the way the sunlight hits the water for sure, but there's danger here too. The water is still, and with no current, it's stagnant, its smell pungent. Mosquitoes cloud above the surface, their bite impossible to avoid. Sitting in the kayak, it feels as if I'm floating in a fibreglass coffin.

After taking a long drink from my own bottle of water, I ask North, 'What happened to the Old Man's brother?'

North says nothing. Takes another gulp of water.

'Did the gators get him?'

'They would have eventually, for sure.'

I hold the water bottle to my forehead, using it to cool my skin. 'Eventually? So what happened?'

North looks uncomfortable. 'It's a private story.'

'Really? We're kind of past private, don't you think?'

He looks down at the water.

I wait. After a long minute he starts to speak.

'It happened in fall 1968. The Bonchese brothers had come of age and the Old Man's father wanted them to prove themselves by setting up a new operation – getting in on the action that was happening here. Word was that the locals had struck a deal with Colombian marijuana barons to smuggle dope out of South America and into the US through the wildest country of the Everglades – the Ten Thousand Islands.'

'I'm guessing the locals didn't much like them muscling in.'

North sucks air in through his teeth. 'Hard to say if it was the locals or the cops who got to the Old Man's brother, Anthony. Things were hazy, the line between who did what – the law or the smugglers – was unclear. Way the Old Man tells it, they flew out to Colombia and made contact with the dope-growers easy enough. The trouble started when they were bringing their first loads back through the Ten Thousand Islands.'

I take in the swamp around us. 'I can understand that.'

'It wasn't the terrain that was the problem – those boys had memorised the route, every twist and turn – it was the patrols: trigger-happy cops and angry locals. None of them wanted a new enterprise – particularly non-local smugglers – taking any of their trade.'

'So what happened?' I ask, taking another swig of my water.

'Anthony was the mastermind behind the plan, him being twenty-two – a year older than Giovanni – and the one in line to take over as head of the family after their father passed. They loaded two shrimping boats with weed, waited until after dark then came into US waters and headed through the Ten Thousand Islands. Giovanni's boat was smaller and more nimble. He made it back before dawn and had the men waiting load the cargo into a couple of trucks and head towards Miami. When they'd gone, he sat down at the waterside and waited for his brother.'

'Who never arrived?'

North nods. 'After the sun came up Giovanni took his boat out, searching for Anthony. Hours later he found his body splayed out on the mangrove roots in the cove we're now heading to. He'd taken a single bullet to the head, and there was no sign of the shrimp boat he'd been sailing.'

I slap a mosquito that's feeding on my arm. 'Well, damn.'

'Yeah. That was the only time the Old Man took dope through the Ten Thousand Islands. After that he started to fly the stuff in. He only ever comes back here for his pilgrimage.' North finishes the last of his water, scrunches the bottle into a cube and tosses it into the bottom of the kayak. 'Mind you, I've heard that every man who crewed the patrol boats that night was murdered before the year was out.'

Well, shit. Seems the whole Bonchese family lived lives doused in blood. 'I can see how that might change a person.'

'Word is, the Old Man would never have got into the family business if it hadn't been for what happened to his brother. He'd always fought against getting involved until that point – only did the dope smuggling to help his brother. But when Anthony died, he was told it was his duty to step up.'

'Who by?'

'Story he tells, it was his mother.' North's jaw tightens. 'From my experiences with her, that doesn't surprise me.'

I think back to the house where I was held just a few days ago. It had a rustic charm to it, the feel of a place that your grandmother might live. 'That's real sad.'

North frowns. 'Don't let that change your thinking on him. It all happened a long time ago – near on fifty years back. Every year he's lived since has hardened him. He might talk like a gentleman and live by the old ways, but he's a ruthless killer, make no mistake.'

I remember how beat up and bruised JT was when he got out of hospital a couple of months ago. The stab wounds he'd received from the shanks of men loyal to the Old Man still raw and freshly stitched. They healed well, but he'll bear those scars forever. It's a miracle he survived. 'Yeah. I know.'

North picks up his oar and gestures towards a narrow gully between the mangroves to our left. 'We need to go through there.'

The gap between the roots seems impossibly small. 'How the hell did he ever get a shrimping boat through here?'

'Like I say, that was a long time ago. The Everglades are always growing. Now the only way in is by kayak.'

I squint at the gap. 'But, really, can we fit? How do—?'

'Paddle towards the gap, and get up some speed. Then tuck your oar lengthways along the kayak, and use the low branches to pull yourself along.'

I do not like the sound of that. 'With my...'

Before I can finish my question, North sets off towards the gully. With a sick feeling in my belly, I take a deep breath and follow. Eight strokes of the oar and I'm at the mouth of the opening. I give one final push, then tuck my oar up into the side of the kayak lengthways.

The little craft only just fits. There's less than an inch of water on either side before the mangroves rise from the water like deformed sentries, barricading us inside. The branches bend over us, forming a water-filled tunnel through the swamp, and blocking all but the most persistent shafts of light.

It feels like we're passing through the gates of hell.

'Grip the branches, Lori,' North calls from a few kayak lengths ahead. 'Check them first, though. You don't want to grab a snake.'

'Yeah, great tip. Thanks so much.' My faked bravado makes my words harsher than intended, but I do as he says. The mangrove tree branches feel damp in places, and kind of slimy to the touch. The sweat runs down my back from the humidity and the effort. Mosquitoes buzz loudly around my face. I stay alert for snakes.

I see none, and for that I'm grateful, as for the last few hundred yards of the gully the trees grow progressively lower over the water, creating a tight, dark shaft. Soon I'm near-on lying backwards in the kayak, propelling myself forwards through the water, with just the branches and North's voice to navigate.

Then I'm out and blinking in the glare of the sun. I take a couple of breaths, letting the kayak slow. The waterway is a few yards wide here. Less claustrophobic.

'Keep going, Lori,' North calls. 'This isn't a good spot to rest.'

The sun's hotter now, but it's less humid in the open than inside the mangrove tunnel. I take a quick gulp of water, my kayak's momentum propelling it on a few yards before stopping.

I feel it then – something brushing the belly of the kayak. There's a loud scraping sound beneath me, and my kayak jerks sideways. I'm powerless as I'm shunted a yard closer to the roots. I let out a sharp cry.

North turns. 'I said don't stop.' He gestures at my arms. 'Keep your elbows the hell in. Have nothing of you sticking out over the water.'

My heart's pounding. Adrenaline pumps through me. I ask the question even though I fear I know the answer well enough. 'What the hell was that?'

'Paddle, Lori. For God's sake!'

Then I see them in the water all around us. Gators, and lots of them, their eyes and nostrils just visible above the surface. Grabbing my oar, I start paddling after North. The gators seem to move with me, gliding silently through the water alongside. Watching. Waiting for me to make a mistake.

My stomach turns and I taste bile in my throat. I try not to think about my last trip to the Everglades; the blood in the water, an arm severed at the elbow floating on the surface.

Try as I might to be cool, my breathing gets faster and more shallow, my movements more erratic. In my haste to catch up with North I stick my oar into the water crooked, and almost lose it to something below the water, unseen.

Panic rises inside me. Has a gator grabbed my oar? I cling on, clutching the oar tighter, and wrestle it free. Then paddle faster. Keeping my eyes on North.

A few minutes later the gators seem to lose interest. My breathing begins to return to normal, and I concentrate on the sounds around me – the splash of our oars and the occasional bird calling above us in the branches. We take a turn, and I catch a glimpse of a white egret, leaning out over the water's edge, looking for food.

'This is it,' North says.

I look towards where he's pointing his oar and see a small area in the mangroves where the roots have been cut back. Laid in the middle of the nook is a bunch of gardenias and a church candle in a mason jar, the wick alive with flame. I turn back to North. 'Where's the Old Man?'

He's opening his mouth to answer when the first shot is fired.

52

SUNDAY, SEPTEMBER 23rd, 09:58

'When we get there, can I take her into dock?' Dakota says. She's standing beside Red at the helm, her hair tucked up into JT's Yankees ballcap.

JT shakes his head as he passes Red a coffee. He's amazed at the resilience of his daughter. Even when he fetched her from the closet where she'd been hiding out during the battle with the mob heavies, and she was shaking and fearful, she raised the penknife he'd given her, blade drawn, ready to fight if he'd turned out to be one of the heavies instead. It was her who found the duct tape they used to patch the fuel line – she'd spotted it in the back of Red's closet when she was hiding. The sharks circling the boat as JT and Red battled to fix the line hadn't fazed her at all. She was a real little trooper, just like her momma; one tough cookie for sure, but sweet with it.

Red thanks JT then smiles at Dakota, steering one-handed as he takes a sip of his coffee while considering her question. 'I'm not too sure on that. But you can captain her now for a little while, if JT here doesn't mind helping you.'

JT scans the ocean. There's no sign of any other crafts; no immediate trouble. 'Sure.'

'Good. Here you go then, Miss Dakota.' Red moves away from the wheel, letting Dakota take it. 'I'm making you captain of this vessel for the next half-hour. I'm going to have me a little nap.'

Dakota takes hold of the wheel with both hands. 'Cool.'

'You look after her well, mind. I'll be checking for scratches when I get back.'

Dakota giggles as Red heads into the cabin.

JT glances towards the back of the *Liberty*, where the mob guy's bullets punched holes clear through the boat's gleaming green-and-gold liveried flanks. Red's not said anything, but JT's seen him over there inspecting the damage, caressing the pockmarked wooden panels. Damage like that isn't the sort easy to claim on insurance.

'When we get to Miami can we go to the beach?' Dakota's voice is bright and full of excitement. 'I love the beach.'

'I'm sorry, sweetheart, but it's not a good idea.'

She frowns.

JT knows he has to keep his resolve. The beach isn't in the plan. It's too hard to be vigilant with all those people around, and unfamiliar territory too. He doesn't know Miami. Wants to limit who sees them. Reduce the risk of being spotted. They need to lie low, stay close to the marina. 'Haven't you had enough adventure for a little while?'

Dakota turns the wheel a little to the right, heading the boat along the crest of a wave. She shakes her head. 'No. Course not. Momma says never say no to adventure. She says girls are just as brave as boys. We can do anything we put our minds to.'

'Is that right?' JT smiles. That sounds like Lori for sure. 'Because I was thinking that this trip has been adventurous already. Things got pretty dangerous yesterday.'

'I've nearly died twice already. I'm not afraid.' Dakota sticks her chin out, defiant. 'You can't ever have too much adventure, and I need lots, so if I get sick again I've got good things to think about when they're giving me the medicine.'

His daughter's illness. They've never much talked about it, him and Lori. The timing's always seemed off. He knows Dakota was diagnosed with leukaemia before her eighth birthday is all. 'Is that right?'

'Yes.'

'Well, that does sound a good reason for adventure.'

Dakota nods, but the smile has disappeared from her face. 'I don't want to get sick again. If I do, and they can't find me a donor, I might die.'

JT frowns. 'Why'd you need a donor?'

'Last time my body didn't get better right away from the medicine. The doctor said I might need a bit of someone else's marrow to heal properly. They tested Momma, but her marrow wasn't right.'

JT clenches his fists. His daughter might have needed a bone-marrow donor, and Lori didn't call him, even once she knew she wasn't a match. She let what happened between them cloud her judgement so bad that she'd have let Dakota die rather than tell him they had a daughter together. He presses his knuckles hard into the boat's wooden panelled side. Tries not to let his tone betray the rage he's feeling. 'That must have been hard.'

Dakota nods, dropping her head as she blinks back tears. Overhead, sea birds call out, wheeling in the sky above the *Liberty*, waiting to be fed.

JT puts a hand on her shoulder. Couldn't bear for anything to happen to her. 'You know, sweetheart, if you did get sick again, you can count on me to give you some of my marrow.'

She looks up at him. 'But you might not have the right kind.'

He forces a smile. 'Don't you go worrying on that. I'm pretty sure that I will.'

Dakota holds his gaze for a beat too long, then reaches for his hand. Squeezing it, she says in a quiet voice, 'Thank you.'

JT nods and looks back out to the ocean.

He can't answer – doesn't trust what he'll say.

He's furious with Lori for not telling him this truth.

53

SUNDAY, SEPTEMBER 23rd, 10:04

This place *is* death. There's no place to take cover.

Bullets ping against the mangrove trees around us, sending bark and roots splintering into the water. Birds screech overhead. Then I hear a shout and footsteps against the roots somewhere to my right, both almost eclipsed by my own heartbeat thumping loud in my ears.

Hunching down over the kayak I paddle back towards the turn. Glance round, scanning the mangroves, trying to work out where the shooter is hiding. I see no one, but, from the sound and angle of the gunfire, I figure they must be somewhere in the mangroves on our right, hiding in the shadows of the trees. Pulling my Wesson Classic Bobtail from my shoulder holster I let off a couple of warning shots in that direction.

I hear a shout. The gunfire ceases. Think maybe I got lucky.

Before I can check it out, a loud splash draws my attention back towards the nook. Shit. North is in trouble.

The back end of his yellow kayak is riddled with bullet holes. It's listing backwards in the water, getting lower by the second. North's fighting to get out one-handed while holding his messenger bag containing the iPad above his head with the other.

Yellow eyes surface around him. First one pair, then three more. I hear a faint splash beside me and look down. A huge gator, at least fifteen feet long, glides past me. Its hide is as gnarled as the mangrove roots surrounding us. Its gaze is set on North.

I've still no clue if I hit the shooter. Could be as soon as I move from this spot, they'll return fire. But I have to do something. If I don't, North's going to be gator food.

Holstering my weapon, I jab my oar against the roots at the side of the waterway to push off and paddle fast towards North. The sudden movement makes the gators dive, but I know it's the surprise rather than my presence that's startled them, and it won't hold them off for long.

Ahead of me, North's gotten his legs free of the kayak and has turned it over, emptying the water that gushed in through the bullet holes so he can use it as a raft. His belly is over it, the messenger bag still held out of the water. But his legs are dangling over the side, from mid thigh down they're beneath the water.

'North, quick.' I bring my kayak alongside him. 'Get in.'

Scowling, he shakes his head. 'It won't hold us both.'

Yellow eyes, four pairs, surface a few yards from us.

'It damn well will.' I scoot forwards as far as I can get inside the kayak, and hook his stricken kayak with my oar as a makeshift way to bind us. I use my strictest mom voice. 'Now get yourself behind me on this kayak right this minute.'

It has the desired effect. He hands me the messenger bag, and I lift the strap over my good shoulder, letting the cargo rest across my chest. Then hold out my free hand, helping North scramble over his kayak and straddle mine. He doesn't fit inside the craft, so he tucks his legs up over the side, his feet crossed around my waist. My kayak sinks lower in the water, but stays afloat.

The gators glide closer. Black vultures circle overhead. My gunshot wound hurts like a bitch.

We need to get out of here.

Passing North my gun, I start paddling towards the mouth of the clearing. 'I might have hit the shooter.' I nod in the direction the shots came from. 'We should check it out.'

'Yep.' North's voice is loaded with fury. 'I want to talk to that son-of-a-bitch.'

I paddle the kayak towards the place I aimed my fire. It's harder work now – North's weight is pulling us lower in the water; we're now just a couple inches from the surface. There's a damp sheen across my skin, and I feel sweat running down my face from the effort. My left arm throbs even more.

We reach the place in the water closest to where I figure the shooter must have been. I butt the kayak against the edge of the mangrove roots and point with my oar in the direction I fired. 'I think he was back through there. Hiding in the shadows.'

North nods, and says the thing I both knew and dreaded. 'We'll need to go across there on foot.'

Suddenly being inside the kayak seems a whole lot nicer situation than climbing across the snake-filled mangrove roots, looking for a shooter. 'Yeah.'

North slides off the back of the kayak then helps me step out. We haul the craft up across the roots, taking care not to damage the bottom of the hull, and leave it buffered against the trucks of two ancient-looking trees.

I pass North the messenger bag, thankful my left shoulder is relieved of its pressure. Leaving him with the gun, I take out my Taser and lead us across the roots in the direction I fired.

We move as quietly as we can. The roots are slippery in places, brittle and prone to snap in others. The stench of death and decay grows thicker in the air as the humidity intensifies. I grit my teeth. Keep watching for snakes. And keep on going.

We've gone maybe fifty yards when a shot rings out. I dive for cover, the bullet slamming into the trunk of a tree to my left. North returns fire.

There's a groan, and I see a spray of red mist plume close to the roots maybe thirty yards ahead. I catch a glimpse of a shaved head. It seems the shooter was already floored. North may have finished him off.

We approach with caution, North first, the gun trained on the shaved-headed guy. He stays down. Doesn't move. When we get to him he's lying, his face planted in the roots, real awkward. North turns to me, and I nod. Reckon he's dead.

North uses his foot to push the guy onto his back. There's a dark patch spreading across the side of his black wife-beater and a crimson stain in the knee of his torn cargo pants. His eyes are open.

He's hit, but he's still breathing.

54

His breathing's getting real laboured, but there's no way in hell North will let him rest. Me neither. Our plan's gone to shit. We need us some answers.

North stands over him. 'You know who I am?'

'Yep.' The guy's voice is a hoarse rasp.

'Good. Where's the Old Man?'

Shaved-headed guy says nothing.

North shakes his head. 'I'm not your enemy. Those wounds have got to hurt. I don't want to add to your pain, but I will if you force me.' He gestures towards me. 'Even if Gabriella wouldn't like that.'

The man grimaces. There's blood in his mouth, bright crimson against the white of his teeth.

Taking the cue from North, I step closer and kneel down beside the guy.

He gasps. Frowns. 'Gabriella? But you're—'

'Won't you help us?' It seems my altered hair, brows and make-up is enough to convince him. I keep my voice soft. Search his face for a sign he might talk. I have to try to make him see that we're not here to hurt the Old Man. 'We just want to talk to him. We have information he needs, and I need him to remove the—'

'Stop.' North's hand is on my shoulder.

I look up at him, confused.

He pulls me to my feet. His expression's grim. 'This man doesn't care about the Old Man and him seeing anything we might want to show him.'

Shaved-head guy wheezes as he forces out his words. 'You're fucked.' His grimace morphs into a smile. 'Both of you.'

North puts his foot over the wound on the man's stomach and presses down. 'Tell me why.'

The guy coughs, choking. Spits up blood. But doesn't speak.

North raises his boot, then stamps down hard.

The man bellows in agony. Writhing beneath North's weight.

'Tell me what Luciano told you to do. Tell. Me. Now.'

I stare at North, surprised. Luciano? I thought the men accompanying the Old Man were his most trusted. How does North know this guy is one of Luciano's and, if he is, how did he come to be here?

The shaved-head guy splutters a volley of cusses and tries to roll onto his side but fails. That's when I see it – the tattoo on the back of his shoulder, half visible beneath the wife-beater. A stylised MM with a serpent in an L-shape around them – Luciano's mark. The man spits out more blood, gasping now.

North changes tack. He leans down beside the guy and lifts his vest, inspecting the wound in his stomach. It looks bad to me, but North looks the guy right in the eye and says, 'You're a mess, but if I get you to a doc, you'll be okay.'

'Why ... would you...?'

'I've seen enough bloodshed,' North's tone is sincere. 'But I'll only help you if you tell me Luciano's plan.'

The shaved-head guy is growing paler. He's losing a lot of blood, and with the hour or so journey back to Everglades City, I really think he's past saving. But the guy nods. It seems that when you're fighting for your life you're inclined to cling to any kind of hope, even if it means betraying your boss.

Gasping between each word, the shaved-head guy speaks. 'The Old Man came here as usual ... brought Klate and me on Luciano's recommendation ... Luciano's smart, he guessed you'd try and get here ... You so sly ... always favourite. Not anymore. We'd wait till you showed then kill you and the Old Man ... tell everyone you killed him.' He lets out a strangled laugh. 'Problem solved.'

North cusses. 'Where is he, then?'

'Old Man got a call this morning ... early. Feds crawling round the big house ... causing trouble...' The guy grimaces. Bugs buzz around his wounds; he tries to bat them away. 'He left with Klate first thing ... You're ... too late.'

That can't be true. I lean over the guy. 'What time did they leave?'

'Seven ... maybe ... but don't make no difference. We had to change up the plan ... Klate will have done it by now.'

I check my watch. It's near on eleven-thirty. If the Old Man's dead there's no way for him to lift the price on me and my family's lives. We're as good as dead too.

North's hand is tight around the gun. The other one is clenching and unclenching at the air. 'Why'd you stay?'

The grimace turns into a grin. 'Klate can handle the Old Man. Luciano wanted one of us ... stay ... case you still showed. Old Man didn't take much persuading ... Guess Luciano was right.' He wheezes. Coughs. 'You're dead, North, just because you're the Old Man's favourite ... don't mean you'll be saved.'

'I've more chance than you.' North raises the gun. Shoots shaved-head guy between the eyes.

I look at North. 'Thought you said you were going to help him.'

He shrugs. 'Sometimes I lie.'

55

SUNDAY, SEPTEMBER 23rd, 11:31

We find the dead man's kayak stowed on the mangrove roots a little ways from his body. I follow North as he carries it back to where we left mine. Both of us are silent, thinking on the shaved-head guy's words and trying to come up with some kind of plan.

If the Old Man is dead already, everything I've done these past few days has been for nothing. There's no way I can get Dakota or JT safe. Even if we get away from Florida, we'll always be looking over our shoulders. I can't let that happen. There must be a way.

We cast our kayaks back into the water. North's still silent. I glance at him. See his jaw's rigid, his expression real determined. He has different reasons from mine, but I know he'll want the Old Man to be alive too.

Right now, living seems a whole lot harder than dying.

As we paddle away, I look up and see the number of vultures wheeling overhead has increased, their shrieks alerting more of their kind to an imminent feast. Nothing here is wasted. This violent, wild environment is nature at her most economical.

North's a half-kayak length ahead. I shout towards him, 'We can't let them kill the Old Man. We have to find them.'

'Yep. I'm thinking the same.'

I paddle harder. Wincing as pain shoots through my left arm. It seems to be worsening and I worry the infection is returning. Maybe the antibiotics North got for me aren't strong enough to fight it off. 'Do you know Luciano's man, Klate? Can you anticipate how he'd do it?'

'I know of him, yes. He's been with the family a long time, but I never knew he was loyal to Luciano.' North shakes his head. There's regret in his voice when he continues. 'It seems a lot's changed since I left.'

'This isn't the time to get sad. We need to find the Old Man. What would he usually do on the trip back?'

'He always takes one rest stop. A little place on the Tamiami Trail, close to the airport.'

I paddle faster. 'Then we need to get there.'

As I draw level with him, North turns to look at me. 'Ain't no point. They've got a four-hour head start on us for a journey that only takes a little more than two hours.'

'But if Klate means to kill the Old Man, it might have taken longer.'

North lets out a long whistle. 'You're clutching at straws, Lori. The best we'll be looking for now is a body.'

I can't accept that. Not now. Not after everything. I grit my teeth. 'We're going to find him.'

North holds my gaze a long moment, then gives a tight smile. 'Well, damn, I guess we are.'

We paddle on in silence through the waterways and back along the mangrove tunnel. After all I know now, the wild country seems a lot more hospitable than the world we call civilised beyond. North is in the lead again, and I see my gun sticking out from the waistband of his pants. I shake my head, thinking that things would be a whole lot better in this life if we could do away with guns.

Back on Lake Placid, we come ashore a half-mile up from Jack's Hire shop. We prop the kayaks around the back of a shrimp shack and head back towards Jack's on foot. As we climb into the Jetta, I feel bad that we've not returned the kayaks to the mulleted attendant in the Hawaiian shirt. But given we lost one of them in the swamp, I'm figuring he'll want to charge us. Right now, we barely have enough cash to pay for the gas we'll need to get us back to Miami.

We take Collier Avenue out of Everglades City and head up Highway 21 towards Carnestown. As soon as I'm out of the town, I dial JT's number on my cellphone. Just like before, it goes straight to voicemail. Shit. Where the hell is he? I try Red's again, then Dakota's, but get voicemail on all counts.

As I drive, my fear for my family increases. Luciano has had near-on every move me and North have made figured out; Missingdon, Carly's place, now the Old Man's pilgrimage. What if he anticipated I'd tell JT to run? What if he guessed I'd tell JT to ask Red to help get Dakota safe? I shudder. Feel sick to my core. What if I've sent my family and friend straight into the predator's mouth?

In the passenger seat beside me, North removes his boots and socks and sticks them into the back. He's dried off from his dunking in the swamp, but smells all kinds of wrong. I open the windows, trying to freshen the air. I know that staying maudlin isn't going to help my family none. If I'm going to save them, if they're still there for the saving and I have to believe that they are – can't bear to think on the alternative – I have to get my head back in the game.

I keep the Jetta cruising along the highway. 'So where next?'

'Stay on this road. We've got a way to go yet. At Carnestown take Highway 41.'

'Okay.' I glance over at North. He's been quiet and pensive-looking ever since the shaved-head guy told us Luciano's plan. I punch him on the arm. 'Don't go bailing on me now.'

He frowns. 'I ain't.'

'You real sure about that? Because you've got the look of a guy who's beat.'

'I'm not beat. I'm thinking.'

'Just make sure that you are, because the smart-mouthed son-of-a-bitch North that I know wouldn't let some sorry-assed mobster stop him doing what's necessary.'

He raises one eyebrow. Cracks a smile. 'Is that right? Well, I guess I've got a lot to live up to.'

'For sure you have.'

He gestures towards the highway. 'You better put your foot down, then.'

I won't let the Old Man be dead. Can't let that happen. I give North a half-smile and speak real determined. 'We're going to find him.'

He nods. And I know that this isn't damn well over.

I stamp on the gas.

56

The *Liberty* is cruising easy at a steady speed. The sea's calm and flat. Dakota's napping. JT and Red are at the helm.

Red's set them on a course to reach Marina 42 near Pompano Beach within the next hour. It's a good thing, too; they're low on fuel, and won't be getting much further without restocking. But that's not what's weighing heavy on JT right now.

'How you doing, JT?' Red's voice breaks him from his thoughts.

He flicks his glance towards the older man standing at the wheel. Confiding in folk, it's not his style, but something about Red's expression makes him decide to share. 'Dakota told me about her illness. Said she could have needed a bone-marrow donor.'

Red nods. Checks his compass and turns the wheel a little to the right. 'Yup. Heard that.'

JT clenches his jaw. Angry Red knew about his daughter's treatment when he didn't even know that she existed. 'Lori kept it from me.'

'Woman had her reasons.'

He rubs his fingers across the stubble on his jaw. 'Reasons enough to let my child die?'

'Dakota didn't die. And she didn't need the transplant neither, not then; maybe not never.' Red holds JT's gaze, his usual laidback calm gone. He's looking real intense. 'If it'd come to that, maybe then Lori'd have gotten in touch. How she'd have afforded the procedure? Well, that's a whole other matter. She'd have found a way for sure, though; she'd do anything for that kid.'

JT shakes his head, the anger building inside him. Lori should have told him anyways. He's Dakota's father; should have been there. 'I had a right to—'

'Did you now?' Red's tone is harder now. Irritated. 'You pretty much threw that woman out when she'd lost everything – her best friend, her home, her livelihood. And worse, she'd just killed a person in self-defence. And not just any person, but a man who'd spent the previous god-knows-how-many years abusing her. She trusted you, and you cast her aside. Made her feel like ... nothing. You think that gives you the right to anything?'

JT bristles. He's been wondering about the relationship between Lori and this man. Why they're so close. Why he knows more about her than him. 'You seem to know an awful lot about our business. There something you're not telling me?'

Red exhales hard. Shaking his head, he says, 'You're way off base. She came out to Florida ten years back with nothing but her go bag and a whole bunch of determination to build a new life. We teamed up on a couple of jobs, helped each other out. She did some legwork for some of my PI cases, and I used my contacts to help her locate the occasional skip trace. She needed a friend is all – even more so when she found out that she was pregnant. Sure it took her a little while to get back on her feet, but she did it. She's strong, smart. Every time life kicks her in the dirt, she gets up and fights back harder.' He pauses. Narrows his eyes. 'Look, it's not my place to tell you about her life. You and her, you're the ones that need to be having that conversation.'

JT's always avoided difficult conversations. 'Not really my thing.'

'And how's that worked out for you so far?'

He avoids Red's gaze.

'Look, you want my ten cents on this?' Red says. 'Talk to her about it. Not right now. Wait until you're clear of this mob business and you've got your heads on straight. Then talk. Don't let it fester; no good ever came of that. And don't ignore it, 'cause it'll come back and bite you on the ass soon enough.'

'Maybe.'

'Your call.' Red gets up, walks across the deck to the cabin door.

Opening it, he looks back at JT. 'But if you act like a jerk, you'll lose the love of a good woman.'

As Red disappears into the cabin, JT looks out across the ocean. The sun's high over the water, the light dancing on the surface, making everything sparkle.

Red's talking a lot of sense. Truths that take a bit of swallowing, but sense all the same. Lori's one hell of a girl, a real good woman, and always has been – even on the day he acted like a fool, turned her out and watched her drive away.

Her gumption and smarts, it's a damn sexy combination. But she's secretive too. And her being secretive on the matter of their daughter's life or death still feels hard to bear.

He keeps staring out at the ocean, fancying that he can see the hazy outline of the Miami coastline way in the distance. Runs his hand through his hair.

Lori and him, they do need to talk this out.

But first they have to survive the Miami Mob.

57

SUNDAY, SEPTEMBER 23rd, 12:17

As we pull off the road into the rest stop he's directed me to, North cusses loud and stamps his foot against the footwell. 'The damn thing's been decommissioned.'

I feel a sinking feeling in my belly. He's right. The gas pumps are sitting idle, the teller's booth boarded up. Across the parking lot, what must have once been a store has been set about by vandals. The windows have been smashed, the door caved in. The scrub surrounding the lot has grown over the blacktop. Bushes have pushed their way up through the cracks, creepers sending out trails towards the teller's booth and winding around the pumps. It's as if nature is trying to reclaim the land.

I stop in the middle of the lot and leave the engine idling. 'Well damn.'

'We should keep going.'

I turn to face North. 'And go where? If we can't get to the Old Man, it's over.'

North's face is ashen. He shakes his head. 'It already is.'

'No.' Opening the car door I climb out into the midday heat. Slam my palm down onto the hood. 'It can't be over. I can't...' I think of Dakota and JT. Clench my fists. 'We can't just give up...'

That's when I see it. At the far end of the parking lot: a glint of metallic silver paintwork and the curve of a truck sticking out a fraction from behind a mass of overgrown bushes.

I bend down, look at North. 'What car would the Old Man have taken to Everglades City?'

'What?' North looks confused.

'Just answer me.'

'He favours a Lincoln. Oftentimes silver.'

'Well, damn.' Moving around the Jetta, I head towards the over-grown area and the spot I saw glinting in the sun. I'm careful to stay shielded by the bushes, unsure what the vehicle is. As I get closer I reach for my Taser.

Be prepared. It's one of JT's rules, and it's mine, too. Important, always.

Staying as low as I can to avoid being seen in the vehicle's mirrors, I peep out from behind the bush. It's my first proper look at the back end of the vehicle. It's a Lincoln Navigator. Silver.

The inside of the rear window is sprayed with blood.

My heart races. My throat goes dry. Are we too late? Is this where Luciano's man, Klate, killed the Old Man? Am I about to find his body?

Turning, I beckon for North to come join me. Then, staying low, I step wide around the car and towards the front. As I get level with the back seat, I raise myself a little so I can see inside. Bite my lip. It looks like a goddamn abattoir.

The cream leather seats and the upholstered roof are splattered with blood and gore. The man on the back seat doesn't have much of a face left, but from the little I can see of it, I know for sure he's not the Old Man.

Then I hear it – groaning coming from the front. Moving forward, my finger on the trigger of my Taser, I peer into the driver's seat. Exhale hard.

A man is slumped sideways against the door. Embedded in his right shoulder, the one furthest from the door, is a knife. It's been sunk all the way up to the hilt, a few inches along from the neck towards the shoulder. It's a miracle he's not dead. It must have somehow just missed the major arteries, but there's still a hell of a lot of blood. Pain too, no doubt.

The man's face is against the window. His usually smoothed-back grey-flecked black hair is plastered over his sweaty forehead. It's the

Old Man himself. As I gasp, he looks back at me and his eyes widen. 'Gabriella? Is that …? No, how can it be, I must be delirious, or dead...'

'You're not dead, and I'm not Gabriella.'

'Then who—?'

'Lori Anderson.'

He grimaces. 'You've come to finish me off, have you?'

'Actually, I've come to help you.'

I can see from his expression that he's as disbelieving that I'm here to help him, as I am that I'm actually doing it. This asshole is responsible for putting a hit out on me and my family, and a big part of me wants to leave him here to rot. It's only when North appears at my side that the Old Man's expression changes and I see hope in his eyes.

North opens the driver's door. The cream leather is smeared with bloody fingerprints. He swallows hard as he views the scene. Still holds himself in a tough-guy stance as he looks at the Old Man, but I can see that there's a muscle twitching in his neck, and I hear disbelief in his tone as he asks, 'What happened here?'

'I was driving. We'd been planning on stopping here but saw on the way down that it was closed. Still, Klate said he wanted to pee, so we stopped. He tried to do me with his pig stick when he got back in.'

North inspects the knife and the wound it's made. He looks at the Old Man real concerned. 'He had a good go I'd say.'

'He got it worse.' The Old Man glances down at his left hand. He's holding a little stub-nosed pistol. He grins at North. Wheezes. 'Didn't figure on me having this.' His expression darkens. There's doubt in his eyes. 'Did you turn Klate? Was this your doing?'

North shakes his head. 'I never betrayed you.'

The Old Man gives him a hard stare. Points the pistol at him. 'A good man would die before agreeing to testify against his family.'

'Luciano isn't any family of mine.'

'He's your—'

'Don't you go telling me he's my brother, because it's not true, and never has been.' Ignoring the snub-nosed pistol, North moves closer to the Old Man. His jaw is clenched, and I can tell that he's biting back the cusses he wants to use. He shakes his head. His tone is laced with anger. 'After I show you the evidence I have on him, and tell you all the things he's done to hurt this family, you'll agree with me. He doesn't deserve to be your son.'

The Old Man lowers the gun. Turns his face away from North. 'I doubt that's true.'

'Fine. You want us to leave you here?'

Fear sparks in the Old Man's eyes before he can suppress it.

'Didn't think so.' North opens the car door as wide as it'll go. 'Then let us get you patched up and out of here.'

The Old Man takes a rasping breath, and exhales loudly. 'Do it. But don't go thinking you're anywhere near forgiven.'

58

I fetch my go bag from the Jetta, looking to fix up the Old Man's shoulder as best I can. I figure I have to take out the knife, but I'm real cautious. I might hate the man, but I need him alive; he's the only person who can take the price off our heads, and bring Luciano to heel.

We keep the Old Man sitting in the driver's seat for now. While I ready my field kit, North holds a bottle of water to the Old Man's lips and he drinks. Beneath his tan he's looking pale. Every few moments he shivers. North and me glance at one another, both fearing that he's going into shock.

'You able to do this?' The Old Man growls. 'Or is it too much for you?'

I clench my jaw. Know we need to be fast so we can get back on the road. Whatever Luciano's planning in Miami, I'm sure it won't end well for me and my family ... assuming they're still alive. My stomach flips. I can't think about JT and Dakota right now. Have to focus on the job in front of me.

I look back at the Old Man. 'I've pulled a bullet from a man's leg before with pliers, and he was someone I cared about, so I sure as hell can do this.'

He winces at my use of a cuss word. I don't care a damn.

The Old Man's dark-grey suit jacket and shirt beneath are bunched around the knife, preventing me from getting a proper view of the wound.

I look him in the eyes. 'I'm going to have to cut your clothes around the knife to see what's going on.'

'It's a two-thousand-dollar suit,' says the Old Man, looking pissed. 'It's worth more than you are.'

I've had enough of his moaning. 'Well, if you want my help, you're going to have to suck it up.'

Still looking pissed, he gives a small nod.

I get to work. Using my nail scissors I cut through the suit fabric and the shirt below, until I've got the knife clear of material. The blade is stuck into the muscle between his neck and shoulder, entering from behind, at a slight angle.

'It looks clear of any main arteries, but it'll most likely bleed like hell when I pull it out.' Ignoring the Old Man's wince at my swear, I look at North and say, 'I'll need you to hold him down when I do it.'

'I'll be fine,' the Old Man growls.

'Can't risk it. It's going to hurt like a bitch. If you start moving when I'm removing it, you could do more damage – maybe make me nick an artery.'

The Old Man scowls at me. Says nothing. I take that as him conceding.

I nod to North and he holds the Old Man still. Then I jump into the Lincoln's cockpit and, with one knee resting on the seat between the Old Man's legs and the other foot braced against the car door, I grab hold of the knife.

It's hot in the car, and my hands feel sweaty around the knife, making the handle slippery. Hoping to hell it's not plugging a hole in an artery, I grasp the knife harder and pull upwards fast.

For a brief moment the blade refuses to budge. Then I feel it release.

The Old Man bucks beneath North's grip, and bellows in pain. I pay him no mind. Cling on, and yank the knife clear. Dropping it onto the passenger seat, I reach for the sanitary napkins I placed there ready and press a wad of them against the wound in the Old Man's shoulder. He writhes beneath me.

Ignoring his squeals, I press down hard.

The Old Man passes out.

North relaxes his grip on him, letting him slump a little to his left against the side of the car. He peers over his body at the wound. 'How is it?'

I keep up the pressure of the napkins against the wound. Try to ignore the pain shooting through my left arm. 'Give it a minute.'

I hold the towels in place for another thirty seconds, then lift them clear. There's no spray, just some normal bleeding, and it's slower than before. 'It's deep, but if we can keep him still and get the bleeding stopped, there's a good chance he'll make it.'

'Just a chance?'

'He's lost a lot of blood.'

'He's a fighter.'

I can think of a whole bunch of less complimentary ways to describe him. I look at the Old Man's ashen face, then at North. 'Considering what we'll likely face when we get to Miami, he'll need to be.' I gesture towards the napkins. 'Keep these pressed against the wound. I need to get the stuff to clean it.'

North does as I say, and I jump down from the Lincoln and back to my go bag. I'm all out of antiseptic and bandages, so I grab a couple of little bottles of bourbon, some cotton wool, a clean dressing and the duct tape.

The Old Man's still out cold, which makes cleaning him up a whole lot easier. I use the alcohol to cleanse the wound, then fasten the dressing over it using the duct tape. It doesn't look pretty, but it's clean and secure, and for now that'll have to be enough.

We're hoisting him onto the back seat of the Jetta when he starts to come to, struggling against our hold until North tells him to ease up. We install him in the back without any further issues, but I'm not so sure that's a good sign.

As North fastens the seat belt across the Old Man's lap, I take a moment to observe him. He's leaning back against the headrest with his eyes closed, his face still real pale beneath his tan. The lines on his face more pronounced than before. His breathing is fast and shallow. His skin's clammy.

As North goes to shut the car door, the Old Man beckons him

closer and murmurs something I can't hear. North nods then steps back, closing the door.

'He's not looking so good,' I say. 'He needs more fluids, and something to help with the shock.'

North's looking troubled. 'What have you got?'

'Half a bottle of water is all.'

'Get it.' North glances back towards the Old Man. 'It'll have to do.'

As I move round to the truck where my go bag is, North asks, 'You got any more of that alcohol?'

'Sure.' I frown, thinking he means to drink it himself. I pass him a couple of bottles. 'That's all I've got.'

'Appreciate it.'

As I head around to the Jetta's driver's seat, North walks back to the Lincoln. He kneels down and unclips the licence plate, and I figure that's what the Old Man whispered for him to do. But he doesn't return back, instead he disappears around the side of the vehicle. For a moment I think he's going to take the dead man, Klate's, ID.

Then I see the flames.

59

SUNDAY, SEPTEMBER 23rd, 13:11

'What the hell did you do that for? You just alerted every cop nearby to the Lincoln.'

'It needed doing.' The Old Man's words drift over from behind me. They have a slight slur to them, but I can still hear the pride in his voice.

North fixes his seatbelt. 'Our fingerprints and DNA were all over that car.'

I step on the gas. The wheels spinning over the blacktop, spitting shingle and other debris from the parking lot in our wake as we lurch back onto the highway. 'But they'll trace the Lincoln back to the Old Man anyways. You've just given away—'

'No.' North takes the Lincoln's plate from beneath his jacket and rests it on his lap. 'They won't trace it fast enough to know before we're back in Miami.'

'Quiet. It's done now.' The Old Man sounds frail, but also determined. 'Show me this evidence you have on my son. Otherwise, the pair of you are as good as dead anyway.'

I grip the steering wheel tighter. Bite back the urge to snap that if it wasn't for me and North, the Old Man would already be dead. I know that if we're to get through the next few hours alive we'll need to play a smart game.

North lifts the messenger bag from the footwell and takes out the iPad. Tapping the screen, he brings up a series of spreadsheets and, twisting round, holds the tablet towards the Old Man so he can see them. 'That young guy didn't kill your accountant. Luciano killed him because he'd discovered the money trail from your accounts to

Luciano's. He's been ciphering off cash for years and using it to run new business that he's kept hidden. The accountant told me what he found on the night he died. I went to see him and saw Luciano leaving. Found the accountant breathing this last. The cops arrived fast, stopped me getting into the accountant's files. So I made a deal with the Feds: said I'd give evidence against Luciano. While I was in protective custody, I got my hands on these files so I could show you. I've always been loyal.'

I glance in the rearview mirror. The Old Man looks sceptical. 'If you suspected all this, why not tell me?'

'Luciano is your son, you'd never believe me without evidence.'

The Old Man exhales, his breath sounds ragged, like it's catching in his throat. 'Is this all of it?'

'No,' North's tone is grave. 'It's only the beginning.'

I stare through the windshield, keep us a few lengths back from the truck in front, listening as North plays each of the videos in turn. The tension inside me builds as I hear the conversation between my husband, Tommy, and Luciano at the fishing lodge a few days before me and JT found Tommy, and I killed him.

When he hears them speaking about taking him out, the Old Man inhales sharply but says nothing.

The video ends. None of us speaks.

The Old Man doesn't cuss, and doesn't posture or try to excuse his son's actions. He just sits in silence.

North puts the iPad back into the messenger bag. I focus on the highway ahead of us and stay below the speed limit.

When the Old Man finally speaks, I can tell from the crack in his voice that he's been crying. 'An eye for an eye, that's the tradition of this family.' I glance in the rearview as he points towards the messenger bag, the iPad. 'That dirty truth on there shows me Luciano needs to learn that lesson for himself.'

North smiles and holds up a cellphone. 'I took this from Klate. Thought we might have ourselves a little chat with Luciano.'

I shake my head, still pissed at him – at the pair of them. 'We need the element of surprise. If the Lincoln burning out gets picked up by the news crews, it'll alert Luciano that his plan hasn't worked.'

'No.' The Old Man's voice is weak, but his tone is still determined. 'What we need is a double bluff.'

Again I look in the mirror at him. For all his injuries, he still expects to be obeyed, and the way North's acting it looks like he'll go along with whatever the Old Man is thinking. That puts me in a vulnerable position.

I make my tone granite hard. 'For all I know that means the pair of you'll be using me as some kind of bait for Luciano now y'all are pally again. Why the hell should I listen to anything you say?'

The Old Man glares at me in the mirror.

But before he can reply, North turns to the Old Man and says, 'There's something else you should see.'

He pulls the iPad back out of the messenger bag and swipes his finger over the screen. I can't see what he's doing, but when he angles the screen towards the Old Man and taps it, I hear a video begin to play.

At first there's just background noise: a kettle whistling on a stove, footsteps over wooden floorboards. Then there's a loud bang, and I flinch. Next I hear JT's voice telling Tommy to stay real still, that he's surrounded. There are the sounds of a scuffle. JT's cusses. Then footsteps running.

My breath catches in my chest. I turn in my seat. 'What the hell *is* that?'

North doesn't look at me. His voice is gruff. 'Keep driving, Lori.'

The video continues. I hear the sound of a window frame being kicked out. Boots running over baked dirt. My heart rate accelerates, and I feel my hands begin to shake. Then my own voice, and the memory of that moment replays in my mind in time with the video.

Tommy drops from the first-storey window and scrambles to his feet. He hasn't seen me. I reach into my holster and draw my gun. Don't want to think on how he's gotten clear of JT. Heart pounding, I step out of the scrub, into the moonlit yard. Say, 'Stop, you're surrounded.'

Tommy freezes.

I feel crazy sick. Know all the bad things Tommy's done, all the evil he's capable of. I can't let him escape. 'Now raise your hands and turn around real slow.'

He turns and squints towards me, all confused.

'I said, raise your hands where I can see them.'

He doesn't raise his hands; he laughs. 'What the hell you doing?'

It feels as if I've taken a roundhouse kick to the chest. I tell myself to hold it together. I have to. I point my gun square at his chest and force myself to meet his gaze. 'I'm taking you to jail.'

He starts walking towards me. 'Don't point that thing at me; you ain't gonna use it.'

'I will,' I say, hating the way my voice trembles, fighting the urge to run. 'You gotta pay for what you did to Sal.'

He stops, but keeps grinning, as if me holding a gun on him is no big deal. Shakes his head. 'Jesus. You still bleating over that two-bit prick tease? Shit, woman, you—'

'Don't call her that.' I keep the gun pointed at him, try to ignore that it's shaking. Tell myself I have to bring Tommy in, for Sal, and for me. I dig my heels into the dirt. Hold my ground.

He laughs again. 'You won't shoot me. I'm your husband.'

I glance towards the lodge, wondering where the hell JT has gotten to. 'We're getting a divorce.'

Tommy's grin fades. 'We ain't. You're mine, and you gonna stay that way, y'hear? Some little whore bleeding out on our floor ain't doing nothing to change that.'

I feel the rage building inside me. He doesn't give a damn about what he's done. 'She was a sweet kid who didn't—'

Tommy steps towards me. 'Shit, woman. You saying I'm a liar?'

I glance again towards the lodge; still no sign of JT. I feel the panic rising in my chest. I don't have long; if Tommy reaches me I'll be in real trouble, unless I can get him cuffed. I have to think fast, plan my next move as I'm talking. 'Yes, I am.'

He looks deflated, suddenly less threatening. 'Well, shit. I didn't want to believe it, but it's true.' His tone is softer, sadder. 'You're the one helping that goddamn bounty hunter?'

'Yes I am.' There's too much pride in my voice, and you know what folks say about that. I reach back to unclip my cuffs from my rig. Lower my gun a fraction. 'And now I'm taking you to—'

'Dumb fucking bitch.' He reaches behind him, pulls a gun from the waistband of his pants, swings it towards me. 'You're going to—'

I don't think, just pure react. Dropping the cuffs, I raise my gun and pull the trigger. Keep pulling it until every bullet is spent.

Tommy drops to the ground, his body jerking as each bullet hits. I know he's dead, he has to be, but I still expect him to put a hand out to break his fall. He doesn't. Just lies there, blood seeping onto the dirt.

I keep the gun pointed right at him, shaking.

Until I hear JT say, 'Put the gun down, Lori.'

I stamp on the brake. Jerk the wheel to the left. The Jetta skids to a halt, half-cocked on the side of the highway. Letting go of the steering wheel, I throw myself across the central console at North. My fist connects with his jaw and I hear a crack. Don't know if it came from him or my knuckles, and don't care either. 'You fucking asshole! You knew how it happened all along. You could have told the truth, shown Old Man Bonchese that it was self-defence, and had the hit taken off JT and me at any time in the past ten years.'

'Lori, I—'

'You selfish fucking fuck. You pretended to be my friend back then, but really you were screwing me over.' I punch him again. 'JT nearly died because of you.'

North's lip splits. He coughs and blood sprays down his chin. Only then does he put his arms up to protect himself. 'Stop, I couldn't. If I'd shared this I'd have had to share everything.'

I glare at him. 'Maybe you should have done. What good has hiding the truth done you? It got your wife killed, and made you a fugitive. You should have told the truth back when you found out. You've—'

'Enough!' The Old Man's voice is a bellow.

I stop, and turn to look at him. North does, too.

'This isn't useful.' He looks from me to North.

'Fuck useful.'

The Old Man shakes his head. 'Don't be so hasty. You're a smart woman and I have a proposition that will work in all our favour.'

'Why should I help you? After everything you've done...' I turn and glare at North. 'After everything you've both done.'

'Because all the men loyal to me still think you and your family are a target, and Luciano framing you and North here for my murder isn't going to help that none.'

I tilt my chin up in defiance. 'So nothing's changed.'

The Old Man shakes his head. 'No. The game's all changed now. You get me home, and you're free.'

I narrow my eyes. Stare at him, disbelieving. 'You'll take the price off our heads?'

He nods as best he can with the wound in his shoulder, wincing from the movement. 'You and your family, the price on you will be gone.'

I say nothing, remembering what North said when we first met – about how I was working for the mob ... and how strongly I denied it. Back then I hadn't been, not in the way that he meant it. But the lines have gotten blurred, and now, just a few days later, his words feel like they've come true. I look from North to the Old Man and nod my agreement. 'Okay. How are we going to get this done?'

60

SUNDAY, SEPTEMBER 23rd, 13:59

The Old Man's compound isn't in downtown Miami but a ways further along the coast, on a small peninsular, sitting pretty on a huge parcel of land that butts up against Biscayne National Park. Screened from the public by a high wall and dense tree cover, the place could have been picked as a site for a medieval fortress. In fact, with what the Old Man has told us about his sentries and firepower, it kind of sounds like a modern-day one.

We pull off the highway a little ways past Fontainebleau at the Mall of the Americas, finding a corner of the parking lot near Home Depot to park up. We've got the radio tuned to the news channel, but so far, although there's been mention of fire-fighters battling to put out a blaze alongside Highway 41 caused by a burning vehicle, there's been no mention of the car's owner or a dead body.

Turning in my seat, I meet the Old Man's gaze. 'Time to put the plan into action?'

Grim-faced, he nods.

North takes the cellphone he took from Klate's body before torching the Lincoln. He works out the password from the finger smears on the screen and taps out a message. He shows it to me and the Old Man:

Old Man done. Car BBQ.

Then he selects Luciano's cell number and presses send. We wait. In less than a minute the cellphone beeps and North shows us Luciano's reply:

Good. Now get back here.

As he reads his son's callous reply, the Old Man swallows hard but gives no other external sign of the impact it has on him.

He looks from me to North. 'Now we need the lay of the land. I can't call my people, in case Luciano has turned them.' He takes a wheezing breath, and gestures at North. 'You can't call because they think you're an enemy. But we need to know exactly what the Feds are doing.'

They both look at me. Shit. Against my better judgement I say, 'I have someone I could call.'

North frowns, no doubt guessing what I'm going to say.

The Old Man raises an eyebrow. 'Who?'

'A Fed, but one that's on my side rather than Special Agent Jackson Peters.'

'The one that warned us about Peters in Jacksonville station?' North says.

'Yeah.'

The Old Man holds my gaze. 'And you trust him?'

I sure as hell don't. He's not a good man, or an honourable one, but he'll give me the intel I need if doing so means he can force me to work his Chicago sting. 'On this, yes,' I say.

The Old Man thinks on it a moment, then nods. 'Do it.'

So I call Monroe. His cellphone rings twice, then he picks up, but doesn't speak.

I wait a beat, then say, 'I need your help.'

'You shouldn't be calling me.'

'I need to get onto Key Biscayne.'

'Well, shit.' His Kentucky drawl seems more pronounced. 'That ain't wise. Jeez, I need you alive, Lori, not going on some damn suicide mission.'

I keep my tone firm. 'If I'm going to stay living so I can help you, I have to do this.'

He doesn't speak.

'Monroe?'

'Look, there's only one way into Key Biscayne – Highway 913. And Peters has a perimeter road block set up there, and another set right outside the entrance gate to the Bonchese place. There's no way you'll get near. It'd be madness to try.'

I glance at the Old Man. Suddenly he's looking real shaky. I know unless I get him back, and he tells his men the hit is off, my family will never be safe. 'I got no choice.'

Monroe cusses under his breath. 'Peters has given the order. If you and North resist arrest, his agents are authorised to shoot to kill.'

'But his team won't enter the compound?'

'They searched the place first thing this morning. As long as Peters has no cause to believe you've gotten inside since then, they'll stay back at the road blocks.'

If we can get inside unseen we have a chance of getting the Old Man to lift the price on our heads, and for him and North to take Luciano out of the game.

'Thanks,' I say, and end the call.

I look at North. 'He says there's no way of getting onto Key Biscayne by road. There's a blockade on the only road in and another outside the compound. The agents are on a shoot-to-kill if we resist arrest.'

North rubs his hand across his face. 'We'll have to go in by water.' He glances at the Old Man. 'But we can't very well swim.'

The Old Man's shivering despite the heat. Every few moments his eyes lose focus and his head rocks back against the headrest. I look back at North and see that he's worried too. 'He needs fluids and medical attention.'

North nods. 'Westchester General isn't far. We can—'

'No.' The Old Man snaps his eyes open and sits up. 'I've got my own physician; she can patch me up when I'm back at the compound. What I need to do first is show my son who the head of this family is, and you're going to help me.'

I can tell I'd be wasting my breath to argue, so I don't say anything more. The Old Man's as stubborn as is he proud, and it's going to be the damnedest thing trying to keep him alive.

The sweat is running down my back. My neck is damp under the fall of my hair. It's baking hot in here without the engine and air conditioning on, and if it's affecting me then it sure isn't helping the Old Man. Opening the Jetta's door I slide out of the driver's seat. 'We're all out of water. I'll go get some.'

At the grocery store on the corner I grab a couple of six-packs of water, a bunch of sandwiches and a few packs of the highest-strength painkillers they have. I use the last of my cash to pay and head back to the car. In the back, the Old Man is leaning against the headrest, his eyes closed. North's watching him, his expression grim.

The only way this will work out is if we all make it to the compound alive. North's right when he says getting there by water is the only real option we've got left, and for that we need a boat. But anything belonging to the Old Man will either be at the compound already, or guarded by Miami Mob guys, who aren't likely to react well to our plan. With the Old Man injured the way he is, from a distance they're likely to assume me and North are the ones that hurt him, and will attack.

Getting back into the Jetta, I pass some sandwiches and water to North. The Old Man opens his eyes and blinks, taking a while to focus. His skin has taken on a greyish hue now, and his breathing has gotten more raggedy. I past him a bottle of water and a pack of painkillers. 'Take these, they'll help.'

Given our situation, there's only one viable way I can think of to get us all across. My stomach flips at the thought, but the Old Man's going downhill fast, and as far as I see it we're all out of other options.

I meet North's eye. 'I know a way to get us a boat.'

61

My mouth goes dry as I tap his number into my drugstore cellphone. Pressing call, I hold my breath, hoping to hell that he picks up this time. For the first time in days it doesn't go straight to voicemail. It rings; twice, four times, all the way to nine and I fear it's some glitch and it'll go to voicemail again.

Then he answers.

'It's Tate.'

'JT?' My voice is breathier, more urgent than usual. 'Are you okay, is Dakota safe?'

'We're fine.' He doesn't sound happy though.

I frown. 'Where are you? I've been trying to call—'

'Mob guys found us at the marina. We had to leave the mooring and head out into the ocean. We made our way around the coastline. Figured Bonchese's men wouldn't be looking for us their side of state.'

My breath catches in my throat. 'But you're all okay?'

'For now, yes. We've just arrived at a marina near Pompano Beach. We're planning to lie low for a little while.'

Relief floods through me. He seems distant ... and kind of mad at me. But he's safe. They all are.

I swallow hard, knowing he won't like what I'm about to say. 'We need to get to the Bonchese compound and there's a roadblock stopping us getting through. I was hoping Red might help.'

JT cusses. His tone's stone hard and full of anger. 'You'd endanger Dakota in that way?'

'No,' I say hastily. 'Because you can stay with her, in someplace safe around where you are.'

He says nothing. In the background I can hear the gentle splash of water against the side of the boat and the call of seabirds.

'If we can get back to the compound, the Old Man will remove the price on our heads. We'll be free of it, JT, isn't that worth a bit of—?'

'Who's we?'

I take a breath. 'Me, North and Giovanni Bonchese.'

JT cusses again, longer and louder.

In a rush I explain what's happened since we last spoke, days back after the shit storm in Missingdon. JT stays quiet as I talk. When I'm done, I can hear him breathing, but still he says nothing.

'JT? Talk to me. You get why I have to do this, don't you?'

He's silent a long moment. Then he says, 'I'll put you on with Red.'

I grip the cellphone tighter. Don't understand why he can't see that I have to do this; how it's the only way to get free of the Miami Mob. 'JT, don't I—?'

But it's too late. I hear rustling on the line. Muffled words that I can't make out.

The next voice I hear is Red's. 'Hello, Miss Lori.'

I smile when I hear his voice, and breathe a little easier, the tension in my chest loosening off a touch. 'Red, I could really use your help.'

'I sure figured as much.' Unlike with JT I can hear a smile in his voice.

So I tell him what I need him to do.

⌒

We rendezvous at the Miami Beach Marina. It's a busy spot for vacationers and weekenders taking out their boats, and we're not dressed for sailing, so I get as close to the visiting-boat moorings as I can before I park up. Like he does everywhere, Red seems to have friends here. Still, I doubt they'd want to know the folks he's taking onto his boat are a couple of fugitives and the head of the most influential crime family in Florida.

I see Red's houseboat approaching, its green-and-gold livery glinting in the sunlight as he manoeuvres it alongside. Turning to North, I glance towards the Old Man. 'We're going to need to move him.'

The Old Man's condition has worsened in the short time since I spoke with JT and Red. Moving him doesn't seem wise, but given his wishes, we don't have any alternative. Climbing out of the car, I put down my go bag and open the back door. Between us, North and me help the Old Man into position, ready to get out. His breathing is erratic.

As Red's boat draws alongside us, I see him at the wheel and wave. His silver-streaked hair is a little longer than when I last saw him, his deep tan looking darker against his white tee and lime-green surf shorts. He raises his hand and cuts the engine. Reaching over, I grab one of the ropes and fasten the boat to the mooring. As I finish, I peer through the windows of the boat for any sign of Dakota and JT but see none.

Red comes around to meet me.

'Thanks for doing this.'

He gives me a hint of his boyish smile. 'That's alright, Miss Lori. The way I see it, you need this finished. If going to that compound is the only way, I best help you get it done.'

'And JT?'

The frown lines between his eyes deepen. 'Best he keeps your little girl safe. They're back at the marina we just came from. Nice place – family friendly. They've taken a room at the motel opposite while I'm gone.'

I nod. Busy myself redoing the knot in the mooring rope. Red's right, of course – Dakota is best as far away from the mob as we can get her. And it was me who told JT to keep her away and look after her. But that doesn't mean I'm not hurting a little that JT left things the way he did.

Red puts a hand on my arm and gives me a kindly smile. 'He needs a bit of time is all.'

'Yeah.' I turn away. Don't want to discuss JT right now. Need to stay focused on what comes next. Catching North's eye I say, 'You ready?'

'I'll need your help.'

I move over to North and help him ease the Old Man out of the Jetta. With my right arm around his waist, and North's left around this shoulders, we support him as he walks to the boat.

As we approach, Red bristles. I don't blame him. Only a matter of weeks ago a couple of Miami Mob heavies beat him real bad – and threatened to do a lot more to him if I didn't play ball. Can't be easy coming face to face with the man who ordered it done. Still, he acts the gentleman, opening the gate and offering his arm to the Old Man to help him over the gap between land and boat, and the step up onto the deck.

The Old Man groans as he sinks down onto the bench seat that runs around the side of the deck. His breathing is worse and there's sweat trickling down the side of his face.

As North turns away his expression is grim. 'We should set the bait.'

I take out my cellphone. 'I'll make the call.'

Leaving North and Red on the boat with the Old Man, I walk away from the mooring until I'm sure the sound of the ocean lapping at the dock won't be audible down the line. Then I dial Luciano's number.

He answers on the second ring. 'Who is this?'

I wait a beat, listening to the noise of men talking in the background, then take a deep breath and let my words come out in rush. 'I'm stuck outside Key Biscayne, but there's no way in. If you want North you're going to have to come and get him.'

Luciano laughs. 'I don't think so. Like I told you before, I want you to kill him.'

'That's not going to happen, so I guess I may as well hand him over to the Feds. It'll be easy for sure, with the road block and all. I'm sure they'll be keen to hear what I've got to say about y'all too.'

The laughter stops real abrupt. 'Where are you?'

'Fontainebleau, near the Mall of the Americas, in the far corner of the parking lot near Home Depot,' I lie.

I hear him bark what I've said to someone near him. They respond a moment later with an ETA. 'I'll be there in thirty minutes. You pull any shit, I'll end you.'

Finishing the call, I walk back towards the boat. I pick up my go bag, carry it onto the deck and sit down beside North and Red. 'It's done.'

As Red goes to the helm of the boat to get us moving, I look out across the ocean in the direction of Key Biscayne and pray to a God I don't believe in that we can make our plan work.

We made for a motley crew: North with my gun, me with a bullet wound and my Taser, and the Old Man pretty much incapacitated. If I were a betting sort, I wouldn't be putting my chips on us, that's for sure.

But, whatever the odds, the stage is set.

How things play out now will be down to a roll of the dice.

62

The sun starts to lower in the sky as we near Key Biscayne via the Cape Florida Channel. Red has the boat moving at full throttle; we don't have long before Luciano realises we've double-crossed him, and we need to be inside the compound before he makes the discovery.

We speed past the residential areas, continuing until the houses are spaced further apart, the plots of land they occupy far vaster. None of us speaks, all lost in our thoughts, hoping our plan will work.

As we get close it's clear to see the Old Man's compound is the biggest property on the island. There's no way to see in due to the high wall that seems to stretch on for miles, but I can see a floating pontoon dock jutting out from the land. I point towards it. 'We can get out here.'

'No.' The Old Man's voice is weak but still has a core of steel. 'Keep going. Further along there's an ancient dock, right up against the wall. It's not used anymore so there's no cameras.' He pats his pocket. 'But I've still got the key for the original entrance gate. I keep it with all the others on my keychain, just to be safe.'

'Got it.' Red pushes the boat faster, the engine roaring as it propels us through the water.

Adrenaline courses through my body. We're in the danger zone now. Although the Old Man told Red how far out he'd need to keep the boat to avoid the cameras that are part of the CCTV security covering the compound, I'm scared that we'll be spotted. If we're stopped before we make it to the residential area of the compound, North and me are as good as dead.

A few minutes later we spot the old dock up ahead, on the edge of the property. The Old Man directs Red, making sure he stays in the CCTV blind spots. North and me check our weapons. I'm leaving my go bag in the boat, but I pass North his messenger bag with the iPad inside. 'You might need this to convince them.'

He takes it from me. 'Thanks.'

There's nothing more to say. We just need to get this done.

Red manoeuvres the boat alongside the dock. Up close I can see that this place must have been abandoned a long while ago – the wood's brittle from age and decay; the mooring rings hang loose from their screws. The boat taps the side of the jetty, and it splinters. Red says a prayer under his breath.

I turn to him. 'There's no place to tie up.'

'Don't fret, Miss Lori. I'll try holding her steady, but you best be quick now.'

The rise and fall of the ocean buffets the boat against the platform, and, despite Red's efforts, the boat drifts away from the edge. It's a risk to get the Old Man across, but we have to try. There's no time to find another way in.

I turn to North. 'We can't wait – we just have to do this.'

He stands, and between us we bring the Old Man to his feet and take him across the boat to the steps. The gap between the boat and the dock is a good yard or so. Glancing down, I see the waves slapping against the platform. The structure looks so rickety it's hard to tell if it'll even hold our weight. Knowing there's no way I can hold the Old Man up alone, I remove my arm from his waist and look at North. 'I'll go over first, test the stability.'

He opens his mouth to disagree, but I turn away and lift my foot to step over the gap onto the dock. As I push off from the boat a swell rises and pushes it away, widening the distance fast. I have to jump to make the platform. The wood creaks under my weight, and the plank closest to the boat falls into the ocean. Thankfully the rest of it holds. Heart pounding, I beckon to North. 'Come on.'

Red revs the boat's engine and gets in a little closer.

North springs across to the dock, helping the Old Man along with him. The Old Man's legs buckle on landing, and I grab his arms and pull him to safety before he unbalances North. Breathing hard, we scramble off the dock onto firm land.

Turning, I raise my hand in thanks to Red. He gives me the thumbs-up, and chugs the boat away from the mooring towards the spot further along the coast where we've agreed he'll wait.

The Old Man hands the key to North and he puts it into the lock on the gate. It's old and covered in rust, but after some coaxing it opens. The three of us slip inside.

This part of the compound is completely unlike the area around the house I was in before. It's dense with tall trees. Cooler. Darker. North gestures away from the wall, through the trees, and I nod. Supporting the Old Man we start down a dirt path.

A few minutes in, the effort is taking its toll on us all. The sun's going down, but the humidity's real high. Sweat runs down my spine. North's face is damp with it. The Old Man slumps in our arms, unconscious.

I cuss under my breath. Glance at North.

Then a man's voice, a little ways from us to our left, barks full of menace. 'Get yourselves face down in the dirt.'

63

We freeze where we are.

'You're outgunned. Do as you're told, don't make me say it twice.'

The sound of my pulse races jackhammer loud in my ears, but I know that voice; it's Growler, the man who held me captive here in the house just a few days ago.

I raise my hands, but don't hit the dirt. Keep my voice calm, clear. 'The Old Man's been attacked by—'

'Get. On. The. Ground.' Growler steps out from the tree line: tall, medium build with cropped hair – it's definitely him. He's not holding a weapon but he's got a bunch of guys behind him, all looking hostile, and each has their gun pointed at us.

'The Old Man's injured bad,' says North. 'He needs medical help.'

'He'll get it. Step away from him.'

North catches my gaze and gives a small shake of his head.

The Old Man is still unconscious. We keep hold of him and stay standing right where we are.

Growler gives a nod and two of his men – one older and bald, one younger with greasy long hair; both muscled and mean-looking – break away from the group and approach us.

I glare at the greasy-haired guy, who's now in front of me. 'Don't you put a hand on me.'

Greasy-haired guy hesitates.

'Traitor,' says the bald muscle guy, squaring up to North. North doesn't response. Frustrated, he spits in North's face. 'For what you've done, you're dead.'

We really need the Old Man to vouch for us right now, but he's slumped in our grasp, his breathing shallow and weak.

Growler shakes his head. 'You shouldn't have come back here.'

I gesture towards the Old Man. 'He didn't give me much of a choice.'

It's a four-way stand-off: Growler's men not wanting to do anything that'll cause the Old Man further injury; North and me unable to go on the attack because that'd mean letting go of the Old Man.

We need to talk our way out of this. And we need to get it done fast. With the time that's passed since the call to Luciano, he will have realised our bluff by now and be racing on back here. A little ways from us, fastened to one of the trees, is a CCTV camera. Our presence here is secret no longer. If we're going to survive we have to make the Old Man's men listen and get on our side, before Luciano returns.

'There's things you don't know about; that's the reason we're here. The Old Man—'

'Shut up,' greasy-headed guy takes a step closer to me.

I play the only move I can without letting go of the Old Man. I lunge forwards, bringing my leg up fast. Direct hit. Toe into balls. The greasy guy goes down.

While he's groaning, curled up all foetal-like in the dirt at my feet, I could use the distraction to my advantage and make a play for Growler, but I don't. To have any chance of this working out without bloodshed, we need a talked-out solution. There's no way for sure to know where Growler and his men's loyalties lie, so I go with my gut.

Raising my free hand, I say, 'I believe that you're loyal to the Old Man, and if that's true you need to hear us out. North's got a video, proving why he spoke to the Feds and why the Old Man here forgave him. You're all in danger right now, you just don't know it.'

Growler lets out a single, sarcastic laugh. 'I think you got that all about face.'

'No,' I say, real firm. 'Luciano is making a move for leadership of the family. If you take me and North off the board, you and your boss here are going to be taken down.'

Growler narrows his eyes. 'Luciano wouldn't do that.'

'He would, and it's not the first time he's planned it.' North reaches slowly into his bag for the iPad. He holds it across the Old Man and says to me. 'Five, six, nine, two.'

Growler watches, saying nothing, his expression still suspicious.

I type the passcode onto the iPad and the screen unlocks, opening on the video of Tommy and Luciano at the fishing lodge ten years ago. I press play, and turn the iPad around to face Growler. 'Watch this.'

As the video plays, and on screen Luciano and Tommy discuss their plan for getting rid of the Old Man permanently, I watch Growler's expression change from sceptical to shock, and finally anger.

He looks back at North. 'Is this all you have?'

North shakes his head. 'No, there's hours of it. I've got the paper trail of all the money Luciano's hived off from the Old Man's business since then, too. The Feds seized the accountant's computer before I could get the files, but I managed to get them while they had me in protective custody.'

I bring up on the screen the spreadsheets and photographed hard-copy documents. Flick through them, one by one, for Growler to see.

'Luciano murdered the accountant because he'd discovered the truth,' North says. 'Then a couple of hours ago, he had Klate try to kill the Old Man on the way back from Everglades City. The Old Man fought back, though, and killed Klate, but not before he'd gotten stabbed. He needs the medic.'

Growler looks at the two men flanking him and gestures towards the Old Man. 'Help him to the house.' He turns back to me and North, his expression determined, his voice filled with fury. 'We need to get inside and decide how we're going to deal with Luciano.'

The two guys take the weight of the Old Man between them, and the greasy-haired guy who came at me limps alongside them, making a poor job at helping.

Growler pulls a walkie from his belt, presses the button on the side and speaks into it fast. 'Friendlies not hostiles. We're heading back to base. Get the medic. Urgent. The Old Man's wife, Juliette, too. ETA: ten minutes.'

As North takes the iPad from me and puts it back safe in the messenger bag the bald guy who spat at him starts to mumble an apology. North turns fast and slams his fist into the guy's face. He goes down hard, blood pouring from his nose.

North shakes his head. There's a look of total disgust on his face. 'You ever spit at me again, I'll kill you.'

With Growler leading the way, we move along the dirt path as fast as the guys carrying the Old Man can manage. After five minutes or so the trees clear, and although the light is fading now, I recognise where we are. To the side of us are the farm buildings – huge barns and warehouses filled with who knows what. I know that the enclosure with the pigs will be on the other side of them, and beyond that there'll be paddocks with horses grazing. Growler leads us along the side of the buildings to the house. As we reach the back door I catch the faint odour of swine and my stomach turns.

Growler reaches for the door and opens it. The guys supporting the Old Man step over the threshold first, already calling for the medic.

I'm just about to follow when I hear it. The roar of a car engine at the front of the house; the sound of gravel spitting out from beneath fast-moving wheels; the squeal of tyres braking hard to a halt.

I look at North, and can tell from his expression that he's thinking exactly what I'm thinking.

Luciano's back.

64

SUNDAY, SEPTEMBER 23rd, 19:42

Growler pushes us into the house and slams and bolts the door. He shouts for the medic. 'Sophia, get in here.'

We stop in the rustic, farmhouse-style kitchen I remember from before; notes on the chalk board, pictures on the dresser. In the centre of the long table is a vase of gardenias, the sweet flowers scenting the air. Our guns and my Taser seems real out of place.

A red-headed woman in blue jeans and a khaki tee hurries into the room, followed closely by an older woman, mid-seventies at a guess, with high cheekbones and grey hair swept back into a French braid. The older woman cries out when she sees us. Throwing herself at the Old Man, she caresses his face, speaking rapid Italian.

'Move back, Juliette, give him some air,' the redhead says gently, her hand on the older woman's shoulder. She looks at the two guys supporting Giovanni and gestures to a battered couch at the back of the kitchen, her voice more authoritative now. 'Let's move him over there.'

North helps and they do as she says. She's Sophia, I assume. The medic.

'This room's our control centre. Get it safe-roomed,' Growler says to his men. As they exit into the hallway at the run, I wonder what the hell they're doing.

Growler pulls the walkie from his belt and barks orders to his other men outside, directing them to defend the house from the attack that we all know is inevitable. There's a burst of static on the walkie, rapid talk, mostly impossible to make out: '...*turned ... guns ... Luciano...*'

Grim-faced, Growler points towards the windows, and I get his meaning. Hustling to them, I yank the drapes shut, scanning the room for something we can use to board them up.

Moments later we hear gunshots. Real close.

Bald guy, Greasy and the other two men return, arms laden with weapons. They dump them onto the flagstones in the middle of the floor and look to Growler for instructions.

I don't wait for more orders. Striding across to one of the dressers, I shout towards the bald guy North punched. 'Here, help me with this.'

Together we pull it across the large double window that faces out over the parking lot. It's barely in place before bullets ping against the window frame and the windowpane shatters.

I flick off the lights. Turning back to the room I shout, 'Everyone get down and away from the windows.'

Sophia's got her medic kit out and is working on the Old Man. The older woman is kneeling beside him, stroking his hand, tears pouring down her face.

Growler barks orders to the men we have in the room. North and the greasy-haired guy pull the kitchen table across the door as a barricade. The other two move one of the other dressers over the door into the hall. We're trapped inside our make-shift safe room, with a whole bunch of weapons for company; but right now it feels far from safe.

The volleys of gunfire continue outside, but most aren't hitting the building. Staying low, I scoot across to the window closest to the parking lot. The dresser blocks most of it, but I'm able to peer around to get a glimpse of what's happening outside.

My breath catches in my throat. It looks like a scene out of an old Western movie. In the darkening night, bloodied bodies are strewn across the gravel lot. Luciano's white Range Rover is jacked across the space, side on to the house. The windows have been shot out and its pearlised white paintwork is riddled with bullet holes. Behind its stricken carcass, I count five men, guns drawn, firing at a barn a ways over to the left. Behind them, shooting from behind the second barn and the other cars in the lot, I count at least another thirty. Thirty-five guns. There are a few men remaining loyal to the Old Men outside, firing back at Luciano's mob. Inside, discounting the Old Man, Juliette and the medic, there are seven of us. Thirty-five to seven, that's real bad odds.

North joins me beside the dresser. 'What's going on out there?'

I turn. 'It's bad.'

He peers through the gap above me and shakes his head. 'We're sitting ducks here. We can't stay cowering; we've got to fight back.'

There's a cry to our left and a young guy close to the house, skinny-looking and barely out of his teens, drops to the ground. He whimpers, convulsing in the dirt. Blood oozes out from his stomach.

North raises his gun and shoots at the men behind the Range Rover. They return fire, then duck down behind the vehicle. As North rises to aim again, the men on the inner entrance gate open fire with their automatic weapons. I count six more men. The odds are getting worse; forty-one to seven.

Bullets thud into the side of the house, the windows, the dresser. Heart racing, I drop to the ground. North and me scramble for the back of the kitchen.

'How many?' shouts Growler above the noise of the gunfire.

'Forty, maybe more,' North says. 'I underestimated how many men Luciano has turned. The men loyal to the Old Man are outnumbered.'

Growler gestures to his four guys, pointing to the positions he wants them to take. 'Get over there and return fire. We're under siege here.'

They do as he says; grabbing weapons from the stash in the middle of the floor, they take up station at the windows. As they fight back against Luciano's men, more bullets pummel the house. Gunfire ricochets through the room. Juliette cries out, Sophia speaks Italian to her in calming tones.

There's a shout, and Greasy drops to the floor, his gun clattering against the flagstones. I hurry to him, but as I roll him over I see he's beyond help. The bullet's gone through his cheek and into his skull, no exit wound. He's gone. Dead.

I rush to the pile of weapons, hesitate a moment. Hate that I'm going to have to do this again – use lethal force. But I know that, in this situation, it's the only way we'll have a chance of staying alive.

I reach for an AK-47.

North grabs my arm. Frowning, he shakes his head. 'It'll take more than that for us to survive this.'

'I can't just stand by and—'

'They outnumber us. We need another plan, a smart one, and fast.'

The bald guy is reloading. The other two let off a series of shots, then pause. Outside all is silent.

'What's going on out there?' Growler shouts into the walkie.

In the kitchen, we're quiet, listening for a response.

The walkie stays silent.

He yells again: 'Answer me. Status update.'

There's a loud burst of static, then Luciano's voice comes through the handset's speaker. His tone's smug. 'They're dead, or they're with me. I'm the head of this family now. It's time for y'all to give it up.'

65

SUNDAY, SEPTEMBER 23rd, 19:49

'We need to go to the bunker,' says North.

Growler nods. 'Take the Old Man and Juliette. We'll hold them off as long as we can.' Picking up one of the AK-47s he moves to join his remaining men at the windows.

As they fire shots out towards Luciano's mob, North glances at me then kneels beside the Old Man. 'I need the key to the bunker.'

The Old Man's regained consciousness, but his eyes seem unable to focus. He peers towards North. Shaking his head he smiles. 'Anthony, you know Papa says we mustn't play in there.'

Damn. He's delirious.

A new volley of bullets pepper the side of the house. More glass shatters. Splinters fly into the air. A red mist sprays from the bald guy's throat as he sprawls backwards from the window.

North tries again, his tone more urgent. 'It's North, sir. You're injured. I need to get you and Juliette safe. Giovanni, please, give me the key.'

The Old Man frowns. He looks bewildered, lost. The man who treated me so callously when he brought me here a few days ago, and the determined man of just a few hours ago, seems to have disappeared. He glances at Juliette. 'I ... what's...?'

She whispers to him in Italian and smiles. Stroking his cheek, she then reaches around his neck and removes a key on a silver chain. She passes it to North. 'This is what you need. Now, get us out of here.'

North opens the pantry door, and starts clearing the freestanding racks holding packets and cans of food from against the back wall. I move after him, helping him shift the racks out of the way, the feet of the metal frames screeching across the flagstones. Then he crouches down and inserts the key into a hole that's low to the ground. I hear a bolt unfasten.

North gives the back wall a hard shove, and it opens to reveal a dark chamber with a spiral staircase leading downwards. 'Come on.'

I don't move. It doesn't make sense. 'An underground bunker? How is that possible? You can't build a basement in Florida.'

'It's not a basement,' North says. 'It's the first level. The ground in this part of the compound is artificially raised.'

'Won't Luciano just come after us? We'll be trapped in there.'

'The Old Man's father had it done, way back in the day. Few people know about it, and Luciano isn't one of them.'

'You'll be boxed in, it's a—'

'I have to.' North glances back at the Old Man. His eyes have rolled back into his head, and he's lost consciousness again. 'He might not last, but I can't let Luciano be the one to finish him.'

'Okay, but I'm staying here. I won't hide in a hole while I'm still fit to fight. I need to finish this and get back to my daughter.'

Before North can argue, I turn and hurry out of the pantry back towards the window. I step over Greasy's body, trying not to look into his sightless eyes and the bloody mass left by the bullet wound, and peep through the gap between the dresser and what's left of the window frame.

I can see Luciano, hunkered down behind his Range Rover. Squinting through the gloom, I use the light of the full moon to count the number of men he still has standing. I have to stop counting at thirty-six; I hit the deck as another barrage of shots pelt against the window.

North calls after me, but I don't respond. If we can't hold Luciano off, they'll kill North and the rest of them in the bunker as easy as shooting fish in a barrel.

I have to do something.

I remember North's words: *We need to be smart.*

He's right. When you're in a tight spot you've got to use whatever you've got to get the job done. This isn't over. There's another play to be had here. Grabbing my cellphone, I dial Monroe's number.

He answers after the first ring.

With the gunfire echoing around me, I shout into the cellphone. 'Tell Jackson Peters me and North are inside the Bonchese compound. Tell him Luciano is making a play for leadership of the Miami Mob.'

Monroe sounds unsure. 'Is it true?'

'Can't you hear it?' I drop to the ground as Growler and his last two men return fire. I know Monroe won't do anything from kindness, only if it benefits him. 'We can't hold them off much longer. If you don't get Peters to intervene you can kiss goodbye to me being around to do that Chicago sting.'

'Hold on.' There's rustling at Monroe's end of the call and footsteps that make it sound like he's running. 'I'm telling him now.'

There's a huge crash and the dresser across the window breaks into pieces and collapses onto the flagstones. Bullets pound against the walls and the floor. I dive for cover in the pantry Growler's close behind me.

Neither of the other two make it. Their bodies jerk as the bullets rip through them. The vase of gardenia blooms shatters.

'Monroe?' I shout into the cellphone.

There's no answer. The call's disconnected.

More bullets spray the kitchen, ricocheting off the flagstones. Gardenia petals whirl in the air, scattering over the fallen men's bodies like funeral pyre ashes. Their blood stains the white petals crimson.

The outline of a man appears in the gaping hole where the window and dresser used to be, silhouetted in the moonlight. I hear a familiar, mocking, laugh; Luciano.

'I'm out of ammo,' Growler whispers.

I don't have a gun, but that doesn't mean that I'm giving up, and I sure as hell won't let Luciano shoot me on the floor of this pantry.

Springing up, I pull my Taser from my holster and wait for him to get within range. He's cocky enough to believe he's untouchable. But no one's untouchable, and in a situation like this, a winning hand can pivot to a losing one in the pull of a trigger.

Luciano steps closer. He's in the middle of the room now. I just need him four paces closer for him to be in the Taser's range.

He whistles like he's calling a dog. Takes another step. 'Lori? I know you're in there, hiding like the bitch you are. I'm going to enjoy—'

From outside, I hear the roar of vehicle engines.

'What the—?' Luciano turns and sprints back to the window gap. He gestures furiously, yelling at his men. 'Fire. Stop them for...' His voice fades as he disappears back out into the lot.

Luciano's men open fire.

I hurry to the window and peer around the wall. A line of police and FBI vehicles, their headlights and spotlights blazing, smash through the entrance gates with one hell of a clatter. The law-enforcement vehicles are armoured, their firepower a whole lot stronger. Luciano's men are the ones who are outnumbered now.

Hitting the ground, I scoot away from the window. Tell myself this was the only play I had left, that Luciano forced my hand, and I didn't have another choice. I know that Luciano will never surrender, and I try not to feel guilty about what I've set in motion.

This will be a fight to the death.

66

SUNDAY, SEPTEMBER 23rd, 20:13

The gunfight seems to go on forever. Law enforcement versus the mob, neither side backing off. I stay hunkered down behind one of the dressers, hoping it'll all soon be over.

There's a pause in the shooting, and I think for a moment it's finished. Then Luciano steps backwards into the kitchen through the hole in the wall where the window once was.

'Luciano Bonchese. You're surrounded.' Special Agent Peters' voice has a tinny echo to it from the megaphone he's using. 'Put your weapon down and come out with your hands on your head.'

'Never,' Luciano shouts. Raising his gun, he fires out towards the parking lot, but all I hear is a trigger click. The gun is out of ammo.

His back is towards me. His focus is on the gun.

This is my chance to end things.

I inch towards him, my Taser drawn. He's almost in range.

Peters' voice booms over the megaphone. 'Luciano Bonchese, this is your last warning. Drop your weapon and come out with your hands on your head.'

Luciano still doesn't notice me. He's cussing loudly. One of his hands is bleeding, and he fumbles with his gun as he tries to reload, dropping bullets in his haste. Cusses more.

Mouth dry. Heart racing.

I take a step towards him, then another. One more and he'll be in range.

Special Agent Peters' voice is firm. The megaphone makes it seem to echo. 'You have until the count of three.'

Luciano's still scrabbling at his pocket for more bullets; he still isn't aware I'm behind him.

'One,' shouts Special Agent Peters.

I take another step closer to Luciano.

'Two.'

Pulling the trigger, I shoot the probes from my X2 Taser into Luciano's back. As they discharge their voltage, he yells out, half turning towards me as he crumples forwards onto his knees. His teeth are set in a grimace, his body convulsing. A damp stain spreads across the front of his pants.

'He's down,' I shout before Peters can count to three. 'I've tasered him.'

'Identify yourself,' Peters shouts in the megaphone.

'Lori Anderson.'

'Is Carlton North with you?'

I know I have to play this real careful. I'm an armed fugitive in the eyes of Special Agent Peters, if he thinks I'm resisting arrest he's just as likely to shoot me as he was Luciano. 'North's in a bunker with the Bonchese family. There's just two of us left in here, sir, plus Luciano, who is immobilised.'

Peters' voice is firm, hard. 'Drop your weapons and come out with your hands raised.'

Given the situation, this treatment is as good as I can hope for right now. I glance over to the pantry, where Growler is hiding. 'You prepared to do this?'

He nods.

'Yes, sir,' I shout. But I don't move, not yet; there's something I need to do first.

Dropping my Taser, I take out my cellphone, and select Red's number. I type a quick message: *North and me fine. Luciano stopped. Feds have control of compound. Get away from here fastest. I'll find you later.*

Pocketing my cell. I put my hands on my head and step around Luciano. He's still jerking about, his nervous system disrupted, and

I know it'll be another few minutes before he's able to think about moving again.

Growler joins me by the gap in the wall.

I glance at him. 'You ready?'

'Yup.'

'We're coming out,' I shout.

Then I step out of the house and into the custody of the FBI.

67

SUNDAY, SEPTEMBER 23rd, 20:28

Two huge spotlights illuminate us, blinding me. I blink into the light. All I can make out are the ghostlike shapes of bullet-ridden vehicles and bodies scattered like litter across the gravel of the parking lot.

It looks like a battlefield.

There's so much death. So much waste.

I bite my lip and try to stay strong, but I fail to stem the tears as the strain of the past few days and my emotions collide. I feel horror at the sight of all these bodies; fear of what comes next. But above all, my overriding emotion is relief, because Red should be well on his way back to the other marina, and Dakota and JT are safe.

SWAT team officers grab me roughly, forcing my hands behind me. I feel the cold bite as metal cuffs are snapped around my wrists. More officers swarm past into the kitchen. They cuff Growler and Luciano. I hear them removing the barricade to the hallway door and continuing on to search the house, yelling 'clear' as they move through the rooms.

A man steps out of the darkness, into the beam of the lights. I recognise him. He's tall and athletic with an FBI ball cap pulled down over his blond hair. Even the fatigue of the past few days as he's been tracking me and North is unable to dim his movie-star good looks. Special Agent Jackson Peters.

He raises his eyebrows. 'Well, Lori Anderson. Finally we meet.'

'I guess we do.'

'Where's North?'

'Still in the bunker, keeping Giovanni Bonchese and two women safe from Luciano.'

'Special Agent Monroe said that you told him Giovanni is injured.'

'He is, badly.'

'How do we access the bunker?'

'I need your word that you won't harm them.'

Peters narrows his eyes then nods. 'So long as they don't fire on my men.'

It's as good a guarantee as I can hope for. I turn, nodding across the kitchen. 'There's a secret passage from the back of that pantry. Follow the stairs down, that's where they went.'

As Peters directs his men towards the pantry, I see another silhouette approaching. I'd recognise it anywhere: tall, lanky, with fly-away hair that's just a touch too long. Special Agent Alex Monroe.

He steps out of the direct light, and his features become clear. His gaze is fixed on Peters. 'You got what you need? We all done here?'

Peters looks from Monroe to me. 'Alex told me what you were doing, that he'd sent you in to gain North's confidence and bust the Miami Mob crime family open.'

I stare at them both, saying nothing, guessing what's happening here. Having worked for Monroe before, I know he'll lie and cheat his way to the result he wants. And right now he wants me to do the Chicago job for him, so he's said what Peters needed to hear in order to prevent me from getting arrested. It means I owe him. And the thought of that makes me shudder.

Peters looks impressed. 'You did good work, Ms Anderson.' He glances at Monroe. 'I just wish Alex would've let me get in on the secret a little earlier.'

Monroe shrugs, and gives a small smile. 'Couldn't have you jeopardising my operation, now, could I?'

'I suppose not.' Peters looks back at me. 'I'm just glad you got out alive.'

Peters nods to the SWAT officer nearby, and he uncuffs me. Rubbing my wrists, I take the bottle of water Monroe offers and take a long drink. It feels like I've not had any liquids in hours.

'You ready to go?' Monroe says.

I nod. 'For sure.'

Monroe walks me out across the parking lot. Gravel scrunches beneath our feet as we navigate a path around the bodies of Luciano's and the Old Man's men. Looking away from their bullet-ridden corpses, I glance over to the SWAT vehicles. The uninjured are being loaded into police transport; the wounded are being tended by medics.

Monroe leads me on past them. Pressing a key fob, the lights flash twice on a black sedan up ahead. 'You did good, Lori. Real good. Hell, you brought down the goddamn Bonchese crime family.'

He sounds impressed, pleased, but that's not how I feel. Sure, I got what I wanted, what I needed. I helped North reveal the deep dirty truth about Luciano, and Tommy. And got the price lifted from me and my family's heads. I achieved my aim for sure. I should feel happy, but I don't.

Before I get into the car, I glance back over my shoulder, at the bodies strewn across the gravel lot, and shudder. An eye for an eye, the Old Man kept on saying; the old way, scores settled with blood. I don't agree. The cost is so high. The lives lost so many. The Miami Mob came after me, and I had to defend myself, but that doesn't change the fact I feel an overwhelming regret that so many are dead.

Monroe glances at me sideways. Raises an eyebrow. 'You're awful quiet.'

'Yeah,' I say. 'What happened here, it doesn't feel good is all.'

68

MONDAY, SEPTEMBER 24th, 01:43

Monroe gives me a ride to the motel where JT and Dakota are staying.

As I go to get out of the car, Monroe puts his hand on my arm. I turn back to look at him. 'Yeah?'

'I'll be in touch,' he says.

I nod. 'I don't doubt it.'

I know what he's talking about, but I don't want to think about the job in Chicago right now.

Climbing out of the car, I slam the door shut and make my way to room seven. When I messaged JT from the car, he said that's where he is with Dakota. I told him I was on my way and he sent me a single word reply: *Okay*.

On the opposite side of the street is the marina where Red's houseboat is temporarily moored up. In the moonlight I can see the masts of yachts and the silhouettes of big tourist cruisers. I fancy I can hear the sea lapping against their hulls, but it's probably in my imagination. A distraction from what might happen next.

As I step along the walkway a knot twists in my belly. I feel more nervous than a girl waiting on her prom date to arrive. Things have been tense between JT and me these past few days. When I spoke to him before going to the compound he was still so mad at me for taking this job, for helping North and the Old Man. The depth of his anger makes me fearful our relationship can't come back from this.

Lifting my hand, I rap my knuckles lightly against the painted green door. A moment later there's a click as the lock releases and the door inches open. I bite my lip.

JT, as big and sexy as ever, steps through the gap onto the walkway and pulls the door closed behind him. He looks at me, his big blues holding my gaze, all intense. His voice hushed. 'Dakota's sleeping, I don't want to wake her.'

'Sure.'

'You changed your hair?'

I don't want to go into details. 'It was a disguise.'

He says nothing. In the silence of the night we stare at each other like two fight-weary boxers hesitating over making the next move.

JT shakes his head. 'Why'd you do it, Lori?'

My heart punches in my chest. I've told him already, but he can't seem to let it go. 'North had to get the Old Man back to the Bonchese compound. Without—'

'You could have been killed.' There's a muscle pulsing in his neck. He seems as angry as he had been when he'd first discovered I hadn't told him he had a daughter and she that she'd been sick. 'Just tell me why it was so damn important to keep that asshole alive.'

'It was the only way for us to be safe.' I explain about Luciano's double-cross, about how North had proof I killed Tommy in self-defence and that Tommy and Luciano had been plotting to overthrow the Old Man. 'If Luciano had won, or the Old Man had died before he'd lifted the price on our heads, we'd have had to run. We'd always have been looking over our shoulder. What kind of life would that have been for our child?'

'You risked everything.' The anger is gone from his voice, but there's still a physical distance between us. 'What happened tonight on the compound ... You could have been killed.'

'I had to keep Dakota safe.'

He nods. He's frowning, but there's pride in his voice. 'She's a strong kid – a survivor. Tough and independent, just like her momma. We talked a lot out on the boat. She told me about her illness, the treatment...'

My breath catches in my throat at the intensity of his stare. I hold my breath. Wait for him to continue.

JT stares at me for a long moment. He looks like he's weighing up what to say next real careful. Then he shakes his head. 'We'll talk more about it some other time.'

'We can talk about it now, if there's something troubling you it's better to be honest with—'

'No.' He steps towards me, closing the distance between us and pulling me to him. 'It can wait.'

I feel his arms around me. Tilt my head up and press my lips against his. I feel the passion in his kiss, the strength in his embrace, and tell myself that everything will be okay.

I'm lying to myself and I know it. There's a problem between us, a secret JT's not willing to share just yet, and I need to know what it is. A niggling voice, deep in the back of my mind, says if I let this fester it'll only get worse and come back to bite me on the ass.

But as JT pulls me closer I melt into him, blocking out my doubts. I've missed this. Missed him. And right now, this is all that matters. JT, Dakota and me, reunited.

We're strong, the three of us. And we've been through so much already.

Surely together we can get through anything?

69

ONE WEEK LATER

It's hard acting normal, but I try real hard for Dakota's sake, because, although the price is off our heads and we've resumed some kind of family routine, the threat of more trouble is getting closer.

I owe Monroe a debt, and he intends for me to repay him in full.

Evenings like tonight help. We're meeting up with Red on board his boat for dinner. Oftentimes it helps me to forget for a little while, but that's not happening tonight.

Just before we drove over here, I got a text from Monroe: *Enough time's passed. We need to act. You leave for Chicago on Monday.*

Now we're sitting around the houseboat's table. The food is delicious – spicy shrimp gumbo – but I've got no kind of appetite. I feel sick to my stomach – dry-mouthed and shaky. I haven't told JT yet. Hate to think on leaving my baby girl Dakota again. But I know Monroe won't back off until I've done the job I owe him.

Dakota's chattering away. JT's ribbing her about her love of shrimp.

Red's watching me closely. He gestures to my untouched plate. 'Not to your taste, Miss Lori?'

I force a smile. 'It's great, thanks, I'm just not hungry.'

He narrows his gaze. 'You hear any more about how things are working out with those Feds and the Miami Mob?'

JT glances at us, then towards Dakota. She's not listening to our conversation though, too intent on getting through her plate of gumbo.

Feeling our gaze, she looks up and grins. 'Can I have seconds?'

I smile. 'Yes, honey, if Red says that's okay.'

'Mr Red, can I?'

Red laughs and ruffles her hair. 'Sure you can. Seconds, thirds, as much as you please.'

Dakota grins, and shovels more gumbo into her mouth, humming as she chews. JT laughs.

Red looks back at me and says, 'So, you were saying?'

'As you know, Luciano and his men were all arrested and charged. They're awaiting trial, but Monroe says the case, especially against Luciano, is watertight.'

I take a gulp of my beer. Hope Red and JT haven't noticed the quiver in my voice. Red nods, and I can tell he wants more details, so I force myself to continue.

'North made a deal. He's given all the dirt he had on Luciano to the Feds and will testify against him in court in return for his freedom.'

'So North's not in jail?' Red asks.

I shake my head. Remember the last conversation I had with North just a few days ago. How he'd thanked me for what I did and told me he'd been in contact with Carly and that she'd survived the attack in her apartment with no permanent damage. If I ever needed the help of the Miami Mob, or Carly's safe house in Tallahassee, I shouldn't hesitate to ask.

'North is head of the Bonchese family now. The Old Man will take a long time to recover. Gabriella's dead, Luciano's locked up, and his other daughter, Maria, has no involvement in the family business, so he's named North his successor.'

Red lets out a long whistle. 'Well, damn.'

JT's eyes are down, focused on the gumbo, but his jaw is tight, his expression a little haunted, the way it is whenever North is mentioned.

'North says things will be different with him in charge, but I'm not so sure. He might draw the line at some of the things Luciano got messed up in, but he's still loyal to the Old Man.'

'He's a powerful man now, and a dangerous one.'

'Yeah.' I haven't figured out whether my relationship with North is a good thing. He might have more honour than most of the Miami Mob, but he's still a gangster. 'At least the price is off our heads.'

Red smiles. 'And your federal friend stopped you getting charged, I'd count that as a win.'

I nod, but it feels as much of a win as a bought-result boxing match. Taking my napkin from my lap, I put it on the table and stand up. 'Could you excuse me for just a moment.'

Red smiles, but there's concern in his eyes. 'Sure, Miss Lori, just don't go too far – there'll be a dessert coming out the oven in a moment.'

'I won't.'

Stepping away from the table, I move out of the cabin onto the deck. Gripping the handrail, I look out to sea. The moon is high overhead, her light twinkling across the surface of the ocean, which tonight is as calm as a millpond. I stare at the dark horizon. Listen to the gentle lapping of the water against the boat and try to stem the panic thinking about what happened at the Miami Mob compound brings on.

'How are you doing?'

I flinch at the sound of JT's voice. Hear him moving across the deck to join me. Turning, I look up into his face. Even though he's right in front of me it still feels like there's this massive distance between us. It's been there since I told him I'd agreed to find North for the Old Man, and rather than getting better now the job's finished, it seems to be worse. I think back to the night I returned from the job. How he started talking about Dakota and her illness, and the real intense look on his face. The bond between him and Dakota strengthens by the day. Maybe he wants to tell her he's her father. Maybe it is time she knew.

I don't know what to do. We've not talked about it, but then talking isn't JT's style. But he's pissed at me, and I don't know how to fix it. And the longer I feel the divide between us, the more I worry that it can't be fixed. We talk about day-to-day things – my bounty-hunting work, Dakota's school, his physical therapy – but we never talk about us. It makes me feel like I can't confide in him now.

'I'm okay.'

'I don't believe you.' He gazes at me, his expression filled with concern. 'Sure, your arm's healing nice, you've dyed your hair back to blonde, and you put on a brave face for Dakota, but you wake up most nights screaming. You'll only take the basic jobs, stuff tadpole rookies do, things that are easy. And you and me haven't—'

'I've got to do another job for the Feds, and they want it started next week.' My words come in a rush, unplanned. My heart's punching against my ribs. 'Monroe wants me to go to Chicago and do a sting to incriminate the head of the Chicago Mob. He says I owe him for getting me free and clear of what happened in Missingdon, and Tallahassee *and* the Bonchese family compound … and he's right. I have to do it. But I don't want to leave Dakota again so soon. I don't want to leave you.'

JT frowns, saying nothing.

Shit. I can guess what he's thinking. I hold my hands up. 'I know, I know. I have to do this, that's what I always say.'

'Yeah, you do, kiddo.' JT smiles. Reaching down, he moves the hair that's fallen across my eye, and tucks it behind my ear. His fingers linger on my cheek. 'I get why, but you're always thinking about how you can protect Dakota and protect me. You always think you have to do the tough stuff alone. You never let anyone look out for *you*.'

I hold his gaze. Know that he's right. I think of having to face up to another set of mobsters, of taking on a new threat, in an unfamiliar city, and my stomach flips.

'Dakota's a tough kid, wise beyond her years. And your friend, Red…' JT glances back towards the cabin. 'Well, he's real good with her. I reckon he'd have no trouble having an extra houseboat guest.'

I get what JT's saying; that Red could look after Dakota for a few days. And he's right. I've seen how great Red is with my baby. I know I can trust him to keep her safe. I gaze up at JT. Remember how good it was to work alongside him, and how great it felt to know he had my six. 'The Chicago job, I don't want to do it alone.'

He leans in, brushes his lips against mine. The scent of him – bourbon and smoke – is as intoxicating as ever, and my stomach flips again for a whole other reason. Then he pulls away a fraction.

JT looks in my eyes with his big old blues and smiles again. 'Then I guess you best tell Monroe that we're both going to Chicago.'